LEARNING
TO FALL

LEARNING TO FALL

A Novel

ANNE CLERMONT

SparkPress, a BookSparks imprint
A Division of SparkPoint Studio, LLC

Published by SparkPress, a BookSparks imprint,
A division of SparkPoint Studio, LLC
Tempe, Arizona, USA, 85281
www.gosparkpress.com

Published [2016]

Printed in the United States of America

ISBN: 978-1-940716-78-7 (pbk)
ISBN: 978-1-940716-79-4 (e-bk)
Library of Congress Control Number: 2016933762

Cover design © Julie Metz, Ltd./metzdesign.com
Author photo © Lisa Dunham of LSD Photography
Formatting by Katherine Lloyd/thedeskonline.com

Author's note:
Everything contained in this book is a work of fiction, and although I tried to be
as true to fact about the details of the sport of show jumping as I could, I did,
at times, take license for the sake of brevity and that of the story.

For Craig,
I thank God and serendipity,
as they led me to you.

1

*A*s if conjuring my dream, the earth shook. My throat closed, and I knew I should run, or duck, or roll—any one of the things I'd been taught since elementary school to do during an earthquake. But I stood rooted, watching the horses gallop up from the creek that bordered the redwood forest—their hooves striking the cracked ground as they flew, their tails raised high, their necks extended, their ears flattened against their heads, desperate to keep up with their herd mates. A cloud of dust rose above the ranch, choking me. I wiped at the grit in my eyes with the heel of my hand.

Then everything settled. The ground. The horses. The dust. The thunderous noise.

And even though I'd been born and raised in earthquake country, and this was not unusual—typical even—from somewhere deep within me, like the tectonic plates colliding beneath the soles of my feet, something shifted and two opposing forces clashed. Courage and fear, logic and absurdity, certainty and fantasy—tearing at me from the inside.

I stood, balancing on the tenuous ground, my helplessness startling me, and I had a sudden urge to taste and smell every bit of our patch of earth. I wanted to touch all the horses, run my hand along the white fence, and pick a few blades of grass, just so the smell would linger on my fingers.

"Come on, Brynn. We don't have all day!" Dad held Jett, my jumper, by a leather lead shank. Pulling a cloth out, the one that always stayed tucked into the waist of his worn jeans, he wiped Jett's face, muttering under his breath. Probably cussing out Derek, our groom and my longtime best friend, for missing a spot.

I hurried over, my hand trembling as if the earth still shook. "Did you feel it?"

"Feel what?"

My pulse pounded in my ears. "The earthquake."

"Must've been a small one." Dad stood back, narrowing his eyes as he assessed Jett, then wiped a speck of dust off of Jett's chest.

The restless herd snorted, their nostrils flaring, their hooves pawing at the dry ground, circling at the gate like they always do when they want to come in. "They must have. They galloped all the way up from the valley."

Dad glanced at the horses. "Nothing we can do about it now." He wiped at the sweat trickling down the back of his neck into the crease of his dusty collar. "Gimme fog over this damned heat any day."

I scanned the barn and house to make sure everything stood as it should. "Should we worry about a larger one?"

"Nah. It was probably nothing. Let's just get them loaded."

I hesitated, but grabbed Jett's lead shank. The task of trailering horses made my stomach clench. It was my least favorite thing in the world: large horses weren't meant to go into small boxes. But we'd owned Jett since he was a foal in utero and he would be fine. He was always fine. I led Jett up the rubber-matted ramp into the three-horse slant-load trailer.

"One of four more shows this season," Dad said.

"Yeah," I said. We were heading to one of the biggest competitions on the West Coast—the Queen Elizabeth II Cup at Spruce Meadows in Calgary. Dad stood behind me, ignoring the long whip that leaned against the trailer. Jett, having ridden in trailers hundreds of times, mostly traveling to shows for competitions, knew we were headed off to another; his tail up, nickering, excited to be loaded, as if to tell me his fearless spirit thirsted for victory.

"Victory by Heart," I said Jett's show name aloud, rubbing the white star on his forehead with my thumb. White hairs mixed with black.

Jett sighed against my cheek.

Dad stood at the bottom of the ramp. "You're not breaking your word on me now, are you? You're going to all of them?" It was more of a statement than a question.

"I said I would." I closed my eyes, praying Dad couldn't read my thoughts. I'd done the unforgivable—chosen vet school over following in Dad's footsteps of becoming a hunter-jumper trainer—but I was still expected to do everything as if I wasn't twenty-three, a grown woman going into my fourth year of vet school, my last, and toughest, year. And even though I'd spent every day this summer on the ranch, riding horses, teaching lessons, grooming horses, mucking stalls—all to help Dad—it didn't make a difference. It still wasn't enough. It was never enough.

I laid my forehead against Jett's. *He* understood me.

"Well, I need to make sure you're still on board. Being a hunter-jumper trainer is where your future's at—it's where his future's at," he said, and gave Jett a rough pat on his rear.

I jerked my head up. "God, Dad. We've gone over this a million times. Being a vet is where my future's at."

"We can talk about it later. Once we've hit the road." Dad turned from me, the conversation over.

I had a sudden urge to yell after him, but I clipped the trailer tie to Jett's halter, adjusted the hay net, then flipped the latch to the stall divider in frustration. Whatever Dad had to say wouldn't make a difference. I would have loved to be a trainer like him, but I didn't have what it took, and school was a much safer bet as far as careers went. I was tired of my dad's constant financial struggles, and tired of the idea of being chained to them.

Our ranch, Redwood Grove Stables, extended over thirty acres of beautiful hills and valleys, down toward a large redwood forest and open space beyond. Situated in Nicasio Valley, it was about forty-five minutes north of San Francisco, and a short drive from the coast. Well, short if I drove. I always sped along the back roads, loving the exhilaration as my little hatchback hugged the curves, taking her to her limits. Mom would have a heart attack if she knew I rounded some of those corners at close to sixty miles per hour. Dad? He'd taught me how to drive like hell on wheels.

I glanced toward our home and wondered whether Mom would come say goodbye. She'd taken on a third part-time job at a retirement community in Santa Rosa, working the night shift. She had a couple more hours before her shift at the Village, a home for the mentally disabled. She also wrote for the local newspaper, a job closer to her real passion: writing a novel, the one she'd been fiddling with for years.

But we still had to load the other two horses.

"Derek! Do you have Sera?" I called, but Derek was nowhere to be seen. "Derek?" He should have been here by now. I walked toward the barn.

Just then, Derek came around the corner, his black curls barely visible above Seraphim's withers. As they neared, Seraphim held her head high, looking around, the soft skin above her eyes pinched in worry. She flung her head up and down, but Derek kept a tight hold on her lead. I could see why Dad had purchased her on his last buying trip to Europe. He'd bought her for Corinne, our best client, as an investment. Corinne owned four of the twelve horses we had in training.

At seven years old, Seraphim was not only stunning, but proving herself to be a contender for future Grand Prix competitions. Her liver chestnut coat gleamed in the morning sun like polished bronze. Her dark mane, short and glossy, fell to the right as if styled. Her sleek muscles rippled over her shoulders and hindquarters as she strutted toward us, lifting each front leg high, painstakingly, like an American Saddlebred.

I had to stifle a laugh. "She doesn't like those, does she?" I nodded at the large pillow wraps.

"God, almighty." Derek shook his head. "Did you feel that earthquake? Man, that's all I needed while trying to get this one out of her stall. She might have talent, but she's got something loose up there . . ." His eyebrows arched over his sunglasses as he circled his finger at the side of his head and mouthed *loco*.

Dad joined us, checking his watch. "C'mon, you two. Let's get this show on the road. We were supposed to be out of here an hour ago."

I lifted an eyebrow at Derek and he hid a smile. According to Dad, we were always slacking.

Forty-five minutes later, Derek, hair pasted to his forehead, grabbed the bucket of grain again, shaking it in front of Seraphim as he walked, clucking and urging her forward while I waved the long whip behind her. We still hadn't been able to load her.

"The hauler who dropped her off last month said she was a bitch to load," Derek said through clenched teeth.

"You actually fell for that? You can't listen to Freddy," Dad said. "He's said that about every horse he's dropped off over the last fifteen years: this one's crazy, that one's wild. Let's just give it another go."

I cracked the whip harder than I meant, the sound splitting the air around us like a thunderclap. Seraphim exploded up the ramp. Dad jumped to grab the stall divider, leaning his body weight against her rear. It only took a moment of Seraphim's hesitation for Dad to latch the stall divider in place. "There you are, mare. There you are," Dad talked more kindly to horses than he ever did to people.

I exhaled.

Seraphim stomped and then calmed, staring out the window between nervous grabs of hay.

"What a freakin' DQ." Derek blew air on the rope burns on his hands. Dressage Queen. Even dressage riders frequently called themselves that.

Dad took off his hat and fanned himself with it. "High maintenance, like her owner, but with a year of decent training she should be worth four times what Corinne paid. A steal at fifty grand, if you ask me." He chuckled. "Should be a hell of a ride at Spruce, too." Of course he'd love the challenge of showing her. He lived for this.

While Derek went to get Cervantes, the last of the three horses, I pulled my ponytail tighter, then took a long drink of water from the hose. I leaned forward, letting water pour over the top of my hair and the back of my neck. I turned the hose off and leaned against the outside of the cedar barn, giving our trailer a once-over. It had seen better days, with spider webs of scratches and dents marring the aluminum exterior. It would be dwarfed at Spruce Meadows by the ones other trainers had, but I was used to that. As a slant load, each horse was loaded on a forty-five-degree angle, one after the next. Dad said horses rode better that way. "Easier for them to balance on those spindly legs."

We could have bought a new trailer this year, but Dad had invested in Cervantes instead. For him, each new horse meant a renewed excitement that this would be *the one*. The one to go to the highest level—the World Cup, maybe even the Olympics. Cervantes, a young gelding he'd found in Europe when shopping for Corinne, was his newest project.

Cervantes gave us no trouble, walking into the trailer without hesitation.

"Are all the supplies in?" I asked, walking toward the side of the trailer.

"In the side compartment, where they always go," Derek said, placing his arm around me. And even though he was barely five six, he was still taller than me. With his broad shoulders, he was like a teddy bear. A big, huggable one.

"What about the Ace?" I asked.

"All in." He tightened his arm around my shoulders. "You wearing your polyester panties or something, B?"

14

"Whatever." I gave his shoulder a playful punch, then I smoothed my hand over my forehead, consciously relaxing the furrows. "Too bad you can't come," I said to him, careful not to let Dad hear. Derek dreamed of going to Spruce Meadows, of becoming a trainer, though he'd never tell Dad that.

"No biggie. Someone's gotta take care of things back here. Besides, Bill would probably throw a fit if I went for that long." Bill was Derek's boyfriend.

I gave him a quick hug. "I promise to post updates." Turning toward the cab of the truck, I went over my checklist. But before I finished, the familiar scent of white musk filled the air.

"Have you forgotten something?" Mom's voice came from around the side of the trailer. Her dark blonde hair, several shades darker than mine, didn't have a wisp out of place—every strand pulled back into a tight chignon. She looked like a teenager, lost in the starchiness of her uniform.

She held out a paper bag. "I had hoped to pack more of a lunch for you, but forgot it was already Saturday." The shadows under her eyes seemed deeper and darker than they had last week.

"Mom, you made it!" I leaned in to embrace her. My mouth watered at the smell of sandwiches.

"I bet you two didn't even bother to grab breakfast." She ran her hand down the back of my hair, touching her nose to mine.

She was right, of course.

Dad came over and took the bag. "We'll sure make good use of these, huh, partner?" He winked at me.

Mom picked at a flake of shavings clinging to the front of his shirt. "Luke, I'm sorry I can't go." She studied her white running shoes. I knew Dad had hoped she would change her mind and come watch us compete. But how could she? Not only was she working three jobs to help support Redwood Grove Stables' up-and-down income, but she'd always been afraid of the horses. Of Dad and I competing. I peered down at the brick pavers, reminded of how important it was to her for me to finish vet school. For me to have an income outside of show jumping. And I wanted nothing more than to see her happy.

"It is what it is." Dad turned her away from Derek and me. "I have a good feeling. I know I'll win, and then we can head up to that place Julia told us about last month. Mendocino, was it?" He tilted her chin up with his finger.

Mom nodded, avoiding his gaze.

Seraphim whinnied and gave a sharp kick, rocking the trailer.

"We better get on the road to settle them," Dad said, his lips brushing hers. Mom pulled him closer.

"Please stay."

"Amelia. Let's not go over this again. This is what I do."

Mom's hand clung to his shirt. I felt for her. I really did. She didn't understand horses and was terrified something would happen to Dad and me, constantly reminding us of Christopher Reeve. She'd grown up on the East Coast, their families socializing in the same circles. They had been good friends, and she'd been there— had seen his accident happen. She wouldn't allow Dad to tell her that that had been a freak accident. That Christopher had been an amateur competing in a cross-country event—a much different sport than show jumping.

"All right, Brynn. Time to go," Dad ushered me toward the truck, his forehead even more creased than before. "Derek, call me with any questions." Dad placed his hands on Derek's shoulders. "I trust you'll take care of things, son."

"Yessir." Derek clicked the heels of his paddock boots and saluted.

We were almost to the truck when Mom caught up to us. "Luke!"

Dad turned back.

Mom reached her arm out to him, then let it drop. "Go show them how it's done."

2

*A*lmost five o'clock.

We'd been driving since eleven in the morning. I couldn't wait to stretch my legs. I closed my equine anatomy book and looked at the GPS for the hundredth time. We were somewhere past Eugene, Oregon. After Oregon we'd go north to Washington, then a short skip through Idaho, and finally across the border into Alberta: thirteen hundred miles in all. Green fields stretched into mountains in the distance.

I glanced over at Dad. His jaw was set in his typical determined fashion as he checked the side mirrors of our Dodge pickup. His slate-blue eyes, so much like mine, narrowed as he concentrated on the road. And even though years spent outdoors in the sun had aged him, his energy and joy for the horses made him seem younger than fifty-five. Luke Seymour, a top hunter-jumper trainer on the West Coast, was a force to be reckoned with, but today he was just my dad—and this would be one of the last times I would drive to Spruce Meadows with him.

I'd have to tell him soon.

The afternoon shadow on his jaw was starting to show, making me want to reach out and touch it, like I used to as a kid. I had loved the sensation of that rough stubble against my cheek as he'd tickle me and throw me in the air.

He never talked much, but when he did, people listened. And he was always thinking, it seemed. I doubt he ever had a spare moment of time to not think—about shows, clients, the farrier, the vet, or about the hay. There were always worries about hay. Its supply. The quality. Rain during harvest. Rain during delivery.

I knew this drive well, having done it every summer for the last ten years. We made pit stops along the way to check on the horses, to give them fresh water, let their legs rest, and then we'd be on the road again. At night we'd sleep in the trailer, in small sleeping quarters built into the gooseneck. Dad said we saved money and time, which there never seemed to be enough of.

Dad looked over at me. "You wanna drive?"

I was too surprised to answer right away. "Sure. We can switch." Dad usually drove the entire way, although the last couple of summers he had let me take the wheel for a spell. "But don't do that thing you always do," I said.

"What thing?"

"You know, watching my every move. Your knuckles get all white and your jaw clenches and then that vein at the side of your neck looks like it'll pop."

Dad wrinkled his forehead, but then his face softened. "I promise I'll be good."

Over my lifetime, we'd probably spent close to six hundred hours in this truck together, driving all over the western United States and Canada interstate highways, pulling our trailer full of jumpers.

For this trip, Dad had hooked up a camera in the trailer. "Amazing technology," he'd said, tapping the monitor. "Now we can watch the horses in the back while traveling in the front. Isn't this great?" He'd laughed and slapped me on the back. On these trips he treated me like a partner, and I liked that.

I'd checked that monitor over a hundred times in the last six hours, gazing at the horses in the trailer:

Jett, Seraphim, and Cervantes. Black, chestnut, and gray. Jett, my baby, always calm and wise. Seraphim, the anxiety freak, who should really be on the equine equivalent of Ritalin, and Cervantes, more of a teenager than I'd ever been—bucking, tearing up the paddock whenever he was turned out.

Most of the time they just munched on the hay hanging in their hay nets. Sometimes they dozed, their heads bobbing with the rhythm of the ride. At one point I laughed aloud, imagining them as little Breyer horses in my plastic trailer that still stood on the shelf in my bedroom. As a child I'd zoomed that plastic truck and trailer around the house with those horses in the back. A familiar scene playing itself out again, one I had done hundreds of times in my imaginary world.

The sun started to set, reflecting from the side mirror straight into my eyes. I pulled my sunglasses down.

"If I haven't told you, I'm glad you're coming." Dad straightened his back as he leaned toward the steering wheel, his hands gripping it with pure excitement. "This is it, Brynn. Cervantes . . . *he's* it. He's the horse of my dreams and I want you to be there. To see us jump. It'll be something, all right. I can't believe he was passed up by all those trainers in Europe." He chuckled. "I tell you, those Belgians don't know a good horse if it was to kick them in the teeth. You watch, with a more forward seat and a lighter hand he'll jump a meter-sixty. Just like he was born to."

Yes. But would he do it in a stadium in front of sixty thousand spectators?

But I smiled and nodded, dutifully, as I'd always done. Dad counted on that first-place prize, his share amounting to nearly $70,000. If Dad did well at this show, the winnings would pay for Cervantes, his shipping from Europe, and most importantly, he'd attract more clients for our training program. Those had been slower to come than he'd hoped.

"Are you excited?" Dad asked.

"That's a rhetorical question." I gazed out at the panoramic view, much greener here this time of year than back home, the fields subdivided into neat rectangular and square shapes.

"But?" Dad pressed.

How was I supposed to explain that I didn't think I'd ever be good enough? And not only that: just like the breeding of a horse limits him, my petite frame would always limit me. At five four and a half, and at just over a hundred pounds, I wasn't strong enough to control Jett, who usually pulled me through the jumps. And there was Mom's fear of me falling, getting hurt, like Christopher Reeve. I knew how terrified she was and had wanted to make her happy. Make her proud of me by going to school.

Maybe I could tell him now? I glanced over at Dad, but he looked lost in thought again. Dad ran his hand through his hair, dislodging a piece of hay that flitted to his shoulder. It reminded me how much I longed for thick hair like his. I placed my hand up to the back of my head and touched my ponytail, pin straight, hanging halfway down my back. Together our heads were like the ebony and ivory of a chessboard.

"I thought you'd be more excited. This is The Queen Elizabeth Cup." He drummed his fingers on the steering wheel. "I know, I know. You'll be jumping in the lower classes, so it's not that big a deal, but it's what you both need. Practice for the Gold Cup."

The Gold Cup. Grand prize: a million dollars. The winner took home a third of the pot, with the rest split among the rest of the top twelve riders. I hadn't a chance in the world to qualify for it, never mind win. It was the highest level of competition on the West Coast. The Gold Cup was Dad's dream. And if that wasn't enough, Dad dreamed of both of us competing at the Olympics. He dreamed of us on the same team: father and daughter, riding for the gold— show jumping was one of only two events in the Olympics in which men and women competed directly against each other. We'd talked about it ever since I could walk, but it was just a silly little dream. Not that I would ever say that in front of Dad. He seriously believed we'd be like the famous Canadian Ian Millar and his kids, or the Belgian Ludo Phillipaerts, who rode with his sons.

What were the odds? Something like one in ten million? But I wasn't going to be the one to ruin that dream for him—at least not yet. I had to keep up an act. Until after this trip. That's when I'd tell him I was quitting riding.

The radio crackled. I searched for a station, finally giving up and turning it completely off.

Dad started in again. "You know, Jett can move up to be a Gold Cup horse, but it's not going to be easy since he doesn't have the raw scope."

Yes. The famous all-inclusive term *scope* that jumper trainers, and every wannabe trainer, used. Scope, defined as natural talent, physical capability, a horse's conformation and spirit in one. His potential. A small word that encompassed so much. Not unlike the word love.

"I know." I folded my feet up on the seat and tore at the threads hanging off the bottom of my worn jeans, letting the string bite into my finger as I wrapped it tighter and tighter. I wished he wouldn't bring up scope. Jett was home-bred and we still weren't sure whether he had enough of it. Plus, he barely reached sixteen hands, which was small for a jumper.

As if reading my mind my dad interjected, "Don't worry. With more hard work and practice, you'll get there." He reached over and patted my knee.

I sighed. "I know, Dad. I know."

I checked the camera. The horses had nodded off. I closed my eyes for a moment and rested my head on the back of the seat, my mind swirling with all the things I really wanted to say—and all the things I never could.

The truck lurched. Then again. My stomach jolted to my throat. We heard a loud bang, and the truck swerved.

"What was that?" I bolted upright, peering over at Dad in the dim light. He surveyed the traffic through his side mirrors. A car passed, then slowed and honked. The driver yelled, waving his arm about. I couldn't make out what he was saying. I looked back to the video monitor. The darkness made it harder to see what the monitor displayed.

Something wasn't right. I saw Seraphim shake her head, wrestling it up. Was she irritated at the lead rope attached to her halter? She started kicking, her body jerking left and right, up and down. The other two horses angled their bodies away from Seraphim, who stood in between them, turning their heads to look at her, as if trying to figure out what was going on. I leaned forward, scrutinizing the small monitor.

"What is it?" Dad asked.

"Not sure. Seraphim's freaking out at something."

"The truck's swerving. Doesn't feel right."

I felt another lurch. "She seems to be getting worse," I said. With that, her kicking jerked and rocked the whole truck. Even at fifty-five miles per hour, I was aware of the fragility of the truck and trailer, knowing that a panicked thirteen-hundred-pound horse could do a lot of damage to the trailer, and to the horses in it with her.

Another car passed, this time slowing to drive next to us. The woman in the passenger seat waved her hand, pointing wildly to the back of the trailer. The kids in the backseat were glued to the rear window, staring at something.

I looked more closely at the monitor.

"I think the back trailer door is open," I said, practically in a whisper.

Dad peered ahead. "I don't see a rest stop anywhere."

I sat up onto my knees, staring out the back window, as if I could do something.

He merged into the far-right lane, slowing down. We passed a sign that read the rest stop was eight miles away. Too far. Much too far.

"I'll have to pull over," he said, and although his voice was calm, I heard it waver.

I started to unbuckle, my heart beating loud, my breath shallow.

"Now don't you dare go into that trailer, Brynn. We'll just stop to settle her down."

I nodded, biting my cuticles.

"And stay away from the freeway, you hear?"

I nodded again.

Dad slowed the truck, the trailer shook with Seraphim's kicking. A large truck zipped by, rattling us even more.

Even before the truck stopped, I was out running. "It's all right, Sera, it's all right," I called. I ran around the trailer to the back, and even before I got there I saw the dented ramp, off the hinges, the trailer door unlatched swinging in the gusts created by the passing trucks. Dad joined me, grabbing the ramp, eyeing the door, trying desperately to shut it.

He eyed the broken latch. "How the hell did this happen?"

A large truck's horn blared as it passed, making me jump. I felt light-headed. I hadn't double-checked the latch. I was supposed to have double-checked the latch. I had been distracted by my own thoughts.

Seraphim kicked even harder.

"We have to calm her." Dad ran along the freeway to the trailer window. "Stay to the side!"

I ran after him. Cars and trucks whizzed by less than five feet from us. Dad climbed on top of the wheel to reach the alum-window gate. Seraphim flung her head every which way, kicking and rearing. A chunk of green froth from her mouth fell on my arm.

"Can we get her out?" I asked.

"Not possible. Where would we put Cervantes?"

"I could hold him while you unload her."

Dad shook his head. "She's too far gone. We couldn't control her. And if she ran onto the freeway . . ." He didn't need to explain. Cars honked, the sound wailing past me. I turned to look behind us just as something flew toward me. I ducked my head but not before a small razor-like rock stung my cheek.

I reached up and felt the warmth of blood on my fingers.

"Brynn! You all right?" Dad was at my side, peering at my face. "We've gotta get off this road!" He pulled me behind the trailer and examined the cut closer, and for that moment I felt safe with his hands on me.

"It's okay, it doesn't hurt," I said. Dad gave me a questioning look, but turned toward Seraphim's window.

"Go grab the Ace," Dad said, then turned to talk to Seraphim in a soothing voice. I ran to get our medical supplies and to fill the syringe with the tranquilizer. We'd need to administer it intravenously if we wanted the effects to kick in sometime in the next fifteen minutes. A panicking horse rarely calmed down until they sensed safety, and Seraphim was overtaken by fear. My fingers shook, and I accidentally stabbed myself with the needle. I sucked on the blood from my finger, telling myself to calm down. I had done plenty of injections over the years, and especially this past year in school. I managed to fill the syringe, then tapped the side to get the air bubbles out.

"How are we going to give it to her? We can't get at her when she's panicking like this. We'll never hold her still enough to find a vein." My voice, unnaturally high, barely rose above the screaming traffic.

"We don't have a choice." Dad kept his voice low. Beads of sweat had formed on his upper lip. I licked my own lips, trying to get the dryness out of my mouth.

"Keep calm, Brynn. Here's what we're gonna do." He grabbed my shoulder, making me face him. "You'll have to help me keep Cervantes from rushing out of the trailer when we undo the back tailgate holding him in. Then I'll go in and try to give her the shot."

I agreed, even though I knew that the chance of Dad hitting a vein when Seraphim was rearing was close to nil.

Dad placed his hand on the tailgate bar. "You ready?"

I wasn't, but I didn't have a choice. With my right hand I felt in my back pocket for the capped syringe.

~

Seraphim was wild with anxiety and fear. Her eyes rolled back in her head, showing her whites like some crazed beast out of a horror movie. She tried to lunge upward but her head, held down by the tie, was contained.

We unlatched the tailgate and instinctively Cervantes pulled back. Dad gave him a pat on his haunches while I held the door slightly closed, trying to prevent him from bolting out of the trailer.

My eyes adjusted to the dimness inside. Jett pawed the ground, but at least he wasn't panicking yet. His black hair shone in the receding light, his tail swished. Seraphim, chestnut coat lathered in her own froth, pawed and kicked. White foam stuck to the roof and sides of the trailer.

Seraphim let out an earsplitting squeal.

I reached up to cover my ears, letting the trailer door go.

It slammed, making Cervantes jump. Terror gripped me, my breath caught in my throat, my lungs burned for air. I grabbed the door. Seraphim had managed to break the snap that attached the rope to the halter. Sensing freedom, she reared as high as she could in the confines of the trailer. As she came down, her foot caught on the stall divider. A spray of red blotted out everything around her. She gave out another piercing squeal, trying to rear again. Blood splattered Cervantes's gray-white coat. My knees buckled.

My eyes sought out Jett; he was calm, almost tranquil. He turned his head toward me, his black eyes met mine, and for a moment I felt his strength, and a fleeting sense of serenity washed over me.

"Okay, Brynn. Latch that door open. You need to be near his head, keep him calm, and hold him in. Cervantes will be fine. Won't you, boy?" Dad placed a hand on Cervantes's haunches. I grappled with the steel clasp, but it kept slipping through my uncooperative fingers. What should have taken me seconds seemed to take minutes. By the time I finished, Dad had undone the back safety bar and had pushed Cervantes's hind end over so that he could get closer to Seraphim. Cervantes's haunches scooted partway down the ramp.

"Dad! The syringe!"

Dad paused, and I reached up to hand it to him. He held it in his teeth, poised, as if carrying a machete through rough waters. Cervantes started pulling back. I worried he'd pull too hard. Every horse person had heard this kind of horror story. Never tie a horse in a way that won't give when the horse pulls back. Without give, the horse can jerk back so hard it might break his neck.

Seraphim bucked and reared, as if unaware of her injury. Dad squeezed between Cervantes and her, wiping away the lather on her neck. Cervantes's fear escalated. He pawed at the floor, pushing his rear toward the ramp, scooting his hind legs under to get more leverage on his halter. Millions of years of instinct weren't easy to override, and if one horse panicked, the rest could too. Evolution had given herbivores one main mechanism to protect themselves and their herds from predators: agility and speed. In fight-or-flight situations, it was almost always flight. Seraphim, one of his herd mates, was panicked. Cervantes had to escape.

Cervantes twisted his body to the left, straining against his tie, trying to step backward out of the trailer. I moved closer to his head, trying to grab his halter.

"Keep him calm!" Dad yelled, but I didn't know how. I pushed on Cervantes's side. He resisted me, stepping another foot out of the trailer. The more I pushed, the more he leaned all of his fourteen hundred pounds against me. I did the only thing I could do: I nudged his flank, the most sensitive area between his belly and hind leg. His skin twitched, sending a ripple from haunches to front, and he moved over to the right. Almost as soon as he did, he took two quick steps back, pushing me to the edge of the ramp. The trailer continued to pitch violently, throwing me off balance.

"Dad!"

"I can't get at her. She won't hold still!"

"I'll move Cervantes out."

"Stick with the plan. I've got this."

But I was already running to grab a lead rope from the storage compartment.

"There, there, Cervantes," I spoke in a calm, soothing voice, balancing myself as the trailer rocked. Horses tended to pick up on your energy, and mine was as out of whack as it could get. Not much horse whispering I could do now.

"If I just keep repeating these words over and over, maybe we'll calm down, huh buddy?" I attached the lead rope to Cervantes's halter, then unhooked him from the trailer. He sensed freedom: he lunged back, stepping off the side of the ramp, knocking me back onto the hard asphalt of the freeway shoulder. The sudden pain seared my spine. My head hit and bounced. Spots blurred my vision. Cervantes pulled backward, my hand tightening on the lead rope instinctively. My shoulder felt like it would tear out of its socket, my hand burning, my finger twisting in an impossible direction, but I held on. I checked the back of my head with my free hand. No blood, thank God.

I managed to get up to my hands and knees, clutching the rope in between my raw fingers. My only thought was to keep him off the freeway.

All of a sudden, the rope jerked me up. Cervantes stood on hind legs, rearing, about to come straight down on top of me.

3

*C*ervantes's hooves struck the asphalt inches from my chest. I ducked and rolled, and let go of the rope. I gaped at the huge mass of animal flesh above me, the darkening blue behind him outlining his gray body, the blood on his coat bright and unreal. For a split second our eyes met, and I thought maybe he'd stay. Then he turned and galloped like a wild stallion, hooves pounding past me, silver tail flying through the air.

"No!" I screamed. But he ran onto the highway.

Tires squealed, metal crashed.

I sat up, wanting to run after him, but all I saw was a flash of white as he disappeared.

I rushed back into the trailer. Dad had unhooked the stall divider to grab Seraphim's head. She reared.

"Shut the doors!" Dad yelled.

I grabbed one of the open doors, prying the metal hook loose. A thud resounded inside the trailer. Seraphim galloped past me, a copper smear. The syringe fell from her neck to my feet.

"Sera!" I ran along the shoulder after her, but knew there was no way I could catch up, so I turned back.

At the entrance to the trailer I stopped. Dad lay on the ground, Jett looming, a dark shadow in the back. Seraphim must have come down on him, just as Cervantes had almost done to me.

"Dad!" I threw myself next to him. The smell of blood, shavings, and manure gagged me as I knelt on the black rubber mat, my throat closing up. Dad stared up at the ceiling as he wheezed for air.

"Daddy . . ." I cradled his head in my arms. His eyes locked with mine, his hand reached toward me. He gulped at the air, his breath rattling in his lungs, an eerie gargling sound in his throat.

"Don't talk." I placed my hand on his cheek, touching that stubble I had wanted to touch just hours before.

"Brynn . . ." He gasped another breath.

I dabbed at the trickle of blood from the corner of his mouth, sticky and hot on my fingers, wiping it off on my jeans, looking for the cloth he always carried. "It's going to be all right," I said, the only words I could think of.

Dad's fingers squeezed around mine. He drank the air in jagged gasps.

"Oh, Daddy, hold on—" I moved to stand, to get my phone, but his fingers closed tighter around mine.

"Don't go . . ." His eyes met mine. "Please . . ."

I squatted again as a car pulled up behind us.

"Promise me, if anything happens, you must take care of the horses, the ranch . . ." He was whispering now, and I could barely understand him, the trailer now still, no longer rocking from the traffic, the headlights splitting the darkness.

"Let me get help—" I tried to stand, but his words stopped me.

"You have to do this—for Mom—for everything we've built . . ."

His hand loosened from around my fingers.

I squeezed my eyes shut, wanting everything to go back to normal. For his rough hands to slap me on the back as he laughed at the way a horse frolicked in pasture; for his harsh look to remind me that I'd forgotten to put away the saddle; for his arm around my shoulders when I rode a great round.

"Promise me . . ."

And I would have promised him anything at that moment. The words rushed out, "Yes, Daddy. Yes. But you have to help me. I can't do it alone."

His breath stopped, then started again. And that's when I knew I was losing him. I began CPR, but couldn't remember how many breaths I should be giving to how many pumps on his chest. I managed to do a slow breath, followed by three pumps. His eyes glazed over, the blood at his mouth as black as Jett's coat.

"No, Daddy," I whispered, tears dripping onto his face as I rocked his limp body in my arms. "No!"

But he didn't respond.

I heard his last breath escape him, like his soul leaving.

It slipped right through my hands.

4

*D*r. Ian Finlay—Uncle Ian to me—a family friend and equine vet, drove up with Derek to get me from the hospital. I spent the night tossing and turning on the unfamiliar pillows and sheets of the motel room, visions of Dad's calloused fingers clutching mine, me screaming, Seraphim running, the needle at my feet.

I buried my head, pushing the pillow over my head, trying to block the visions out, trying to forget Uncle Ian's words, "Cervantes—he didn't make it, Lassie."

Cervantes hadn't made it. Dad's horse. His new prospect. His soon-to-be superstar. "No one else was hurt," Uncle Ian said, holding me to him.

I'd stared at him, not comprehending.

"This is good news, ay? Good news . . . no one else was hurt . . ."

His Scottish burr had trailed off as he held me by my shoulders, his hooded eyes staring deep into mine. The neon motel sign reflected off his glasses, reminding me of the ambulance siren.

The next morning, I tried to block it all, refusing to talk about any of it. Maybe after I got home I'd think of a way to handle it.

Uncle Ian drove us home while Derek stayed in Oregon, helping with the search for Seraphim. She'd managed to jump a fence farther up along the highway, and they hadn't been able to track her yet. Uncle Ian and I barely exchanged two words on the drive back to the Bay Area. He respected my space and I respected his in return. He and Dad had been best friends for years. I knew he was coping with his own grief.

But what I dreaded most was seeing Mom.

I wasn't sure how I would face her. My eyes blurred at the thought of her. The police had notified her of the accident the night before, but I hadn't been able to speak to her on the phone. My voice had seized up. This was her biggest nightmare, and now it had come true. As we got closer to home, I pulled at the bits of skin on my cuticles, digging deeper and deeper, until they bled.

Uncle Ian turned into our circular drive, which led around a meticulously planned rock garden full of native grasses and flowers, one Aunt Julia, Uncle Ian's wife, had helped design when my parents had first built the house. Built of California cedar and accented with masonry, the house was set back about two hundred feet from the road that lead toward Devon Creek.

Uncle Ian shut off the engine. Silence filled the pickup cab, louder than the radio that had just been on. The keys jangled, then his hand rested on my knee. He gave it a squeeze, then moved to open the door. I was thankful for that small amount of physical contact. I felt empty and alone. What would I tell Mom? How could I ever tell her I hadn't double-checked the latch? Dad would still be alive if it hadn't been for my carelessness.

As I stepped into the sun, the sound of the waterfall, cascading through the rock garden into the small koi pond, greeted me—a sound that normally served to soothe me and remind me I was home. But today I trudged up the stone steps, toward the smoky-glass front door, as if headed to an inquisition.

The house blended with the valley, contemporary, yet natural, both inside and out. It was older now, but still had grace. Mom sat on the worn sage-colored couch in the living room, bent over, her head in her lap. Although it was midafternoon, inside it was dim and she looked minute with the large vaulted ceiling looming above her. Subira, our twelve-year-old Irish Setter, lay at Mom's feet. The tip of her tail and brow lifted up at me in greeting, but she showed no other signs of affection, almost as if she understood what had happened and was already in mourning.

Aunt Julia greeted us. "Brynn, dear." She came forward and kissed my cheek, embracing me, her nose red, her eyes puffy. "I'm so, so truly sorry."

I squeezed my eyes shut, holding my tears in. Once I'd regained control I looked at Mom. I forced myself to move as softly as I could across the pine floor, afraid that she would startle, like a wild horse. I stopped at the sheepskin rug in front of the couch and fell to my knees, wrapping my arms around her.

Mom looked up, her eyes red-rimmed, the tears accentuating the lines around her eyes. The fatigue had been replaced by a pain that seemed to run as deep as her soul.

"Brynn. Oh God, Brynn." She moaned, gasping as if in pain. "God, no! Brynn, bring him back, Brynn!" She sobbed, her arms around me in a fierce grip, her pain squeezing my heart like a fist. I wished I could turn back the clock. I wished I had checked the latch. I wished I could make Dad come back. But I couldn't do any of those things. The only thing I knew, right then, was that I would never live a day and not feel this pain. I would never forgive myself as long as I lived.

"Good news!"

Sheriff Malcolm's voice resounded in my ear. My heart skipped a beat, and I wondered for a moment whether he would tell me it was all a mistake—that Dad was alive and well, and on his way home.

"A local dairy farmer found your horse, ma'am," he said. "The ol' guy saw the eleven o'clock news story last night. He spotted him in his field! Whatcha make of that?"

Two days since the accident. All I remembered of Sheriff Malcolm was his peppermint breath, his tan-colored shirt with the coffee stain near the front pocket, and the missing button near his belt as he questioned me that night. Now I stood in the kitchen, staring out at the milky gray landscape that concealed the barn and valley below. I held the phone in one hand, gripping the windowsill with the other. His voice didn't belong here. Dad belonged here. We should be planning the day together, schooling the horses, showing together, celebrating his and Cervantes's win.

"Sure as the mornin' sun, I tell you, ol' guy was eatin' his eggs, looked out his kitchen window, and there he was."

"She . . . ," I said, under my breath. "Seraphim." But he didn't hear me, rambling on.

I wondered what the dairy farmer had thought, seeing a remarkable mare—a show jumper—standing in cow manure, her chestnut hair masking the rust-colored blood, eating hay right alongside his heifers.

I spent the day wandering through the empty rooms of the house, waiting for Derek to come home with Jett and Seraphim. I checked on Mom but she'd stayed in bed all afternoon, sleeping fitfully. I was glad that Uncle Ian had left a sedative for her. Derek told me they had to tranquilize Seraphim to get her into the trailer, but that Jett never panicked.

He told me they'd found the latch on the back door broken off. "They said it snapped. Too much rust," Derek had said quietly on the phone. I didn't respond, not believing. I should have checked the latch and I didn't. I got caught up in other things. How could I ever make a good vet? How could anyone ever trust me again?

"Brynn, latches break. Horses freak out. It's just the nature of working with them . . ." I didn't even listen to the rest.

In the sitting room I ran my finger along the spines of Dad's books. I picked up and flipped through the last horse magazine he'd read, but Dad's sweater, the one he'd tossed across the back of his favorite chair just the night before we'd left for Spruce Meadows, beckoned me. I sat, curling my toes into the worn leather of the chair, and even though the fog had burned off and outside the temperature had reached into the seventies, I laid the sweater over my shoulders, the wool scratchy around my neck. It smelled of leather and sweat and hay. I imagined Dad walking in and wrapping his arms around me, telling me everything would be all right.

The sound of a diesel truck startled me from an uncomfortable dream. I'd dozed off and now the walnut clock chimed eight. I glanced out the window. The sun hung low above the Pacific. The truck and trailer crawled to a stop in front of the barn.

"Come here," Derek said as I practically ran toward him. We hugged for a long time. His fleece would have probably absorbed many tears, if I had cried—but I didn't. Empty, I breathed against the terrible tightness pressing down on my chest.

"I'm going to miss him so much," I managed to choke out.

"Me too, B. Me too."

Derek was the closest thing I had to a brother. He'd been working for my dad since he was eighteen, when I'd met him at a Southern California horse show. Derek's father was in the Air Force, and Derek had lived a nomadic life, moving every couple of years, sometimes more frequently. His father, who had never accepted his son as gay, expected Derek to attend West Point. Problem was, Derek wanted to be a horse trainer. Derek had lost his family, but he'd gained another one in ours.

I breathed in Derek's familiar scent, citrus mixed with a tinge of patchouli. Then I pulled away from him, rubbing my face with my palms, composing myself. "How's Bill?"

"Good. He'll be here for the funeral, of course. Wants to know if there's anything he can do."

"Right . . ." As if anyone could do anything. I walked around to the back of the trailer.

I stopped. Frozen.

The trailer doors loomed toward me.

"Derek—" I nearly doubled over as I grabbed onto his thick arm.

"You head on up to the house," Derek said, holding me.

I walked back on rubber legs, but not fast enough. I stooped near the pink and purple hydrangea, grasping at my knees as I doubled over, dry-heaving before my stomach settled.

5

$\mathcal{S}$aturday, 11:00 a.m. Six days since Dad's death. The day of the Queen Elizabeth II Cup at Spruce Meadows. The day Dad was supposed to have been winning on Cervantes. From the podium, I looked out at the wooden pews of the small white stucco Catholic church, minutes up the road from our house. I was chosen to give the eulogy, God knows why. Shouldn't it have been someone else? Someone with more experience at this sort of thing?

I tugged at the mid-length hem of the simple gabardine black dress I'd rushed to buy yesterday. Black looked terrible on me, washing out my pale eyes and complexion, but I had nothing else that was appropriate, my closet full of sweatshirts and polos and jeans. I hated wearing dresses. They showed off my bony knees and my twig-like legs. I wore my hair in a simple bun, which hung low at the nape of my neck. I lifted my hand to play with the gold horseshoe pendant at my throat. Dad had given it to me on my sixteenth birthday.

Mom sat in the front pew, in a black pantsuit, a string of pearls adorning her neck, the bones of her clavicles prominent, her eyes red-rimmed and puffy. The two of us, drifting in a daze like lost souls, waiting for someone or something to step in to take charge. I stared at all the expectant faces and wished I was anywhere but here.

"Dear friends . . ." My throat constricted, and only a grunt of sorts reached the small microphone positioned close to my mouth. I clutched the podium, steadying myself as the smell of incense, mothballs, and perfume hit me.

Derek gestured for me to continue. Then Uncle Ian stood and walked toward me.

He covered the microphone. "You okay, Lassie?" I stared at his plaid tie, his shock of white-gray hair. "I got this. You go on and grab a seat."

The church was full. Most of our small Devon Creek community were there, along with our eight clients. Corinne and her two daughters, but not her husband. Helena, my favorite, with her daughter, Payton, resting her head on Helena's shoulder, and her husband, who kept sneaking his phone out of his pocket, likely checking the 49ers game. Petite Mai, second-generation Japanese American, a recent divorcée, and her daughter Lani, who reminded me of me when I was her age, her nose always in a book. Our token male rider, Stuart, a medical doctor who decided to take up riding at the age of fifty but had time to ride only once a week, though he owned two horses. And the three little peas, as Dad had called them, Pam, Patty, and Peggy. I could count on them every Tuesday to come brush their horses. Always together, driven to our farm by their retirement-home driver.

"Luke was a husband, a father, and a dear friend," Uncle Ian's voice echoed through the church. I gripped the seat of the pew. "He was like a billie to me. A brother. Able and kind . . ." Uncle Ian cleared his throat, then continued, his words floating away with the dust motes.

I peered at the pew next to us, my gaze stopping at the man sitting in the front row next to Aunt Julia, holding her hand. His brown hair fell below his ears, and his slightly crooked nose and unshaved jaw gave him a roughened look, as if he were trying to downplay the chiseled cheekbones and fine jaw structure. His eyes, light green and yellow, like peridot and amber, glinted beneath a thick brow that extended straight across then arched, as if he were pondering something.

His eyes met mine, and although I wanted to look away, I

couldn't. I inhaled, tilting my head down. A sense of connectedness, understanding, washed over me.

Uncle Ian's voice interrupted my thoughts. "Luke will live in all of our minds. Ay, that he will."

The priest said, "Amen." The people responded, then silence filled the church. Everyone bowed their heads. Uncle Ian made his way down. I searched Mom's face for a sign of emotion, but she gave me no encouragement, no emotional support. I wanted her to reach out to me. To touch me. To say it was going to be all right. I reached over and held her hand, but it was limp. Lifeless.

The mass continued. I couldn't focus on anything, my mind wandering to a million places. A stream of light filtered through the stained glass windows, lighting up a statue of Mary. Her head tilted toward a figure of a boy Jesus. Mary watched her son die, with dignity and strength—I had to muster strength too. But how could I? I balled my fists, shut my eyes.

The church was old and I hadn't been here in years. As a child I couldn't wait for church to end. I had wanted nothing more than to run outside to play with my ponies.

In a way, nothing had changed.

After the burial, I went down to the barn to see Jett. It was a short hello. I fed him a couple of carrots; he nudged my pocket for more. I stood, stroking his neck while he ate his hay. I looked in on each of the thirteen horses, the way Dad had done every day he was home— morning, afternoon, and a late-night check. It's always about the horses, he'd said. When I reached Seraphim's stall, I paused. Her stall was dark and I had to peer in to make out her shadow. She stood with her back toward me, her tail hanging low, and if she'd been a dog she might have tucked it between her legs. Her front leg had sustained serious injuries and Uncle Ian predicted that she'd be on stall rest for at least two months.

Uncle Ian came twice a day to change her bandages, and the last time I'd seen him at the barn, he even hinted for me to help. Said it would be nothing more than changing the bandages, monitoring the wound. But it wasn't about the injuries, and I wished he understood that it had nothing to do with blood—I just couldn't bring myself to be with her. I closed my eyes for a moment, and the earth seemed to sway. Seraphim turned, eyeing me, beckoning me to go to her, her eyes soft, as if asking for forgiveness. But I turned and walked out of the barn and up the hill to the house.

Dozens of people milled about as I entered the foyer. I ducked into the kitchen where Derek was busy with Bill setting out the dishes people had brought, and handing out drinks. I poured a glass of wine and waded through the crowd, avoiding eye contact. Aunt Julia and Uncle Ian came over as soon as they saw me.

"How are you, my dear?" Aunt Julia asked. "You look like you've lost weight." She held me at arm's length, tsk-tsking at me as she ran her hands down my back.

"It's just the dress." I forced a smile.

"I'll stop by with a casserole tomorrow. Ian, we need to come over tomorrow."

"We'll be fine. There's bound to be plenty of leftovers."

"We looked for you earlier but couldn't find you. I wanted to introduce you to Jason Lander—a good family friend and someone close to your dad. He was sitting next to me at the funeral."

The mystery man. "I was down at the barn . . ." I wiped at the condensation that had collected on my glass of wine, trying to remember if Dad had ever mentioned him, but couldn't. Jason Lander's name sounded familiar though.

"Aye, your dad and him go years back. He was a bit of a project back then. Might you have met him when you were a wee lass? Spruce Meadows, was it? Julia, do you remember?"

Aunt Julia nodded her head. "Yes, I think that was it."

"He's a good lad. A great rider too. One of the best. Won the

World Cup. Twice. The youngest ever to do so. Such a shame he's not showing anymore. Gone to India or some such thing."

I ran a finger over the rough skin of my cuticles. Of course! *The* Jason Lander. I hadn't heard much about him lately, and I still couldn't recall meeting him. "What is he doing now?"

"Some yoga thing. A waste of good talent, if you ask me. Don't know why he'd give it up."

"Well, it doesn't surprise me, with his history and all," Aunt Julia said, but Uncle Ian shook his head slightly and she said no more.

We all got quiet then, and I glanced down at my feet, trying to think of an excuse to escape, telling them I needed to grab some food. That satisfied Aunt Julia.

I lost myself in the crowd, keeping my gaze down, trying to keep any conversations at bay. I realized that even though we had many friends, none were family. Mom was an only child; her parents still lived in Manhattan. I'd never met them. I'd never met any of my family beyond my parents. My grandparents on both sides had been against the marriage, the families as different as Icelandic ponies and Arabians. Mom's had never quite disowned her, just acted like it, trying to gain her back through manipulation and money.

Mom's dowry was spent on this land, the building of our home, and Redwood Grove Stables. Stella and Mike Kowalski, her parents, made it a point to never visit us, even though my grandfather flew regularly to San Francisco from New York on business. After one or two visits with me as a baby to the East Coast, Mom had refused to give into their "scare tactics," as she'd called them, and remained in California. "Let them live their bitter lives alone," I'd heard Mom say to Dad one night. "I'm tired of the bullying. About us, religion, horses, politics, everything. I married you, a horse trainer, not the Wall Street tycoon they wanted, but that's tough for them. Brynn is the only blood they've got and they'll accept my life here, with you, or they'll never see her again."

I was old enough now to understand what the repercussions were—Mom working three jobs to help support Dad's struggling horse business, never following her passion of penning a novel, living a life she wasn't accustomed to.

A picture of Dad as a child in Montana caught my eye. I had thought his brother might finally appear. I had only heard about him through Mom, who'd told me snippets of information while pointing out strangers in faded family photos, the photos in the brown shoebox hidden in the least attended part of the attic. From what I gathered, they never left their ranch outside of Great Falls, and Dad had been too busy running ours to visit them.

Out on the back deck, small lanterns danced in the breeze along the balustrade, waiting for the night. Melancholic Diana Krall songs drifted through the central sound system. I longed for everyone to go home so that I could get out of this dress and into my yoga pants. Subira found me and pressed against my leg, nervous of the crowd. I leaned my elbows on the redwood deck railing, taking in the valley and hills that stretched toward the Pacific Ocean.

"We'll take care of things, won't we?" I whispered to Subira, digging my fingers into her warm fur.

"Brynn, there you are."

The suddenness of the words startled me. I turned to see Vivian Young, a local trainer, towering over me in high heels. I smiled a hello.

"I'm sorry about your father." Vivian leaned in to embrace me. Spicy perfume filled my senses. "He was a good man," she said, a hint of nostalgia in her voice. "Taught me a lot when I was a kid."

"All the way through juniors and barn management too," I added. He'd taught her everything she knew. She'd ridden at our ranch since she was a child, and later worked for my dad as an assistant trainer for several years before starting her own training business.

"Yeah," she added as if an afterthought. She reached down and ran a finger along the swooped neckline of her black and gold dress. Always a knockout, I thought. Even at a wake.

A clamor of laughter rose behind me, as people's voices surged, one above the other.

"You must find that hurtful." Vivian studied me over the rim of her glass of red wine.

I shrugged, reaching down to pet Subira's head. "I would rather this than everyone crying. At least they're being honest, right?"

"I bet this is the last place you want to be. I bet you'd rather spend the night in the barn."

I looked up at her in surprise. Her dark hair spilled around her shoulders, her green eyes glinted against the metallic shine of her dress. Did she know me? I'd always tried to stay in the background, keep to myself. She'd been in her late twenties when she'd left my dad to start her own business. That had been five years ago. I had looked up to her, and wanted to be like her when I was younger. She was a great rider, and had the looks, the confidence, the resonant laugh, and the force of will to get what she wanted. Well, except my dad. He never seemed to fall under her spell. In fact he'd always shaken his head when he'd seen her at horse shows after she'd left him, saying that he thought she was choosing the wrong path—but I'd thought he was overly judgmental, figuring he'd been mad that she'd left to strike out on her own.

"I'm glad they're all having a good time," I said, gazing out at the valley below. The hills had turned golden brown from the summer sun, the California oak trees dotting the fields of grass which disappeared at the edge of the lush forest and stream below. A crescent moon hung above in the darkening sky, Jupiter sparkling bright just below it.

"That's no excuse," she said, an indignant look crossing her face. "Disrespectful."

The song changed to something by Chopin. Mom's favorite composer. Mom used to reminisce about her days of going to the New York City Philharmonic Orchestra with her parents, where they had season tickets. As time wore on, she mentioned it less and less frequently. Almost as if that part of her life hadn't happened. The only time I heard her Chopin CD play was when she was writing—though that had been years ago.

"I'm sorry I couldn't make it to the service earlier. I had a lot on my plate at the barn this morning." Vivian leaned her elbows on the railing next to me. "I'm here because I was thinking about you, and how hard it all must be. I heard you saw it happen."

Prickles ran down my spine and I closed my eyes.

She gave me a sidelong glance. "Well, anyway." Vivian patted my arm. "I wanted to offer my help. Anything I can do, I'd be more than happy to. Just say the word."

"Thank you," I said, my head suddenly starting to ache.

"And if you need help with clients, teaching or riding horses . . ." Her voice drifted as she reached down to pet Subira's head. Subira pressed more tightly against my leg. "I know you're heading back to school soon. Last year of vet school, right? Your mom must be so proud. I know she's always wanted you to do that."

A coldness swept through me. Clients? Business? Lessons? I hadn't even thought about any of it.

"Well, anything at all." She placed her arm around my shoulder, and squeezed. "It's the least I can do after all your dad did for me." Her smile revealed crow's feet and lines around her lips. She was getting older. Somehow I never pictured her old.

"Thanks, Vivian," I said, the throbbing in my temples increasing. "At least you know the ropes around here . . . ," I added absentmindedly, my thoughts racing in every direction. School, clients, barn.

"It's not an easy business, what with the unpredictability of the economy, the clients . . . but anyway. It's not important." She pinched her nose, closing her eyes momentarily.

"Is everything all right?" I asked.

"Yeah, of course. It's just tough, you know? The clients are never easy. And fickle as shit. Sometimes I worry about things not working out for me."

"Oh. I didn't realize." She'd done the tough thing—set up her own business. And done it well too.

Vivian said her goodbyes, asking me to call, and I was left with the sudden realization that somehow another hurdle had been raised—bigger than I'd ever jumped before.

6

A couple of weeks later, Vivian's offer of help still hung in the air. With taking care of Mom, the house and the horses, I had pushed the decision to the back of my mind. I walked around in a daze as I helped Derek out at the barn, planning the lesson and riding schedules, organizing the hay deliveries and the farrier, and opening the bills that had started to pile up. Dad's request weighed heavily on my mind too. To take care of Mom, the barn, the horses—to take Jett higher.

Then Seth Armstrong, our accountant, left an urgent message with me asking Mom to call him right away. She hadn't been returning his calls and we needed to come in to discuss the estate.

When I told Mom about it, she said that I shouldn't worry, but I could come if I wanted to. I was determined to go.

Devon Creek was a unique mixture of Gold Rush and eighteenth-century Spanish architecture. Seth's office, on Main Street, was a two-storied, vanilla-white stucco building, accented by cappuccino-brown beams and a brown shingle roof. Mom and I sat in the quaint office waiting room, on wooden chairs, similar in discomfort to the church pews we'd sat on not too long ago.

The secretary's high-pitched voice grated on my nerves. I watched the slow rotations of the fan above, listening to the whoosh as the blades cut through the hot air. No air conditioning. Most Bay Area offices didn't have any, given the moderate climate.

Seth appeared a few minutes later, filling the small waiting area with his presence. "Amelia. Brynn. Please come in." He gestured to the office behind him. We followed him in. An arched window, that stretched almost as high as the ceiling, overlooked Main Street. It smelled of coffee and wood, stale and musty.

"Amelia, please accept my deepest condolences." He extended his hand, grasping hers in both of his. "Luke was not only a client, but a well-respected member of the community."

Mom nodded, and mumbled a thank-you under her breath.

"Now. The reason I asked you here—your accounts." We sat as he shuffled some papers on his desk, then folded his hands together, as if in prayer. "Luke took out a second mortgage on the property two years ago."

"Oh?" Mom's voice wavered.

The vibration of a passing car's stereo reverberated through me.

"Amelia." He leaned toward us across his mahogany desk. It gleamed, and besides the folder of papers with a purple Seymour sticker on the tab, not a single paper or pen lay out of place. A hint of salsa wafted toward me from across the desk. "He took out a second mortgage after he'd already taken out a large line of credit just twelve months before."

She wound her fingers together, pressing them harder in her lap. "I see."

I reached up and pried my shirt away from my back. I peered up at the fan, which wasn't giving much relief in the heat.

"Your funds are overdrawn, and at this point, you might lose the land unless you earn at least as much as you have been. Actually, you need to earn at least thirty-five thousand more per year just to stay afloat. You see, he hasn't made the last three months' payments—"

"What?" I moved to the edge of my chair, my hands gripping the edge of the desk. "I don't understand. Shouldn't we have almost completely paid off the property by now? Dad's been in the business for thirty years. Why the second mortgage?"

Seth looked at me, then my mom, almost as if unsure whether

he should be answering me. "This isn't the first time he's done this, Brynn. He's taken out mortgages multiple times throughout the years—at least five times since he first bought the land. Your mortgage is now underwater." Seth's eyes, even smaller behind his thick glasses, bored into me. I could see the large pores on his nose. I cleared my throat, realizing he was telling us we were worse than broke. We'd always gotten by with old tack, the old trailer, never taking a vacation, Mom working any job she could find, but now we were absolutely and positively broke.

"How much do we owe?" I asked pointedly.

Mom twitched a little bit in her chair.

Seth removed his wire-rimmed glasses. A bead of sweat trickled down his forehead. "More than the ranch is worth."

I stood up, my fists clenching and unclenching.

"Why wasn't my mother aware of this?"

Seth shifted uncomfortably in his chair.

"I don't know how to answer that, Brynn."

We both looked at Mom. The telephone in the waiting room rang. The secretary laughed. The fan above us whooshed.

"Of course I was aware of this, dear," Mom said under her breath. I had to lean in to hear her. "Let's just get going, darling. We'll figure it out." She looked up, her eyes meeting mine, her cheeks pale, her hand trembling.

"How could he let this happen?" My words came as a whisper, as my eyes searched hers.

"Let's talk about this at home." She glanced at Seth, her cheeks flushing.

I sensed the blood drain from my face as I turned to Seth, his white shirt heavy on the starch, his collar a size too small. "How much time do we have?" My voice sounded small now.

"Well . . ." Seth looked down at the papers again, shuffling them around until he found what he was looking for. "You have a couple of months before the bank files an NOD." Seeing my quizzical look, he quickly added: "A Notice of Default. Maybe longer . . . depends. Then you still have ninety days to catch up, to make a payment. So I'd say you have until the spring. And then of course you'll have to keep making the payments on the mortgage."

He looked at us again. Mom had pulled out her notebook and was scribbling something, her eyes glazed over. It was her writing notebook, her escape from anything that stressed her. I'd seen her do this whenever any conversation with Dad got tense.

"Oh . . ." I peered down at my lap, winding my fingers together. "So what are we supposed to do?"

The secretary's giggle filtered through the door. Seth looked down at his desk.

"I . . ." He cleared his throat. "I'm not sure what to say . . ."

He had no advice. We had no one else to rely on now. No one to help us make decisions, or to tell us the best course of action.

7

*S*ilence filled the small confines of my Honda Civic on the drive home. Mom kept her eyes straight ahead as I drove, leaning over only long enough to change the station to NPR. She sat, knees pressed together, her hands folded over her purse, Michael Krasny's voice filling my car. I wanted to discuss the situation, but the dabbing at her eyes with her tissue told me this wasn't the right time.

Once home, I got into my riding clothes and darted outside with Subira trying to keep pace. I slowed, tapping my leg. "Come on, old girl. Let's go."

Right after the accident Derek had told me he'd called a hiatus on lessons, and it crossed my mind that I had to organize a meeting with everyone. But I'd deal with that tomorrow. I made my way along the dim aisle of the barn, pausing at Cervantes's empty stall, grabbing onto a stall bar for support. Cervantes, Dad's dream horse. I closed my eyes and pictured Cervantes's white mane, his forelock, the dark gray dapples on his hind quarters, the graciousness of his gallop as Dad took him around the arena. Dad's shoulders hunched, his arms soft, his face drawn in concentration as he rode. The sweat lathering between Cervantes's hind legs, Cervantes foaming at the bit, his neck arched, his legs extending with each stride. Then Dad's smile as he took Cervantes over the jumps, and Cervantes's buck as he acted out. Dad always smiled when jumping. No matter how good or bad the horse was, no matter his worth, Dad loved each one. Each horse has their own spirit, their own unique talent they bring to the world, Dad would say. I wish we could have seen Cervantes's scope.

The horses were out in pastures and paddocks. I should have known it was still early, but the day had gotten away from me and I had no idea what time it was now. Noon? Four? I peered into Jett's stall to confirm. Most show horses stayed in their stalls for a majority of the day, but ours had all-day turnout. Dad had always been proud that he had been able to give the horses fresh air, a chance to socialize, to graze in the large pastures, where they could stretch their legs, jump, and frolic. *They need this too, you know?* he'd said.

Turning to head back outside I accidentally knocked over a bucket, the sound echoing in the silence of the barn. Derek stuck his head out from the office.

"It's just me." I returned the bucket to its rightful spot.

"Wasn't expecting you down here. Thought you were gone all day."

"You and me both," I mumbled.

Derek walked toward me, the light behind him outlining his stocky build. "Did you want me to get Jett?"

"I'd rather do it myself." I feigned a smile.

Derek nodded, pressing a hand on my shoulder, then walked back to the office. Dad's office. Where I still hadn't been able to bring myself to go. It was too painful, Dad's presence still too strong.

I leaned against Jett's stall door, inhaling the scent of shavings, fly spray, horses. My shoulders relaxed. This was my place. This was my sanctuary. And for a moment I felt better.

Outside, I followed the path to the turnouts. Jett stood in the pasture under the large oak. Gleaming black coat, white star, one white sock. He wasn't a beautiful horse. Solid, masculine, handsome even, but definitely not beautiful. I whistled quietly. His head popped up from the hay, his ears pricked forward. With his head held high, he commanded attention, like one of those horses pictured in the art books on the shelves in our sitting room. To me, he was *the* most beautiful horse.

Jett's forelock fell between his eyes. His mane, much too long and in need of pulling, fell to either side of his neck. A wave of guilt washed over me. In the last three weeks I hadn't taken care of him as much as I should have.

Jett stared at me, his liquid eyes spoke of knowing, of understanding, a bond we'd shared for years. He didn't care about his mane. What mattered was this. This unspoken love. If horses could smile, he'd be smiling now. My heart filled with warmth, blood surging through my veins. No one could steal moments like this from me. "Come on, buddy. Let's go for a ride. Just you and me."

I talked nonsense to Jett as I put on his halter and led him back toward the barn. I savored each brush stroke while grooming him, carefully picking out his feet, gently wiping his face, all as if they were my last. I ran my hand along his body, loving the softness of his hair, the thick muscles rippling beneath. I knew him almost as well as I knew myself. His snorts. His nickers. The way he nodded his head up and down when he begged for treats. I pressed my cheek against his warm neck, inhaling his scent. Everything faded.

I wrapped my arm around his neck, playing with the wiry thick hair of his mane. "We'll figure things out . . ."

Once in the outdoor arena, I needed to gallop. With a single flex of my calf, Jett cantered. I pushed him faster, craving the speed, the feel of him beneath me, the wind rushing through my ears, my breath merging with his, replacing every thought in my head. We rode and rode, until Jett's nostrils flared and my breath came short. Sweat dripped into my eyes, and lather coated his neck from where the reins rubbed against it. I don't know how long we rode, but oh, how good it felt to be one with him, to feel him, to ride as if we could ride together indefinitely. Once we'd slowed, I sunk heavy in the saddle. Spent.

Jett and I came around the corner and the ranch came into view. My head reeled, and I had to grab onto Jett's mane for support. How had Dad taken out additional mortgages? Why hadn't Mom stopped him? Had she known?

Dad had worked for years to build up the training program: eight clients, twelve horses. Their trust fell to me now, even if I'd only been an assistant trainer to my dad, and only during summers and the occasional weekends, and holidays. That didn't qualify me as a trainer. Or did it?

I was the individual silver medalist for Young Riders, and our team had won gold. No small feat, it was an award prestigious enough that our clients should take me seriously. With Derek's help, maybe there was a chance?

No. No way.

My final year of vet school would be more demanding than the previous three, which had me burned out as it was. The professors had warned us to be ready for no social life. For life spent in the field, on call, or in the library. I couldn't possibly come here every weekend to train. And who would ride the horses during the week? Who would teach the afternoon lessons?

I hopped off Jett. I needed to talk to Mom. We had to resolve this. We had to figure things out.

"Hey." Derek stood at the entrance to the barn, as if he'd been waiting for me. He wiped his hands on his shirt and chewed his lip for a moment. "I don't mean to bother you, but, umm . . ." He cleared his throat, then grabbed the halter I was reaching for and passed it to me.

"What's going on?" I asked, not really wanting to know.

"Helena, Corinne, and Mai were just in the office, and they're a bit concerned about the show."

"The show?"

"Yeah. Your dad was supposed to take them to a show in a couple of weeks. They, um, wanted to know whether we're still going."

I heaved the sweaty saddle pad and saddle off Jett. "What did you tell them?"

"I told them you were still thinking about it," Derek said, taking the saddle from me. "Is that all right?"

"Yes. Yes, of course. I'm thinking about it." I hadn't been. I didn't even remember it. I unclipped Jett from the cross ties, pressing my hand against the sweat stain left beneath the saddle pad—slick and wet and warm. "So, which show was this again?"

"Woodside."

"Right . . ." I led Jett outside toward the wash rack, buying time. Jett's shoes clip-clopped as we walked down the asphalt of the aisle, marking time, like the beat of my heart. The show. How could I have forgotten about the goddamned show?

Derek followed me outside. "So what do you want me to say?"

I sprayed Jett, top to bottom. Sweat, thick and soapy, slid down with the jet stream, leaving his coat black again. By accident I squeezed the nozzle harder and Jett pranced, but then settled.

"Tell them the show's on," I said. "*I'll* take them."

Derek didn't move.

"I said, tell them I'll take them." I faced Derek this time, straightening my back, trying to make myself taller.

Derek clicked his heels and walked away. I couldn't help but notice he didn't do it with as much gumption as he normally did with Dad. I knew Derek wasn't ready to trust me as the head of the barn. I was like his younger sister, after all.

I led Jett to a patch of grass around the side of the barn, tucking the hair that had fallen out of my ponytail behind my ears. Derek would have to get used to it. And this was the right thing to do. This was the *only* thing to do. I had to take the clients to the show—it would buy me precious time to figure out what to do next.

"Brynn." A young male voice. Not Derek's.

Startled, I pulled Jett to a stop. "Chris!"

Chris Peterson sat on one of the oak tables in the courtyard.

"Holy shit! You scared the crap out of me."

"You know me. I like the element of surprise." Chris, my first love. He walked toward me, smiling. I hadn't seen him in close to a year, when he'd moved back east to train and compete with McLain

Ward, an elite hunter-jumper trainer. When he reached me, we embraced, him kissing my cheek. "I heard about your dad. I'm really sorry I wasn't here."

Chris's voice cracked a bit. He was only a few inches taller than me, and, like most professional riders, lean. As my hands wrapped around him, I inhaled the scent of high-end stores: Gucci, Armani. I closed my eyes, carried back in time, my cheek pressed into his freshly ironed shirt. He'd always be my first love, even though the timing never seemed right.

Chris pulled away, eyeing me. "I heard you were there."

I didn't meet his gaze. I couldn't. So I changed the topic. "What are you doing here? Last we talked you were headed to a show in Florida."

"Well, here's the thing," he said, clearing his throat. "There's been a change of plans. I've moved back."

"What?" I stepped back, taking him in, his designer jeans and black shiny shoes, his hair styled in that perpetually mussed-up look. "Moving back? I thought this was the best opportunity of your life?"

"It was. It just wasn't for me, you know?" Then he smiled, revealing that little gap between his teeth that had driven me crazy. Me, and all the girls on the West Coast hunter-jumper circuit. "Sometimes things aren't what they appear to be. And I guess I miscalculated how much I'd miss California. Miss you."

He'd always been a flirt, though his romantic interests always involved girls with a modeling background. Not girls like me. "Your mother must be excited to have you back."

Chris suddenly found interest in a piece of lint on his shirt. "Actually, I'm staying at the old Hendricks Ranch."

I laughed, but Chris's head shot up and the look he gave me was anything but funny. "You're kidding, right?" He had to be. The ranch had been through a number of trainers in the last twenty or so years. The owners weren't horse people; they just hired trainers to manage the business. It was a far cry from the typical show barn Chris would normally ride at, and he'd never stoop to training other people or their horses for money. Prestige? Maybe. Riding with McLain Ward? Definitely. But not working out of a dump like the Hendricks Ranch. His parents' pockets were too deep for him to ever have to do that.

"Hey! Don't be a snob. It's a decent place. And you'd be surprised. They've really fixed it up. Even added this awesome loft that's part of the deal."

I couldn't decide if he was telling the truth. I pulled at my ponytail, my eyes drawn to his freckles, evenly spaced, a handful on each cheek. They gave him an irresistible, innocent look. Memories of days playing on our ponies, laughing together at shows, spending evenings at his parents' estate, hiding out in their guest cottage ran through my mind.

"So you'll come visit me, right? I'm around tonight."

I shook my head. "I'm taking clients to Woodside. I've gotta get the entries in by tonight."

Chris pouted, sticking his bottom lip out, giving me his puppy-eye look. I laughed. Chris stood straighter, and wrapped his arms around me again. "Next week, then? Promise?"

"I'll try." Though really I knew I was lying.

8

*T*he day before the Woodside show, Derek and I packed all the required supplies for the horses plus the items needed to create a spa-like atmosphere for the clients: water and grain buckets, grooming and first-aid kits, tack, blankets, trunks, a water fountain, a patio set, an awning, and decorations for the stalls. I called in an order for sod. The deliveryman promised it would be there the next day.

Through it all, I didn't get stressed, or frustrated, or sad. I didn't yell at Derek or Subira the way Dad always did the night before a show. I actually liked it. I liked all the details.

"It's the OCD in you," Derek said.

Over my Cup-o-Noodles I read the show schedule, making sure I had each class and rider combination memorized. And I listened for Mom. It had been days since I'd seen her eating, and I'd started to worry. I'd heard her call in sick to work all week. I listened for a sound, a whisper, a creak, but only silence greeted me. I needed to talk to her so we could figure out our plan.

As I walked down her hall, I was five again, giggles and murmurs drifting toward me on the dust motes released like blowing dandelions into the air. Dad and Mom lay in bed, their legs intertwined with the steel-colored covers, a mix of rough and smooth, of white and bronze. I remembered how Dad's face had appeared above the duvet. His eyes shone with the sparkle reserved only for jumping horses. Mom's tousled hair, normally always in place, spilled around her face in messy waves. I thought she was the loveliest woman. Alive and full of laughter.

Now I crept down the endless hallway, the redwood floor stretched before me, overlaid with the same blue runner, meticulously woven but now faded and worn. Photos, framed in ebony, lined the hall. Photos of Mom and Dad at her graduation; the three of us at Tahoe; Dad competing at a show; and my favorite: me, about four years old, atop Valkyrie, a nearly eighteen-hand dappled gray. Dad's first Grand Prix jumper. In the photo Dad had his arms around me, his smile wide and sure. I could almost taste his pride. The memories hung on the walls in the same place they'd been for years, but their meaning seemed misplaced now.

My steps didn't make a sound on the silk runner as I hurried beyond the ghosts of the past. I paused outside her door, my hand resting on the doorknob, my pulse pounding in my ears. I wanted to see my parents in bed again, laughing, giggling. I closed my eyes and pushed the door open.

"Mom?"

Silence greeted me. My voice faded in the dank air. The damask curtains hung closed, their blue diminished to black.

"Are you awake?"

My eyes adjusted. Her running shoes lay in the middle of the room, disorderly in comparison to the rest of the room. The brush strokes of the painting above their bed softened the severity of the windows on either side.

The sheets on Dad's side of the bed were tucked under the mattress, the way Mom had taught me. Dad's pillow lay untouched, as if waiting for him to fill its deep recesses. Mom's side was almost as well made, except for the long, narrow bump, the outline of her body.

"Mom?" I asked again, afraid to startle her. I knelt beside the bed, the floor unforgiving. I placed my hand on her arm, like a porcelain doll's atop the duvet.

My eyes gravitated toward the nightstand on the other side of the bed. Dad's reading glasses rested on top of several carelessly placed books, as if he'd laid them down only last night before falling asleep.

"Where do we go from here?" Her voice, barely a whisper, sounded unrecognizable.

"It's just a little setback," I said quietly, trying to lift her spirits. It was something Dad had always said whenever something went wrong.

She didn't respond.

I stood and tugged at one of the curtains, the ones I used to hide behind while playing hide-and-seek.

She cringed at the small amount of light filtering into the room. I pushed the window open. The room had always been filled with the scent of blooming hyacinths and roses and lilacs that had grown just outside her window. Now the garden stood bare, the air in the room thick.

"I never wanted it to be like this," she said.

Her face matched the grayness of her sheets. Her hair hung in clumps. Unwashed.

"I asked him years ago to stop riding. To figure out a new way. But you know your father—always knew best." Her lips twisted up into a smile. "Such a stubborn, annoying old trainer."

I wrapped my arms around myself.

"It was all a foolish dream," she continued, her eyes still fixed ahead. "I was so in love . . . and when he drove me out here, to this land, he stood proud, like a young prince. He knelt, and placed dirt in my hands." She squeezed her eyes shut. The curtain fluttered.

"I trusted him. His passion. His vision. It was contagious. I fell in love with this land too. And I wanted him to be happy. For *us* to be happy. I gave up everything. My family. New York. My writing. And it would have been fine. I was glad to do it. Your father,"—her voice wavered—"he promised me the world. I believed him."

Mom breathed heavily, her chest rising and falling rapidly. "And maybe it wasn't perfect, but we were together. But I was always afraid of him riding. Of you riding. I begged him so many times to stay put." She closed her eyes, a stream of tears running down her cheek. "How could I, though? How could I ask that of him? How could I ask a horse person to give up the one thing that made his blood course? But I don't know if I can forgive him."

I sat, the mattress sinking beneath me. A prescription bottle lay on its side on the nightstand, white and blue pills sprinkled around like Tic Tacs. My hands shook like they did when I had too much coffee as I reached for the bottle.

"Don't worry. They're for depression. Or anxiety. Or both. Something to numb the pain. I didn't take too many."

I closed my eyes with relief.

"How could he leave me? We were going to travel, we were going to see Paris. He was going to travel with me on book tours. He promised." Her fingers clutched at her nightgown, as if it was choking her. "And . . . how could he keep me in the dark about the ranch?"

"So you didn't know?"

Her eyelid twitched. She reached up as if to still it, her chipped nail polish splotchy against her nail beds. "I didn't know, Brynn. God, I just didn't know. I worked so hard—so many hours to try to make ends meet. Why would he do that?"

He hadn't told her.

"He promised. 'Just one more horse. This is the one. Just a win or two, and you'll see,' he'd said. I wanted him to be happy. I always put my needs second. He made me believe."

For a second I thought I heard the water running in the bathroom. I turned, expecting to see Dad shaving, getting ready. He would come out any minute now and this nightmare would disappear.

I was thankful for the fresh air coming in through the window.

"I'll make it work," I said. "I promise." I linked my fingers around her arm—that's how small she now was.

I clicked the door of her room shut behind me and I leaned against it. I slid down, sinking onto the worn silk rug, and placed my hands over my face. There was no one to turn to but me.

9

I stood at the edge of a hunter arena, my foot propped up on the low white railing, reading over the posted courses for the classes in which my young riders would be competing. I had been at Woodside since a quarter to six in the morning and had already ridden two of the ponies. Scanning the printouts stapled to the board outside the arena, I memorized all four courses. Satisfied, I noted they were all straightforward.

The first class was scheduled to begin at eight. I inhaled the smell of sand, trees, and horses, pulling the lapel of my jacket tighter around me, enjoying the silence before the heat and fatigue of the day that was sure to follow. The show grounds were still coming to life. A jump crew set up elaborate obstacles in the higher-level hunter arena, ones that resembled hunt fields—coops, walls, gates. The bright flowers contrasted with the natural colors of the rails and standards. Two girls, eight or so, ran across the empty arena, pretending to be horses. A crew member pulled up at the entrance with a water truck. The girls squealed and ran out, the truck's water spray barely missing them. The tractor with an arena harrow would follow to smooth the footing. On the horizon to the east lay the heart of Silicon Valley; I could just make out the white Stanford Clock Tower. To the west, a panorama of tree-blanketed hills stretched from north to south.

Derek had offered to trailer Corinne's, Helena's, and Mai's horses and ponies from our barn to the show on Monday, suggesting that I drive my car so that we could go back and forth in it, giving me the much-needed out. Without saying a word, I'd hugged him, grateful that I didn't have to load the horses and ponies, nor drive the truck and trailer to the show.

I'd been riding and showing our clients' horses and ponies for three days now, doing one of the trainer's jobs: to prepare the horses and help adjust them to a horse show setting. Today would be the first day of the week the clients themselves showed. I glanced down at my smartphone and adjusted my sun hat, which never left my head at the shows. Seven twenty-five, and I still hadn't spotted any of my clients. Derek knew to have the ponies tacked up and ready, but it wasn't him I was worried about. It was the rest of our barn. I'd told the parents to consider staying at a local hotel, even with home only about an hour and a half away, so that they'd be here on time. They had to put their boots on, find their crops, their helmets. A flurry of activity would ensue: *"Where are my spurs? Mom, have you seen my spurs? I know I left them right here yesterday!"* Panic would set in as trunks opened and shut while busy hands searched for pieces of misplaced equipment. Grooms would be grilled. Moms' normally quiet voices would rise. Boots would be polished, hairnets placed over bobby-pinned hair, helmets put on.

"Brynn!" A woman sitting in a golf cart called, waving wildly, as if I weren't the only person within a hundred feet. The rising sun hit my eyes, and I had to squint to make her out.

Ruth Stubbs, a trainer from the valley. She and her white golf cart were a fixture at the local shows, and had been for the past thirty years.

"Did you take a look at the course yet?" Ruth inclined her sun visor toward the arena.

"Yup. Really straightforward."

"Good, good." She hesitated, picking something off her tightly stretched polo shirt. "I'm glad you're here. I wanted to talk to you." Ruth rubbed her palms on her jeans.

"I was just heading over to get some coffee before the first class."

"I'd love a cup myself." She heaved her heavy bottom from the golf cart with a grunt. Little clouds of dust puffed up as her brown paddock boots hit the ground.

"How are things?" she asked as we walked toward the food tent.

"All right." I kept my gaze straight ahead.

"I've wanted to tell you how sorry I am about your dad. Seems I haven't had a moment . . ." Ruth's voice trailed off as she gave me a sidelong glance. She kicked a few wood chips. The scent of cedar wafted up toward me. "I was at the funeral, but had to leave early."

Here we go again, I thought. Everyone was sorry and I sure as heck didn't know how to respond to sympathy.

Ruth continued, "It's such a shame." A horse show judge walked by and nodded at us. He nursed his complimentary cup of coffee as he rubbed the sleep from his eyes. I nodded back. "But you know, Brynn, these crazy things happen. None of it makes sense, I know, but horses are large, unpredictable beasts."

An assortment of riders passed by, young and old, tall and short, dressed in show breeches, long colorful socks, polo shirts and dress shirts, bundled in sweatshirts or jackets, chatting as they checked their schedules and courses.

"Dad always thought highly of you and he always considered you a friend."

"We go way back, Luke and I." She gave a throaty laugh. "When your dad first came to California he was just a kid, you know. He'd work at any stable, as long as they gave him a meal and a place to lay his head. Well, he'd go to all the shows, even the bad ones." She shook her head. "Luke was such a crazy fool. The craziest I ever met. He'd ride anything. And not just to make a buck, but for the challenge. God, he loved a challenge. There was no stopping him."

"That's my Dad for you." I smiled, imagining him as a teen, following trainers, riding any horse he could get his hands on.

"But he changed. I don't know when, but he changed. Well,

I reckon I know . . ." She paused and glanced at me. "It was after he had you. He grew careful. Well, maybe I'm wrong. Maybe he would've been that way anyway. Anyhow, if you need anything, just give me a holler." We split apart as a young groom walked between us, leading a frisky horse. "I owe him." She removed her sunglasses to peer directly at me.

"What do you mean?"

"Oh, I don't know. He'd help with tough horses at shows, or by dropping my name to people he'd heard might be moving down my way so that I could pick up a client or two. He was a good guy, your dad." She nodded. "Not like half this other muck running around."

She stopped and took me by my arm. "You gotta watch your back." Ruth looked past me, as if seeing herself and my dad when they were young, and she smiled and lifted the heel of her age-spotted hand to her pale eyes, rubbing them. "You just watch your back."

A loudspeaker above me crackled, then boomed. "Pony hunters in Hunter Ring Two. Pony hunters in Hunter Ring Two."

Startled, I spilled coffee over the show schedule printouts. "Dammit!" I shook the coffee off my papers.

"Let's go, people. I don't see a single soul warming up here. We start at eight on the dot, so get your kids and ponies out here!"

I rushed toward the ring, but as I rounded the corner Vivian caught my eye. She stood behind the show trailer, stubbing out a cigarette. Our eyes met, and she smiled and waved and I remembered I hadn't called her yet about her offer to help. I waved a quick hello, then ducked away before she could ask me again, too embarrassed to tell her that I couldn't afford her even if I wanted to.

"Danny in one, Kennedy in two, Samantha in three."

I nodded toward the gate announcer's small booth at the entrance to the arena, letting him know I'd heard. Kennedy, Corinne's daughter, was up after the boy ready to head in.

Where the hell are they?? I texted Derek.

On their way, Derek texted back.

I crossed my arms. We wouldn't have enough time to warm up. I noticed other clients of ours—Stuart and Peggy, Patty, and Pam—were here to watch. I waved and smiled, trying to appear calm.

Vivian and her riders approached the arena. She walked tall and proud, her client moms obediently walking behind the five ponies and riders, like a group of goslings. I had to find out her secret. Clearly I couldn't even get our clients to show up on time.

Finally, I picked out Payton, Kennedy, and Lani as they rode toward me in descending order of pony height: large, medium, small. I should have been relieved, but my heart raced and I regretted drinking that second cup of coffee.

The girls, ages ranging ten to thirteen, were similar, yet their personalities clashed as much as their looks. Kennedy the relaxed, lazy kid. Payton, the anxious tall reed of a girl, opposite of her mother, and Lani, a shy, nerdy kid, who seemed to need more time outside than studying. But they all had one thing in common: their love of horses. And in this world, that's all they needed to be best of friends.

Danny, a boy around eleven years old or so, rode in. Derek busied himself with wiping the girls' tall boots, while they held their feet out for him from their stirrups. Once finished, he leaned down and scraped the caked-on dirt off the outside of each pony's hooves with a hoof pick. For the finishing touch, he coated the hooves with hoof polish—which would become encrusted with sand in a matter of seconds of riding in the arena. But the judge might notice such details, so who was I to question the rules of the hunter ring.

A rail crashed. I jerked around just in time to see that the pony had slid to a stop in front of the rail, but still had a lot of momentum. Danny leaned back and kicked the pony. Trying to obey, the pony bunny-hopped over the jump, but in the process, dislodged the boy onto the pony's neck. The rails toppled behind them. The pony, ears pinned, spooked and bolted, then took off in a mad gallop.

Mai screamed. Danny's trainer ran into the arena, yelling, "Sit up, sit up!" The saddle slid over to the side as Danny's weight pulled the saddle with him. I gripped the railing of the fence, praying to God that Danny didn't get caught under the pony's legs, then realized the pony had turned away from the trainer and was headed straight toward the open gate.

Running, I dropped the schedule and jumped the rail, headed for the gate, stretching my arms out, blocking the exit. Several people followed suit, herding the spooked pony. The pony galloped, tail streaming, and I was reminded of Mom's fear about horses that always gripped her. How would it feel to see someone you knew, and cared for, injured? How would it feel if it was your child? I waved my arms at the pony that headed straight for me. Finally, the pony slowed enough that the boy could slide off the saddle. He rolled and jumped up. I caught the pony's reins, and the spooked pony—nostrils flaring, ears like radar dishes, ribs heaving from exertion—pranced in place. "It's all right, boy," I said. "It's going to be all right."

Danny started crying. The trainer and his parents ran over, but he pushed past them, wiped his nose with the sleeve of his show jacket, and pulled his shoulders back. Handing the reins over to him, I patted him on his back. "Great emergency dismount," I said. His eyes met mine, his chin raised a little higher. The small crowd clapped and I stepped back toward the fence, opening the space in my lungs again, regaining my balance.

Kennedy was next. I swallowed hard, trying to get my adrenaline under control. Just like Cervantes had picked up on Seraphim's fear, Best of Luck could have too.

"All right, Kennedy. Just ride how we always do at home. Keep your head up, shoulders back, and heels down. Make sure you take the turns wide, and whatever you do, don't look down at the jump."

"Mhmm." Her little head bobbed up and down, although her

brown eyes glazed over. I had to close my eyes for a moment and count to three.

"Earth to Kennedy." I knocked on her black Charles Owen show helmet. Even though she was mounted, the pony was small enough that she was barely taller than me.

"I'm here, okay? You don't have to be so pushy." Her pouty pink lips jutted out at me. She slouched as she sat atop her dappled gray pony, Best of Luck. I shook my head. Ten years old and more attitude than I'd ever been allowed. Dad would have put me to work mucking stalls. But as I knew from teaching her in the summer, Kennedy lost interest easily, and she'd whine about riding in the heat if it was above seventy, and the cold if it was below sixty. She did such a poor job of grooming her pony, taking twice as long as any other kid, that Corinne requested help. Now Derek did it instead. Corinne kept her kids busy with a packed schedule of activities, and I sometimes wished she would take Kennedy to a Get Over Your Attitude class.

I tucked a brown defiant curl back into Kennedy's hairnet and pushed both up under the helmet. "Okay, then. Can you tell me your course one more time?"

Kennedy waved her arm about as she pointed to the jumps, describing her course, while I checked her girth. I did a once-over of her attire, inspecting her breeches for dirt, dusting specks off her navy blue show jacket, adjusting her rider number to the center of her back.

I led Kennedy on Best of Luck toward the in-gate. "You're ready. Now just relax and breathe. Get in there and show them what you've got!" The pony's tail swished back and forth as they rode in.

Corinne stood under the awning next to the arena, drumming her fingers on the fence, biting her lip. Her older daughter stood next to her. Kennedy yawned as she rode into the arena. I closed my eyes and counted to three. Patience . . .

"Watch your heels!" Corinne called, leaning against the waist-high arena fence, her knuckles white as she clutched her professional camera.

Damn that woman. Dad and I were always having to remind her not to interfere with lessons and shows. Kennedy was to focus only on her trainer. Not her mother. I turned away, making a mental note to have another discussion with Corinne later. She'd already tried to convince me that Seraphim should go back to showing as soon as possible. The mare still hadn't been cleared off stall rest, her injury requiring at least another month off.

The announcer's voice brought me back to the show. "And now, in the ring we have Kennedy Schultz from Mill Valley, California, atop Best of Luck, owned by Corinne Schultz."

I reached up to bite at my cuticles, my heart suddenly beating faster. I hoped she woke up. She had thirty seconds to get focused.

Mai, a newbie to the show world, came to stand next to me by the arena entrance. She loved to learn, but the side effect was incessant questions. A recent divorcée, she spent time with Lani at the barn, and in the evenings she hunted for a new husband using Table for Six and other dating services. "So tell me again what we're looking for?" she asked, as I scrutinized Kennedy's every move. Kennedy started to trot a large circle. She pulled her leg back an inch and picked up her canter in a smooth, fluid indiscernible motion.

I clucked at the pony. "Pace, Kennedy. Pick up the pace," I quietly called as she rode past me toward the first jump.

"So pretty!" Mai clasped her hands under her chin. This was Lani's first show. Not a good time for me to talk, but I didn't have a choice.

At the hunter-jumper shows, there were two ways to be judged: on style, performance, and soundness, also called "hunters over fences"; and on speed and agility of the horse, called "jumpers." Only jumpers were considered an Olympic sport. I wasn't fond of hunters because of the subjective judging, but I wasn't about to tell Mai that. Most kids started in hunters.

"She's good, isn't she?" Mai asked, watching Kennedy. "Do you think Lani can do that?" Her words stumbled over themselves, then she blushed, as if she had been too forward.

"Yes. Definitely. With practice," I said, clapping, smiling at the out-of-breath Kennedy as she walked Best of Luck out of the arena. Mai smiled, covering her mouth with her hand.

"You did great!" I said, grabbing the pony's reins and patting his neck. He nosed my pocket. I pulled a sugar cube out and gave it to him. He moved his lips over my hand, satisfied, once he found what he was searching for.

"Let's move out of the way and talk about your round." I led Kennedy and Best of Luck away from the arena. Corinne waited at a distance. At least she had learned not to approach until I'd had my time.

"So, I loved how well you remembered your course, Kennedy, and your ability to make it through that diagonal line at the right speed. But do you know what I noticed?"

"Um, no . . ." But it appeared that she actually was thinking about it.

"You forgot to go into your corner at the back of that ring. That will cost you points. You also didn't steady Lucky enough to the last jump, and so he rushed it. Overall, it was a fantastic round. Now I better go get Payton warmed up."

Kennedy nodded. "Hey, Brynn?"

I scanned the dozen or so kids atop their ponies for Payton. "Yeah?"

She bowed her head and mumbled, "I really like riding with you."

I had to turn my head up at Kennedy, still atop Best of Luck. I studied her face. "Everything okay?"

"Yeah. I just love how you always explain things so clearly to me, you know? And you never get mad at me. Even when I screw up."

"That's my job."

"Well, it's just that you don't even seem to care if I win or not. Mom . . . she's always pushing me for those blue ribbons. Sometimes, well, I, ummm, I feel I disappoint her." She played with her reins, then lay forward on top of Best of Luck's neck, hugging him.

Well, there was that side to Corinne. She seemed to expect the worst, always analyzing and calculating everything. Once she'd even presented Dad with Excel spreadsheets reviewing classes and points—for Kennedy and each of her competitors. I had laughed when Dad had told me about it, though he hadn't found it funny.

"You know what, kiddo?" I said, lifting Kennedy's chin up. "All I care about is that you're listening to me, improving, and—most importantly—you're having fun. Isn't that why you're here?"

"Yeah. I guess. It's just not as fun as riding the ponies back at the barn out in the field. I like that much more." She glanced around, as if to make sure her mother wasn't within earshot.

I leaned toward her. "Sometimes, I like that best too."

Her eyes rounded in surprise.

"Shhh. It'll be our little secret, okay?"

She nodded again, and I saw a spark in her I hadn't detected before.

"Now you go wait over there with your mother and sister. And if you do well this weekend, maybe I'll give you and the other girls a bareback lesson back at the ranch. What do you say?"

Her big smile said it all. Maybe Kennedy wasn't such a brat after all. Maybe I could teach these kids a life beyond their day-to-day luxuries. A life of caring about animals and teamwork. Competition.

As I walked with Payton toward the arena, I noticed that instead of talking to Kennedy, Corinne was watching Vivian warm up her clients over the jump.

10

*K*ennedy ended up with a coveted first place in one of her rounds. With fourteen kids or more in each class, that was quite an accomplishment. Corinne said she deserved a reward from one of the traveling tack shops. Helena's daughter, Payton, got a fourth, and Lani got an eighth. Mai had taken about thirty pictures of Lani and the girls, Lani and the pony, Lani and the girls and the pony and me, in every configuration, until I told her the ponies had to go back to their stalls.

As I led Best of Luck, Vivian and her group passed me, her mouth drawn into a tight line.

"You guys need to smarten up," she said to them. "If you're going to ride with my barn, you better get it right or not even bother."

The kids slumped in their saddles. The moms trailed behind, their hands carrying only cameras and no ribbons.

"Got it?"

The girls nodded.

Back at the stalls Derek came over to give me a hug of congratulations. "Hellacious job, B. And your first time as the head trainer too."

"Oh, please. Like I haven't helped Dad at these shows for years," I muttered, then sat in one of the cushioned patio chairs, trying to shake off the tightness in my neck from the earlier incident. To distract myself I polished the arena dirt from my boots for the second time that day. As if there was anything to be proud of. It's not like

I'd won a Grand Prix, or anything. That would be something to feel proud of. I shook my head. Where had that thought come from? Graduating vet school. That was something to be proud of.

Our barn awning and seating area faced the main corridor where people walked back and forth with horses, to and from the show rings. Helena walked over and sat down across from me.

"Where's Payton?" I asked.

"She went with Corinne and Kennedy to the tack shop. I told her she could look around." Helena had been riding on the A circuit herself since the age of thirteen or so. She never went overboard buying hundreds of dollars' worth of gear. Payton was always "pleases" and "thank-yous."

"This is the best advertising for you. Right here," Helena said, leaning back on the couch, placing her arms up behind her head, piling her curly strawberry-blonde hair on top. She reminded me of Goldie Hawn, but with gray eyes. "Everyone who walks by will catch sight of our barn and all the ribbons."

She was right. Our show stalls were located along the horse show throughway. It was all here: people walking, others riding their horses to and from the show rings, grooms leading done-up horses covered in sheer netted fabric with barn logos—and of course the golf carts. It wouldn't be a show without the dozens of golf carts zipping by, loaded down with excited kids, teens, moms, and trainers traveling between the show office, show rings, and stables. Between now and Sunday hearts would soar and hearts would break. People would vow never to come back. In the end, they always did. They craved the adrenaline rush of the competition—and the camaraderie. There was something to be said about being with people who shared the same passion as you.

"Speaking of which." I turned and hung up the new ribbons on the side of our show tent, right above the Redwood Grove Stables banner.

"We'll collect plenty more over the next three days," Helena said. "I'm happy, though I think Payton wanted a blue." Helena's voice held a hint of melancholy.

I watched her from under my hat. "There are plenty of chances for her to get one . . ." I hesitated. "You're a pro, Helena. You've done the show thing. You know what it's like. She probably won't win any classes at this show."

Helena lifted her feet up and rested them on the coffee table. "I know." She picked up a copy of *Riding* magazine and started flipping through it. "Although it sure would be nice . . ."

Here we go. It was time to have another talk. Dad had already had one with her a few months ago, but now I would have to go at it alone.

"It's not that she's not a good rider, Helena—"

"Oh, I know. It's that she doesn't have the six-figure pony." She smirked, as she continued to flip through the magazine. I couldn't see her eyes behind her sunglasses, but I knew they were hard. An exemplary corporate wife, married to the successful CEO of a booming biotech company.

"Exactly. You know how this works."

"I refuse to do that. I refuse to buy her a pony that costs more than a car." She sat up and threw the magazine on the table. "And it's not the money, Brynn. You know that. I just think she should be judged on her skill, not how expensive her pony is. I want her to learn to win based on merit, not on money."

"And I don't blame you." A pause filled the air, as I pondered how to make her feel better. "Jumpers will be good for her," I finally said. "As soon as she's ready, we'll put her in those classes. Her personality will suit that better, anyway."

Helena exhaled. "Yeah. You're right."

And even though outwardly Helena agreed, part of me worried. When a client started wishing for the blue ribbons, yet didn't want to spend the money on a horse that could make those possible, problems followed. All I could do was hope that she meant what she said—and that she really did care more about skill than ribbons.

I made my way down our row of stalls, checking on each horse and pony, making sure none were exhibiting signs of colic. The horses swished their braided tails and munched their hay. I went into Dolce's stall, fixed up a loose braid. Then I sat on one of the eight tack trunks that stood in front of one our horses' stalls, closing my eyes, happy for this reprieve before the next wave of classes, the next bout of craziness with my adult lady-riders.

The women were more demanding than the children in many ways. Luckily Stuart wasn't showing yet, since he was a complete beginner and his goal was to trail-ride around the property within the next year. But the ladies? They'd lose their confidence at the last minute, panic, forget their courses, pretty much forget how to ride. With time they would get better, but sometimes I compared watching their show to watching some reality-TV disaster, and when the older ones fell, they never bounced back as easily as the little boy had.

The sound of the grooms chatting filtered toward me from the stalls behind our row. Their voices mixed with the sound of a Spanish song on the crackling radio made me smile. Shows were a home away from home and I half-expected Dad to round the corner, yelling at me to hurry up because I was in the next class.

"Not this time," I whispered. I wouldn't be riding in shows anytime soon.

Mom and I had finally had our talk last week. She wasn't back to normal yet, but she was up and about. We sat at the oak kitchen table overlooking the barn and rolling hills. I brought out my notebook, filled with numbers and calculations and ideas, and laid out my plan. I would do both: go to school and train the clients on the weekend. Derek would ride the ponies and horses Monday through Thursday, and I'd come home on Friday and ride, teach a few lessons, then do the same on Saturday and Sunday. Derek would get Sundays off, and me . . . well, I told her I didn't need any time off. Just being home with the horses would be break enough for me. I didn't tell her that I wasn't sure how my professors would handle the news that I couldn't be on call during the weekends.

"This way," I said, "I can finish school and run the business."

Mom looked down at her hands, circling her thumbs round and round each other. "I don't want you to ride anymore, Brynn. There's too much risk—remember Christopher—"

I had to cut her off. To stop her from going down that path, the path that would likely lead to more tears. "Yes, Mom. I know. It's terribly sad, but accidents happen."

Mom shook her head, placing her head in her hands. "Brynn, darling. Let's make it work some other way. There has to be another way."

"There isn't, Mom. And it'll work. You'll see. I'll handle the accounting side of things, too. I know you don't have time for all of that—but I promise to keep you updated. I'll work with Mr. Armstrong to try to keep things on track." I tried not to let my eyes meet hers, in case she sensed the doubt and fear I felt with this plan. I had to make it seem like I was really on board. Like I knew what I was doing.

Mom bit at her lower lip. "I don't like it, you know. I always wanted you to focus on school," she finally said. "I wanted you to make something of yourself, to make money on your own terms. To be safe on the ground. I really don't like this at all."

I took her hand. "Give me a chance, Mom. I owe Dad this—"

"You don't owe him anything. He should have planned better for you. For me. I gave up my entire life for him, and what has he done? He left us. He didn't love me enough to quit this sport. Even though I begged." I had to calm her, getting her a prescription pill, helping her into bed. I told her we'd be fine. That I could handle it. That it was only temporary. I would graduate at the end of the year, and all would be back on track. We could figure things out from there. And then I prayed she couldn't hear how my heart fluttered or sense how much I wanted to run away from it all.

The dressing room was a converted stall filled with a portable clothes stand, a wardrobe, a full-length mirror, a rug, and a few pictures to add warmth. A couple of chairs stood in opposite corners for the comfort of the clients. I checked my white polo in the mirror for horse goop, and confirmed my tan britches were still clean. I had on my favorite blue belt, silver thread weaved through, and although I didn't follow fashion, I always knew the latest trends in the hunter-jumper world. I readjusted my large-brimmed sun hat, and forced a smile, telling myself that I had to keep up appearances for only a bit longer. The day was almost done.

A horse neighed, then another. The conversations the horses held between each other amused me. Sometimes I would imagine they remembered each other from previous barns or shows, checking in how the other had fared since they'd last seen each other: some complained about their owners, others raved and bragged about how good they had it. Most had nothing to complain about, especially on show days, where the owners had nothing to do but spend extra time and money pampering them.

A male voice drifted toward me, followed by a laugh. *That* laugh. Chris. He'd sent several text messages asking me to dinner, and I wanted to see him, but I needed to get through this day without any distractions, and he was always a distraction for me. Always wanting to have fun, never understanding I had work or school or some responsibility, and I couldn't allow myself to get pulled into that right now.

11

aturday afternoon I glanced at my phone. Four thirty. I rubbed my hands over my face trying to wake myself up. My arms and legs felt like rubber that had been left out in the sun too long. Besides having to manage the worries of the clients, avoiding Chris had taken its toll.

At least all the adult riders did well in their classes. Helena and her horse d'Artagnan had scored enough points to place her in second for the Amateur Owner Hunter division. We still had a day of showing, so she could walk away with a Reserve Champion, maybe even a Champion ribbon. Corinne on Dolce had won a first in her Equitation over fences class, but was disqualified from her Low Adult Amateur Hunter over fences class for forgetting her course. That had soured her mood, and no matter what I said, she seemed too upset at herself to be consoled. It had been a relief when Derek had come over to grab Dolce and fawn over her first-place ribbon.

One more day. Then we pack up the horses, their corresponding supplies, and of course, the tent, patio set, planters, signs, and fountain to head home.

School started in two weeks.

I called the braider to confirm he was still on for the night. Each night he braided the manes and tails of the hunter horses and ponies, and the next day, Derek would take them out as soon as the classes were done. Every day they had to be redone. Frizz or rubbed-out braids were cause for docked points in the eyes of the judges. I double-checked the entries for the next day's classes, then made my way toward the office to adjust a few before the five o'clock deadline. I was a couple of hours away from my shower, a pair of comfy yoga pants, and the new Barbara Kingsolver book that Aunt Julia had dropped off for me—not that I was likely to stay awake for longer than fifteen minutes.

As I passed the food tent, smells of hamburgers and french fries made my stomach rumble. I realized I hadn't eaten lunch yet. I pulled out my phone and called Helena. "You ladies hungry?"

"We're going to go watch the Grand Prix—it starts in ten minutes. Aren't you coming?" Helena asked.

"Right . . ." With everything else going on I'd forgotten.

"Why don't you come watch with us?"

"Nah. I'm fine. But have a great time. I'll see you first thing tomorrow." I hung up and walked back to the stalls. I'd find something to eat at home. I checked the horses one more time and headed out.

Walking toward my car, I spotted Chris chatting with a group of girl riders who were brandishing hips and doe eyes, and taking selfies with him. He was beyond handsome in his navy blue dress shirt, white tie, and white riding breeches, the kind reserved only for Grand Prix and the highest amateur classes. A tightness grew in my chest as I remembered what it was like to walk through here with him, talking about strategy for classes, laughing, hanging out together. I shook my head. Until I figured things out on my own, I couldn't have him clouding my judgment.

I pivoted on my heel to walk up a different path before he noticed me. The turn took me past the Grand Prix complex. A small crowd gathered near the in-gate and in the stands. Corinne, Helena, Mai, and the girls were easy to spot. I made my way past the warm-up arena, where Ruth was parking her golf cart. Her straw-like hair escaped from under her sun visor in wisps.

"He's handsome, isn't he?" she said as I passed.

"Who?"

"Devil's Slide, the chestnut there." She nodded toward the red-haired horse going over warm-up jumps. I recognized the rider, Roman Kuzara, one of the best on the West Coast. Roman was rumored to be a party animal and a ladies' man—supposedly having moved to America after meeting an American rider in France at a World Cup competition. She dumped him shortly after. He said he loved America too much to go back to Poland.

"He is nice," I said, trying to act interested, yet wanting to get home.

"He's by Darco. Quite fancy. Roman's client picked him up at Spruce Meadows last week. Lucky ass," she added almost as if in afterthought, obviously referring to the trainer. She rubbed her hands on her jeans, then hooked her thumbs through her belt loops.

My curiosity got the best of me. I loved Darco, an amazing stallion. He'd been to the Olympics, and had been the winner of the World Cup on two occasions. Dad and Uncle Ian had always kept an eye out for his foals.

"Roman's doing a good job with him," I said. "How old is he?"

"Only seven, I reckon."

"And he's taking him in the Grand Prix?"

"It's a pretty low one."

I whistled quietly. "Still . . ."

"They like to start them young now, you know? Most of them over in Europe are showing at this age. They don't wait around for them to get old."

The conversation made me think of Dad's question before he died. What about Jett? What was his future? He was eleven, and he still hadn't gone into a real Grand Prix. I might have been showing him in Grand Prix last year if I wasn't in vet school.

"Are you headin' up to watch?" Ruth asked.

I shook my head. "Just walking to my car."

"Next time," she said, nodding a goodbye, getting out of her cart.

"Next time." I moved closer to the entrance of the warm-up arena, studying Devil's Slide. What a name. He wasn't tall, but taller than Jett. I put him at 16.3 hands. He had four white socks, a large white crooked blaze down his face, and a heavy, long body. He knocked a rail in the warm-up round, then immediately bucked. Roman took control of him, pulling firmly on his reins. Obviously Devil's Slide didn't like hitting rails, and would probably jump better the next time around. I watched, and sure enough, as Roman took him around to the jump again, he cleared it by six inches. He didn't show any sign of strain, and looked more like a cat pouncing than a horse making a five-foot jump.

Vivian walked out of the Grand Prix arena atop a bay mare, Love's First Trip. It had won many Grand Prix for Vivian. Vivian breathed heavily, her face scrunched. She hopped off the mare like a puma, throwing the reins at her groom. The groom flinched, then grabbed them.

Vivian stretched tall and pulled off her helmet, her hair net along with it. She tossed both at her groom, who struggled to catch them while trying to keep the wired horse under control. Vivian's dark long hair spilled out toward the small of her back, her gold belt flashing above her white britches. Her breath steadied, and she appeared like she hadn't even broken a sweat.

"Vivian. Great round!" A pimple-faced teenager with braces jogged past me toward her.

Vivian eyed the teenager who stood with her hands clasped together, as if she were praying to an idol, her eyes round, full of eagerness.

"I just love watching you ride!" the girl said.

"Thank you," Vivian said and walked toward the in-gate.

"I ride at Oak Hill Riding Academy in Napa, but my parents said that if I continue to keep up my grades they might let me take lessons with you!" The girl jabbered on, following Vivian. Vivian paused, and the girl almost ran into her back. "Oh! I'm soo sorry!"

Vivian turned around to eye the girl up and down. "So you think you might come train with me?" She propped her sunglasses on top of her head and squinted at the girl. "That's really nice. But I'm only taking on clients in full training."

"I'm not sure that we would be able to do that right away—"

"And I need to be frank with you. I'm fully booked, so if you're interested in riding with my barn, we require you purchase a horse worth at minimum, forty thousand. Is that in your parents' budget?"

The girl's shoulders sagged, her eyes filling with tears. Vivian had taken complete account of the girl, deducing she had no money. The girl wore cheap cotton breeches. Her boots were muddy, probably an off-the-shelf brand unlike the custom leather ones Vivian wore. The polo shirt was crumpled and untucked, the girl's pudgy belly spilling out over her breeches like a Winnie the Pooh bear. No belt. The girl's lips made a round circle, but no sound came out.

"I suggest you stay where you're at, or move to a less expensive barn. But, I'm sure you'll do perfectly fine with your current trainer." Vivian turned her back on the girl, and stood at the entrance of the VIP tent filled with dinner tables.

My heart went out to the girl. I debated whether I should go say something, but instead I hovered next to the warm-up ring. This was the harsh reality of the show world. The part I despised. The part I wished I could change somehow. But it had always been like that. Ever since I was a child, and no doubt since my dad was a child.

I'd always known it had been a stretch for both Dad and me to show. Now, I knew by how much: Dad had been willing to go into immense debt. We never splurged on fancy show gear. My saddles were always hand-me-downs, but they'd taught me how to keep a good seat, and stay modest. Still, when I was younger, I'd resented Dad for the cheap tack, the cheap boots.

Vivian had come from a broken home, but somehow she'd managed to get to the top—now she had the clients with fancy gear, the fancy barn. But my dad had been her first instructor, giving her free lessons in exchange for work around the barn. How could she treat this girl like this? I was reminded again of Dad, telling me he didn't like the choices he saw her make.

I turned and glanced over at my group of clients. They were a good gang. They weren't focused on image or money, not as much as some anyway, otherwise they wouldn't be riding with my dad and—let's face it—now me. Vivian stopped at the entrance of the Grand Prix arena, wishing Roman good luck as he walked in. Roman smiled and she blew him a kiss.

As I was about to walk away, I noticed her wave, then smile, at my group of clients.

Suddenly, my yoga pants could wait; I needed to talk to Corinne, Helena, and Mai. By the time I walked up to the Grand Prix arena stands, Vivian was already laughing with them. I put on what I thought was my warmest smile. "Are you ladies ready for a glass of wine?"

"Brynn! You decided to stay!" Helena beamed, reminding me how important these functions were. It wasn't just about teaching an exceptional lesson or riding to the best of my ability. I had to socialize afterward too.

"I wouldn't want to miss hanging out with all of you!" I put my hand on Corinne's shoulder.

"Brynn!" Vivian smiled and leaned in to give me a kiss on the cheek. "So nice to see you! I was surprised to hear you were at the show after all."

A silence fell over the group. Helena called to the kids to come closer.

Corinne gestured toward the arena. "We were just chatting about Roman's skill at taking that young stallion over the jumps." Roman atop Devil's Slide jumped on the far side of the Grand Prix arena.

"Vivian had some great observations. She thinks he should be sending that horse higher. He's only seven! Can you believe it?" Helena added. I was grateful for their steering the topic away from my dad, but my cheeks still burned. It wasn't Vivian's place to talk to my clients about riding.

"Brynn, did you know that Vivian's trained with George Morris?" Corinne asked. All eyes turned toward me to see what I thought of this revelation. Kennedy, who'd been playing with the other girls, came to stand next to me. George Morris had been the Chef d'Equipe for the US Equestrian Show jumping team since 2005. A gold medal winner at the Pan American Games in 1959 and a silver medal winner at the 1960 Olympic Games. He was one of the most celebrated and respected trainers in the country.

I wished I had kept walking to my car and had never stopped in to say hello. I felt as young and inexperienced as little Kennedy next to me. "Oh, I didn't realize you'd trained with him. Wasn't that just a clinic?"

"It was held over a long weekend . . ." Vivian twirled the crop she still carried from her ride. "Well, I better get to the VIP tent. Best not to keep my clients waiting." Then she leaned in toward me and lowered her voice. "We got the table for the week at a steal. Twenty-five hundred for the eight of us." Mai's and Corinne's eyes widened, either in envy or shock, I couldn't tell. Vivian straightened, speaking louder now. "Are you ladies going to have dinner inside?"

"Um, well we don't have a table," Helena said, flushing.

"Oh, I'm sorry," Vivian said, then turned and mouthed, "Sorry" toward me. "What a pleasure meeting you all!" Vivian smiled, the whiteness of her teeth contrasting against her red lipstick. "Brynn, let's catch up at the next show. I'd love to discuss the possibility of us working together again."

"Sure." I had to sound convincing in front of my clients to save face, but after her performance, there was no way in hell I'd ever work with this woman.

"It was wonderful to meet you too," Corinne said, shaking Vivian's hand. "It really is a pleasure to meet the undefeated champion"—Corinne paused, tapping her chin for a moment—"of two years, right?"

"Two and a half, actually, but who's counting?" Vivian said, then laughed. The group joined in. "Have a nice evening, ladies!"

We couldn't help but watch Vivian's lithe frame retreat.

"She's surprisingly nice. Isn't she? I don't know what I expected, but she's always come across as standoffish. Goes to show, don't judge a book—" Helena said.

"She's so talented!" Mai said.

"What's this about you two working together?" Corinne asked.

"Oh, it's nothing."

"Wouldn't that be wonderful?" Corinne said.

"I'd love to work with her," Helena added. "I'm sure she'd have some great tips for me."

A murmur of agreement went through the group.

"Hey, let's get that drink, ladies. I'm sure we could find a bottle and have a drink back at the tent."

A silence greeted me. "I don't mind paying to get in tonight," Corinne said.

"Me neither. Let's go!" Helena added.

"I don't think we can get in, but sure. If you all want to," I said, though my insides churned, knowing we'd likely be turned away.

The VIP tent was the place to be, where all the best riders sat and ate in between their classes, where all the beautifully dressed ladies sat when they watched the big events. All the laughter that filtered from the tent seemed louder, and the people always appeared to have more fun.

My dad would have never spent our customers' money on glitz and glamour, so VIP tents were always out of the question, though I had eyed them longingly as a little girl. Now that I was older, I wasn't as drawn in, knowing that the laughter and joy was brought on by the free-flowing champagne.

A hostess greeted us at the entrance to the tent. "Names, please."

"Brynn Seymour. Redwood Grove Stables."

She scanned a paper in front of her. "I don't have you on the list."

"We'd like a table just for this evening."

"I'm sorry. We're all sold out." The woman went back to scribbling something on a pad.

"I see an empty table right there." Corinne gestured toward a table, front and center, facing the ring.

"It's booked," the woman said, barely glancing up from her ledger.

I leaned in toward her. "I understand, but you see"—I peered directly into her eyes—"my family's been supporting these shows for years, and it would be such a shame if we weren't able to make the show a little more money by spending some here tonight." I gave her a big smile, wishing I had better skills at charming people. "I'm sure that Erika would be ever so grateful!" I hated to drop names, but Erika knew our family well, so why not use it to my advantage? I needed to keep the clients happy.

As I thought she would, the woman softened at the sound of Erika's name. Erika was all about making a profit. Any potential revenue lost had to be accounted for at the end of the show meetings. Erika wanted her VIP tent to be renowned in the show-jumping world.

"I'm sorry." The woman's pale blue eyes darted toward the empty table. "I just can't break the rules."

I turned toward my group of riders. "I'm so sorry, ladies, but I promise to make it up to you. Let's go someplace after the Grand Prix." I wanted to crawl behind the tent.

"What's wrong, Brynn?" Vivian stood in front of us.

"It's nothing," I said.

"They won't let us in," Kennedy replied. "Brynn can't convince them and we don't have a table."

I *knew* she was a brat, I thought.

"Seriously? Come on, Lesley. They're with me!"

The lady, whose name apparently was Lesley, looked between Vivian and our group. "I don't have them on the list," she said, but with a lot less conviction than before.

"You don't? How strange!" Vivian grabbed the papers from Lesley's hands, scanning them with her finger, a look of shock on her face. "I went to talk to Erika about this earlier today. This list must not be updated." A bit of hostility entered her tone. "I'll call her right now—and hopefully this doesn't happen again. I'd hate for someone else to be embarrassed like this."

She turned toward us, beaming. She looped her arm through mine and turned me toward the entrance of the tent. "Let's go, ladies. The best riders are still to come."

A breeze picked up; the white tent billowed on three sides. The long side of the tent faced the Grand Prix arena. Twenty or so round tables, seating about a dozen people each, filled the tent. Once seated, I rested my hands in my lap, my fingers clenched and sweaty. Why had I ever walked up to this tent? We could have easily popped a bottle of wine back at our barn's tent, drinking out of plastic cups the way we'd always done it with Dad. And now here we were at Vivian's table, getting the VIP treatment because of her. I should have felt grateful, but instead my stomach was in knots.

Strangely, not one of Vivian's clients was in the tent. Had she been sitting here alone? Though the way she yelled at them earlier, maybe it wasn't that much of a surprise.

The enthusiastic voice of the announcer boomed through the speakers. "And now, ladies and gentlemen, a longtime local favorite, Chriiiis Peterson!" The small crowd cheered, while music blared. Shit. I had done so well avoiding him, and now he'd be showing right in front of me. I used to love nothing more than watching his smooth and elegant riding skills. For a moment I imagined being in his bedroom, between soft sheets, his hips pressing against mine.

Chris stopped in front of the tent, directly below our table. "Brynn." He circled De Salle, his bay, the color of a boulder opal. "You haven't called!"

I wanted to crawl under the table. Everyone in the tent and stands was watching now.

"Chris, just ride." My face was on fire. This was ridiculous, but just so . . . Chris.

His eyes met mine until I looked away, nodding my head at the clock tower. Chris didn't seem fazed. "Call me," he finally said. He and De Salle galloped off and made the first jump with under a second to spare.

I leaned back, sucking in a breath.

"Well, well. Looks like you two have something going on." Vivian gave a half smile. Helena rolled her eyes at me, knowing not to prod.

"He's so cute!" Kennedy giggled and Corinne gave her a sharp look.

Gratefully, a waiter came over. Helena ordered a bottle of red to go with the food. "A nice one," she whispered in my ear. "We deserve a celebration!"

I sat forward in my chair, analyzing each jump Chris and De Salle took. Countless times watching Grand Prix with Dad flashed through my mind. The best were the ones in which he had competed. Dad would always explain what was going on, telling me how many strides each horse should have taken, analyzing the strategies the riders took, spelling out what he agreed with and with what he didn't. Now, the horse's hooves pounded past us, De Salle's breath loud, his nostrils wide, flaring for air. A pang went through me, not just from seeing Chris.

A small part of me thought I should be out there. I'd ridden at higher heights than this when I competed at Young Riders at Spruce

Meadows. My dad had stood at the gate, calling instructions out to me, and the team coach had let him. And our team had done it. We'd won silver. During that victory, as I'd stood on the podium with the other three riders on our team, just for a moment I thought I could achieve anything, that I *could* actually ride with my Dad at the World Cup—damn, even at the Olympics. But that feeling soon faded and I went back to my day-to-day life, thinking it was all a fluke. I worried that I'd fail Dad, and in some ways, I'd fail Mom too. She didn't want me to ride. She wanted me to be a vet. She wanted me to make an independent life for myself. So I never allowed myself to imagine I'd compete at that level again.

And now, even if I wanted to, I had lost my best trainer.

I sensed eyes on me and turned. Vivian was sipping her wine. She nodded and smiled, raising her glass to me. I raised my glass in return, thankful she'd stepped in to help us get into the VIP tent, but wondering how she expected me to repay her. In my experience, nothing ever came for free. As I turned back to the arena, Chris and De Salle took the lead.

12

The next night, after getting home and helping Derek put the tack and show supplies away, I double-checked on the horses. Seraphim's head hung out of the stall into the barn, her ears pricked toward me down the dim aisle. The other horses were busy eating. Only the occasional tail swish or foot stomp resounded in the barn. The light was already off and the sunset had brought with it the evening wind. Seraphim and I stared at each other; she seemed to beckon me, as if she wanted to speak to me through those deep brown eyes.

I walked toward her, my stomach twisting with each step, my breath slowing. She remained still. As I neared, she gave a little nicker and swung her head up and down.

"Hey Sera," I whispered so as not to disturb the silence. She stopped nodding her head, her eye staring deep into mine. "Derek said your leg is all better."

Hot air from her nostril tickled my arm.

"I saw you in turnout the other day."

She nickered again, a throaty sound, then moved her head up and down like a pendulum. I brought my trembling hand up to her muzzle and she searched my open palm with her strong lips, her trimmed lip hairs prickling my hand.

"I don't have a treat for you." I smiled, my hand moving to her forehead, rubbing in between her ears. She lowered her head, her lids half closed.

She was eight years old, ready for jumping higher this year. The breeders in Belgium had already shown her in a decent-height Grand Prix.

"She's ready for you," Derek said from behind. Seraphim's head jerked up at the sound of his voice, then relaxed, realizing it was only Derek.

"I know," I said, not turning to look at him. Seraphim leaned into me, begging me to continue rubbing her face.

"I can tack her up." He moved to Seraphim's other side, picking out a piece of shavings from her mane.

I shook my head. "No. I'm fine." Sera shifted, exposing her neck. I used my nails to scratch deep through the gold and red hair that glistened like burnished brass in the darkening light. "It's been a long day wrapping up after the show. Why don't you head out?"

"You sure?" He was slipping into my dad's caretaking role. I took care of the business, and he took care of the horses—and me.

I nodded.

"All right." His hand rested on my shoulder, and I leaned my cheek toward his hand, enjoying its warmth. I turned and smiled at him, hoping he knew how much I appreciated him.

"You go." I put on my bravest smile. "Have a good night."

Derek stood by my side for a while longer. Finally he said, "I'll see you tomorrow." Then he walked down the aisle, turning once to look back at Seraphim and me.

I stood for a long time with Seraphim, but I couldn't do it. I just wasn't ready to ride her again. I hadn't forgiven her yet.

It was Labor Day. The day before vet school started. My last day teaching before heading up to Davis. Corinne and Helena stood by the fence, observing the three girls cooling out their ponies after their lesson.

"This brings back memories of my childhood," Helena said. "In the summers, my sister and I would spend time at our grandparents' house. They had horses, and we'd go out in the back hills of New Hampshire and ride for hours. My grandma was fine, as long as we got home before sunset. Half the time we didn't, and she'd get so angry—by golly—you could hear her screaming at us for miles. She had this old straw broom at the back of the veranda and she'd swing it at us, threatening to beat us silly."

Helena's laugh rang out, her shoulders shaking with laughter.

Corinne laughed too. "God, I wish I'd had that opportunity. All I did as a kid was amble from one friend's house to another. We grew up in Boston, and there weren't many horses to be found." A wistful far-off look crossed Corinne's face. She was in her forties, but she looked younger, her features prominent, strong cheekbones as if an artist had drawn them into place. She adjusted her sun hat over her stylish bob.

"Those were the best days of my life," Helena said. Her strawberry-blonde hair, looped through her tan baseball cap, accentuated her heart-shaped face. "Brynn, thank you for setting this up. I'm so glad you're able to give them this opportunity."

I smiled in response. Kennedy, Payton, and Lani had just finished their lesson when I remembered the promise I'd made to Kennedy.

"Oh, girls! I told Kennedy you'd get to ride bareback today if you did well in your lesson. I'd say we can call your lesson a success. What do you think?"

A chorus of cheers and squeals greeted me. The girls busied themselves with removing the saddles while I walked over to the moms.

Mai approached me. "Are you sure they're ready?" she asked in a hushed voice.

"They're going to be fine, Mai. They jump courses, they can ride bareback. These ponies are sweethearts, plus they're tired out." I patted her shoulder.

"Keep your heels down, even with no stirrups!" I called. "And don't forget to keep your distance from the other ponies!" Back on their horses, the girls picked up their canter. Kennedy's long blonde ponytail flopped in rhythm with Best of Luck's tail, both blowing behind them in the wind like a pair of sails. Payton laughed the whole time, her mouth wide.

"Watch out you don't catch any flies!" Helena called.

The girls' joy filled me with a huge sense of accomplishment. A few minutes later they asked us if they could take their ponies out for a trail ride, to cool them out.

"I don't see a problem with it as long as Brynn is fine with that," answered Corinne.

I nodded my approval. "Get your saddles back on and stay on the trail around the back field. But no cantering!"

The ladies and I walked to the round oak table. The fragrance of the flowers in the earthenware pots surrounding the courtyard filled the air. Helena had brought some cheese, bread, and fruit for a snack. Her freckled arms were always busy doing something. I poured freshly brewed coffee. Horses neighed in the barn as Derek wheeled in the afternoon hay. The sharp, sweet smell and sound of the cart always brought the horses to excitement.

Corinne tore off a piece of French bread. "So Brynn, have you called Chris yet?" Of course she'd ask. She always wanted to know everything and wouldn't allow for anyone else to get the news first. I was surprised it took her this long.

"Corinne!" Helena looked over at her friend, clearly surprised by her forward question.

All eyes turned toward me.

"Nope." I didn't want to feed the rumor mill, so I hoped my one-word answer would shut it down. I stared out into the distance, keeping an eye on the three ponies and their riders.

"Well, I guess it's none of my business, but everyone's speculating about why he left the East Coast," Mai chimed in.

"Ladies, I think we better leave the gossip out," I said, holding my hand up.

"Well, he is a handsome catch—I wish I were young enough to scoop that one up!" Helena laughed. Mai and Corinne joined in.

"If Brynn doesn't want to hear the gossip, she doesn't need to." Corinne cocked her head sideways, and I was almost lured into asking what she knew, but I bit my lip and turned my head. It wouldn't be that easy. Corinne, noting I didn't take the bait, tossed a grape in her mouth. "So, who's got a good erotica book recommendation?"

"Ooh! I read a juicy one last week," Mai leaned in, peering over her shoulder before continuing.

I stood up, grabbing the coffeepot. "It's been wonderful afternoon, ladies, but I've got to get to Davis tonight. First day of school is tomorrow, and I want to make sure I have everything ready at my apartment."

"We'll see you next Friday!" Helena replied and the others nodded, wishing me a happy first week of school. Their voices trailed off behind me as I walked to the barn.

My cell phone chimed. Text message from Chris. *Still waiting. Stop by my place tonite.*

I stared at the cell phone, my thumb running over the text. Maybe I needed the distraction after all.

13

After taking a shower and packing for Davis, I took one last glance at my dresser to see if I'd missed anything. My musical jewelry box lay hidden beneath the silk scarf draped over my dresser mirror. I picked up the box, my fingers grazing the silver unicorn stitched into the lid. Inside were items I'd collected as a little girl: a strand of my first pony's hair tied with a pink ribbon, a wallet-sized picture of Mom and Dad with me and my pony at my first show, the heart pendant from Dad, goofy photo-booth pictures with Derek, and the beaded necklace Chris had given me at our first show at Del Mar.

I hesitated only a moment before texting him that I'd stop by. His place was on my way to Davis, and it wouldn't take me more than an hour to get to my apartment from there.

I placed my two suitcases and a duffle bag into the trunk of my car, gave Subira one last pet goodbye, and went back into the house.

"I packed a little something," Mom said, holding out a basket for me. It held a jar of my favorite jam, a container of tomato soup, and my favorite sweet bread from the local deli. I gave her a kiss on the cheek, and she pulled me in for an embrace. She said she'd do better next weekend, and she'd go shopping for more of the things I liked.

"This is more than I expected," I said. It had always been an elaborate dance, me leaving for school at the end of August, Mom packing food and supplies for my apartment, filling the trunk of my car with a couple of throw cushions and a fleece blanket, "for those long nights studying," she would say. She was more excited than me at the start of each semester. "You're going to have that DVM behind your name soon," she'd chirp. "You just wait and see. It'll feel so good to have your own freedom. To be independent. To follow your dreams." Dad would wait for me to go down to the barn to say goodbye, busy with riding or teaching or working at his desk, making sure I knew how displeased he was that I was leaving. I was caught in between their dance steps—a third wheel in a cumbersome waltz. But I knew they had both wanted the best for me. Today it all seemed like a hasty rendition of that dance, a mock performance, but at least she was out and about, her depression seeming to lift—and that's all I needed to keep moving forward. I had to fulfill my duty. I had to be the good girl.

My last moment before heading off to school, I had to finally confront Chris.

Driving, I started reminiscing, how I'd met Chris at a show in third grade, how we'd been friends for years, going to Del Mar and other horse shows as friends and teammates. What stuck out in my mind most was a moment during the summer after I turned seventeen. Chris and I sat leaning behind a barn at the Spruce Meadows show where we had competed for the West Coast Young Riders Team, when he lit up and passed me a joint. I wanted to say no, but I also wanted to spend time with him like we used to, to feel like his girlfriend. Before I knew it, we started kissing, his hands slowly moving up my shirt. Our kiss made my head reel, though looking back it was probably the pot, and by the time we fell back on the ground, I said I wanted him.

Chris pulled away from me, holding me at arm's distance, staring at me as if seeing me for the first time. He told me I was the most innocent and precious person he'd ever known, and he would never spoil that by sleeping with me. I felt like someone had punched me in the gut. We walked back to the party, and he talked and laughed with all the riders, and pretended like nothing had happened, and we never brought it up again.

After that, I was busy with college, then vet school, and the last thing I needed was the complication of a relationship. Not that he was interested. Until now.

As I drove through the gate I had to pause to make sure I was at the right address. The old Hendricks Ranch had been transformed. It had always been one of the barns where weeds grew taller than the fence, and the paint chips gave eye splinters to anyone driving by. Now the asphalt reflected the mauve sky, the barns gleamed with a fresh coat of white paint, and the barn entrances, adorned with wisteria, reminded me of a Spanish hacienda. The footing in the arena had only ever been good enough for growing crops, but now the white silica sand glared back at me as two riders walked their horses side by side, chatting. The place belonged on the cover of some sort of *Architectural Digest* for barns.

I pulled up to the last of the three barns on the left and stepped out of my car. A staircase wound to the apartment above the barn, and as I climbed, my hesitation grew. The girls riding in the arena stared at me, making my climb intolerable. My pet peeve about this business, again—the gossip. No doubt they knew who I was, and by tomorrow rumors would be flying. The hunter-jumper community left no place for privacy.

"Brynn! God, it's good to see you!" Chris pulled me toward him as soon as he opened the door. We hugged for a moment, his scent reminiscent of tall city skyscrapers and the surf, of a Ralph Lauren ad. His hair fell over his forehead and I resisted an urge to brush it aside. Instead I ran a hand through my own hair, which I wore down for the occasion, feeling out of place in my plain blue jeans and UC Davis sweatshirt.

He wore the necklace I had given him when we were at Del Mar, the sister necklace to the one back in my jewelry box. We'd exchanged them at our first Young Riders competition. I ignored the sudden tightness in my throat.

He came close, as if to give me another hug, but I turned to take in the apartment.

The loft had exposed wooden beams, arched windows with blue tiled accents recessed into the white adobe walls. Skylights streamed in ribbons of the setting sun. A ladder led up to a second split level. The smell of fresh paint and brand-new carpet filled the room. The oak cabinets in the kitchen appeared new, and though the apartment was small, it didn't seem crowded due to the sparse contemporary furnishings, which were, not surprisingly, well organized. Chris had always been a neat freak.

"Wow. They did a great job fixing this place up. Last I remember it was a hay barn."

"You like? It's not quite finished, and obviously it's a bit small and needs a certain *je ne sais quoi*." He pointed to several boxes on the floor. "A woman's touch, maybe?"

"I'm sure you won't have a problem finding that." I walked toward the leather couch, running my hand along the back.

He followed me. "I can show you upstairs. It's right here." He gestured toward the wooden ladder steps. Seeing the look on my face, Chris laughed. "Well, come on. Have a seat and I'll bring out the grub."

I sat on the sofa. "This is nice, but why in the world didn't you finish your year with McLain Ward? And why didn't you move into your parents' guesthouse?" His parents owned a three-acre estate in Tiburon, and the guesthouse spanned almost two thousand square feet.

"It's not far enough away from my mother," he called from the kitchen, his voice muffled as he poked his head in the fridge.

"Besides, being here works out perfectly, since this is where De Salle is stabled. I don't have to wake up too early to train. Want one?" He held up a bottle of beer.

"No thanks. I'm driving to Davis, remember?"

I picked up an East Coast–based show jumping magazine from the coffee table, interested in the fresh faces and big shot names of riders who didn't frequent the West Coast shows. A story titled *The Benefits of Ayurveda and Yoga for Hunter Jumper Riders*, by Jason Lander, caught my eye. Ayurveda and yoga for riders? I peered at the small photo insert of the author who stood in a field of wildflowers, his arm around a gray horse, yellow sun lightening the field behind them. Uncle Ian's friend, the man at the funeral whose eyes I hadn't been able to get out of my head.

I turned the page. Photos of Chris going over a huge black-and-gold jump, a close-up of him laughing with his hair ruffled, and one of him with a group of people at a party took up a two-page spread titled *The Jumper Rider to Look Out for Next Year*.

"Hey! You're in here, Chris!"

"Oh, that. Whatever. It's nothing." He carried in a tray of food and drinks. He sat next to me, his face clouded.

His lack of interest surprised me. Normally he'd be bragging about this kind of thing. "What are you talking about? This is so amazing!"

"Seriously. It's nothing." He grabbed the magazine out of my hand and tossed it on the end table. "Mother's having a conniption fit that I want to switch to jumpers. As if I ever wanted to be a hunter rider to begin with. It was always *her* dream. But, whatever. It's time for some dinner." He placed the tray of rolls in front of me. "I haven't had good sushi like this since I left California."

Our eyes met, and he seemed to lean in. I could almost feel his breath. He reached and brushed my hair behind my ear. "So now you know the real reason for my coming back."

I held my breath.

"It's the sushi!" He sat back up and laughed.

I closed my eyes. I hadn't realized how much my body would react to his. And I thought that if I let myself, I could have fun and be young with him. But how could I, when so much responsibility lay on me? I sat up and picked up a piece of a rainbow roll with my chopsticks.

"Shit. I forgot the music!" Chris jumped up, almost dropping his plate, and turned on the surround sound. A Train song filled the room. I leaned back and with the sound of the music, Chris's laugh, and the sushi, the past few weeks faded. I curled my feet up on the couch, wanting to hide from the world in this loft.

After dinner, in the bathroom, I stared at myself in the mirror. My eyes sparkled, my cheeks had color, my complexion glowed. *Take it down a notch, Brynn,* I told myself.

I dried my hands, scanning the shelves for hand cream. His bathroom had more salon shampoos, conditioners, and moisturizers than I ever used. Having a tough time finding a simple lotion, I picked the closest one. Its musky scent reminded me of Chris, and a part of me wished he'd ask me to go upstairs again. This time I'd say yes.

When I got back, Chris had already put away the sushi tray and plates. He tapped the sofa next to him. "Don't go yet. Let's talk about your plans." He cleared his throat and added, "What with your dad gone and all . . ."

I felt the blood drain from my face. I didn't want to talk about my plans. I'd have preferred to go upstairs instead, to not analyze, to not think. I picked at the ends of my hair, tearing apart a split end. "You still haven't answered my question. Why are you back?"

Chris eyed me for a minute, leaning in, brushing my hair off my shoulder. "Let's just say it was best."

"Best? For what?"

Chris stood, and busied himself with wiping the counter. "Can we not talk about it?"

"Chris. It's me. Brynn. Remember?"

"Don't worry about it. It was nothing. Just got mixed up with the wrong crowd, that's all."

"What the hell? Did you get caught smoking weed or something?"

"Just drop it." He moved across the room, his fists clenched at his side, his jaw tight.

"Fine." I stood. "It's probably time I get going anyway."

We said our goodbyes, and Chris asked me to stop by the following week. He gave me a cool kiss on the cheek, and whatever I'd felt between us had dissipated.

I wound my way down the stairs. "Is that you, Brynn? What are you doing here?"

I squinted into the darkness. "Vivian?"

"Funny to find you here." She glanced at the stairs leading to Chris's apartment and I felt heat rising in my cheeks.

"Visiting an old friend," I said.

Vivian nodded, then walked closer. "I teach lessons here sometimes."

I gave her a questioning look.

"Yeah, I know. Weird. But the last trainer left in the middle of the night, and the Hendricks were desperate to fill the instructor position. I finally caved, and told them I'd fill in until they found someone. You can imagine my surprise when Chris got the job." She laughed.

"I'm sure." I jangled the keys to my car, wishing I could get to Davis.

"Have you given some thought to me helping you out?"

My sweatshirt suddenly seemed too warm, and I pulled at the neckline, wishing the breeze would kick up. I stood up straighter, asserting myself. "I haven't had time to think about it yet."

A rider exited the arena, his horse's shoes clip-clopping on the asphalt as he walked the horse toward the barn.

"But I promise I'll get back to you soon. Well, I still have a long drive." I tried to move past her.

"Davis?"

I nodded and opened the driver's side door.

"You should be careful around him," Vivian said as I threw my purse onto the passenger seat.

I paused, my foot resting on the edge of the car. "What?"

"It's not really my place to interfere, but"—she hesitated—"we're friends." Vivian looked at me, as if awaiting confirmation.

I nodded, despite doubts about her motives.

"You might want to find out what happened back East." She tilted her head up at the loft. "I hear he's caused some, shall we say, problems?"

I wanted desperately to get in the car, to not listen to her.

"Well, I sure hope it's only a rumor. I've known Chris as long as you have, maybe longer," Vivian said, putting her hair up. "And I love him like a brother. He means a lot to me. Well, you know. We've *all* known each other a lifetime."

The light inside the car turned off, leaving us in darkness. I looked down at the ground, chewing on my lip.

"Well, goodnight, Brynn. I hope this helps. I'm just looking out for you. Us girls, we have to stick together. Girl power, and all that."

I wasn't sure whether to believe her and whether she really was looking out for me. What would be in it for her?

"I'll call you," Vivian said. "And don't worry. It's probably nothing."

14

I sat in the barn office, staring at the calendar hanging on the wall. Wild mustangs ran through a river, water splashing around them, their manes and tails flowing: gray, black, and pinto-colored horses, wild as their ancestors. Saturday, October 13. Six weeks since school had started. Over three months since Dad died. I surveyed the office: the bookcases laden with horse nutrition and training books, the wall of ribbons and photos. Dad's leather chair and his mahogany desk. I ran my fingers along the armrest of the chair, the cracks in the dark leather so much like wrinkled skin.

I wondered how long I could keep going like this. The circles under my eyes continued to darken as my skin grew paler. My head throbbed, and the tightness in my neck wouldn't go away even with extra-strength Advil. The crazy schedule of driving to Davis on Sunday nights, studying, going on-call in the middle of the night, driving back to the ranch on Friday afternoons, teaching and riding Friday through Sunday were all taking their toll. I knew I didn't have much choice but to keep moving forward, but I wondered what would happen next year. And the year after. Would I be able to find a job as a vet? And how much money could I make the first year? From the statistics I'd seen, not much.

According to Seth Armstrong, we had until February at the latest to catch up with the missed mortgage payments. Dad had purchased the lowest-cost life insurance policy possible, and twenty percent of it had already been used up by funeral expenses. The

Farmington Public Library
SelfCheck Out Receipt (5)

Customer ID: ****9067

Items that you checked out

Title: Learning to fall : a novel
ID: 002000550338
Due: Friday, February 07, 2020

Title: This house is mine
ID: 002000438975
Due: Friday, February 07, 2020

Title: Waiting for Bojangles : a novel
ID: 002000508178
Due: Friday, February 07, 2020

Total items: 3
1/10/2020 4:57 PM
Checked out: 4
Ready for pickup: 0

For a complete schedule of events at the
Farmington Public Library, be sure to check the
calendar at www.infoway.org

#ReadFarmington

remainder had paid for two months' worth of expenses for the farm, and one month of the past-due mortgage. We had until spring to be in the clear. I closed my eyes, not able to imagine what life would be like without the ranch, our home, to not be able to ride Jett, to not see him every weekend.

"Hey." Derek stood at the desk. I hadn't even heard him come in.

"Hey." I straightened my shoulders, trying to paste on a smile.

"Do you want Jett out now or later?" Derek looked younger than me now, his cheeks still golden brown, and now he sported a small goatee.

"Later's good." I wanted to wait until everyone had gone home, to be alone with Jett, alone with my thoughts. I went back to staring at the computer screen, leaning forward over my keyboard to give the appearance of being busy. Derek kept standing in front of me.

"I know you have a lot going on, and I don't mean to bug you about this, but . . ." He drew the "but" out, and I didn't like where this was heading. "It's Seraphim." Derek's voice trailed off. "Did you want to ride her this week?" As the trainer, it was now my job to ride her, to train her to be a show jumper. To the level at which Dad had planned to show her.

I didn't take my eyes off the blank computer screen. "Well, I think she's doing fine under your care, don't you?" My eyes flitted to him, then I squinted, pretending to read something carefully on the screen. She was still in rehab and Derek was doing well training her on the flat.

"Yeah, yeah. She's doing great. She's really coming along. I just thought—"

"Hey, Derek. I really have to get to this e-mail." I tapped a nail on the desk. "So, just keep using the Eurociser and stick with the exercise plan Uncle Ian created. Okay?" I felt stifled, desperate to open a window.

"Yeah. Of course. No problem." He smoothed his goatee. "And just a reminder I'm heading out early today. Bill and I have tickets to the Giants game. You know, box seats and all. Lots of booze, and great food beforehand, too. So even though it's not really our bag, it's a freaking Giants game. Can't be all bad. You want to join? We have an extra ticket." He smiled, raising his brow, trying to get me to smile back.

"Nah, I've got a lot of things to catch up on, then a bunch of clinical studies to read through for a class next week. But say hi to Bill."

"Sure. Well, thanks for letting me go. Bill's been such a crab, lately. Constantly grumbling about my long days, that he never sees me, yadda, yadda, yadda." Derek ran his hand through his dark hair, scratching his scalp.

"What's going on?"

"Nothing. Just *relationship* stuff." Derek threw me his most charming smile. "Nothing to worry about. You get some rest, B. You look like you need it."

After Derek left I rubbed my temples with my middle and index fingers in slow circles, putting pressure on the pain. I checked the barn schedule on my smartphone. One more lesson, and then I could ride Jett.

I was managing to ride Jett only once a week now. If I was lucky. I tried to pretend that didn't bother me, but in reality every time I was with him now I felt that I should be showing him, not just keeping him as a glorified pet. Dad had wanted more from Jett, and definitely more from me, but I'd never known how to tell him that I didn't have the courage. I was afraid of failing, of losing, of disappointing him. It was much easier to pursue being a vet, something I knew I could do well. All I had to do was follow the prescribed courses, study hard, and I'd end up with a degree at the end. A lot more predictable. A lot more chance of success. Then Mom could quit one of her jobs. Maybe she'd get back to working on her novel. She could finally pursue her dreams.

The retirement-home driver had just picked up Pam, Patty, and Peggy, who'd come to brush their horses, and I was finally alone at the barn.

"I'm sorry I haven't been around, buddy." I cleaned Jett's face thoroughly with a damp terry cloth, making sure to wipe around his eyes, up and around his nostrils and his lips. Jett nuzzled my arm, trying to stick his head under it. "I know you could do a lot more. You could still have a whole jumping career ahead of you."

I mounted him outside and opted to ride on the trails around the property instead of in the arena. The trees and shrubs had taken on a hint of pink, reflecting the light in the sky as the sun went down. Wisps of fog filtered through the trees, like a scene from *Lord of the Rings*. I heard a hawk's high-pitched, long *kee-eeeee-arr* sound above, looked up, and saw it plunge toward something below us. The speed of a hawk's flight always amazed me. It reminded me of the rush of going over jumps.

I hadn't yet taken down the small three-foot course I'd set up for Helena's lesson. I trotted back to the arena, then cantered Jett around the ring. The combination of the setting sun in the distance, the cool breeze, and the wonder at being alone lifted me to a place I hadn't been at in a long time. My soul seemed to connect with Jett's, with the hawk's, with the surrounding light. There was nothing like it in the world.

I picked up my right lead and pushed Jett forward over the twelve-jump course. He barely made an effort as we flew over them. The course was too easy for him; we'd first jumped fences this height years ago. He didn't even arch his back. I laughed, the sound startling me.

Jett nickered, and I laughed again, throwing my arms around him. His breath came slower now, his heat radiating, warming me from the inside. I knew in that instant that no matter what happened, I needed to keep Jett and this land.

I hosed him down in the outdoor wash rack. The water droplets caught the setting sun's rays, like diamonds falling through the air. Jett's wet coat reflected blue, gold, and red, like a drape of silk over his body. I used the sweat scraper to get most of the water off, then grazed him in the grass.

I looked up just in time to see Corinne placing a saddle into the back of her black SUV.

"Corinne!" I called toward her. She had the driver's side door open, hesitating.

"Oh, hi Brynn. Just, um, forgot Kennedy's school bag." She walked slowly toward me and Jett, a waft of her vibrant perfume drifting on the breeze. "That reminds me, she's got a ton of homework this week. I was going to e-mail you. She won't be riding in lessons." Corinne began to tap her foot, clad in a gold ballet flat. With her white capris, she didn't belong anywhere near a horse barn.

"There's that show at the end of October coming up, so it would be good if she got to practice more," I said, letting Jett graze in the grass next to me.

"She's in junior high now, at the Lycée—you know how tough it is to get in there—and it's such a challenging program. Really was a wonder she got in, what with her lackadaisical attitude. And you know how it is with kids these days, they have to prove themselves or they won't get in to the right high school, then won't get in to the right college, then won't get the right job." Corinne played with the pendant of her necklace, pulling it back and forth.

"Of course," I said, patting Jett.

"Well, I need to run. Dinner to pick up and all that. But I'll see you later." She smoothed her hair absentmindedly, her eyes shifting away.

"Yes, of course," I said again. "Don't forget the lesson on Friday and Saturday."

"Yes, yes. We'll be here," she said, turning toward her car.

"Good night then," I said, and placed my hand on Jett's back, his muscles moving ever so slightly as he grazed.

I watched her taillights recede, blurred by the tendrils of fog rolling in.

I put Jett back in his stall and walked down the barn aisle, peeking into every stall, checking on each horse as they settled in for the night. I might as well have been tucking children in, these creatures in my care, my responsibility. I turned off the lights, then pulled the cedar doors of the barn shut to ward off the dampness and cold of the fog. I wondered about dinner, not looking forward to eating alone again. Mom had been back to work, night shifts twice a week and day shifts four days a week.

I turned to walk up toward the house and was startled by a man's outline leaning against the oak table. I jumped back, looking behind me, wishing I had something with me for protection.

Then I recognized him, the moon behind him, its light filtering through the mist, casting shadows on his face.

Chris walked toward me.

"God, you scared me," I said.

Chris moved closer, a sheepish smile on his face. "I've missed you," he said, holding out a bouquet of red roses. "I'm sorry for being so weird last time. The move, everything, it's all just getting to me."

I pressed my nose into the silky rose petals, inhaling. "I've missed you too," I said, suddenly longing for a connection. I wanted to belong. I was an empty vase, and the roses weren't enough to fill me. I needed his touch. I wanted to be held, to have someone's arms wrapped around me.

Chris grabbed me, his hands on the small of my back, tugging me toward him. The flowers crumpled between us as his lips crushed mine. I entwined my fingers in his hair, pulling his head tighter to mine. His lips sought mine, his tongue warm inside my mouth. He tasted of dark chocolate and raspberries. The air filled with the scent of roses and Giorgio, and before I knew it, I asked him to come to my room.

We hurried inside. I dropped the roses on my dresser, my jeans and shirt on the ground. Chris took his time, undressing slowly, watching me watch him, then he placed his clothes neatly on top of the bench in front of my bed. How long had I wanted this? Years, I decided. Definitely years. I stood exposed in my bra and panties, crossing my arms over my chest, suddenly shy, even as my heart and body filled with a desire to feel him, to love him.

"You're fucking exquisite," he murmured.

He pressed his body into mine. We fell on the bed, and all my hesitation disappeared, my guilt, my fear. I silenced my conscience. I needed this. As Chris moved above me, I lost my need to analyze and understand, and instead, gave in to the moment.

I woke the next morning with a smile on my lips, the smell of sex, musky and sweet, all over me, the bed. Chris was gone. I stretched, realizing that this was the first time I had slept well in months. No nightmares, no waking up at three in the morning trying to force myself back to sleep. I ran my finger along my lips, remembering Chris's kisses, his tongue, his body pressed into mine.

My cell phone chimed. I tried to find my phone among my clothes and the wilting rose petals that had fallen to the ground. Text message from Chris: *Be ready in 20. Taking you to brkfst.*

I did a Charlie Chaplin jump, letting out a small whoop, wrestling with my iPhone to get music on. Hurriedly, I showered and dressed.

When I heard his car pull into the drive I checked the phone. Right on time. I twirled out the door, locking it behind me. Chris bound up the steps toward me, two at time.

"Hello, gorgeous!" He leaned in, wrapped his arms around me, then dipped me. He gazed into my eyes, his nose brushing against mine, kissing me in a dramatic gesture. I had to laugh.

As we walked toward the car I stopped, letting out a whistle. "Holy shit, Chris!" I walked closer to the blue Porsche convertible sitting in the driveway.

"Killer, isn't she?" Chris walked around the car, leaning on the hood. "You'd look perfect right here, baby." He patted the hood.

I couldn't help rolling my eyes. He really did make me laugh, and I'd forgotten what that was like. "What about your Lexus? As I recall, that was a perfect ride too, wasn't it?"

"It got old. I'd had it for three years. It's time for a change. Fresh start, and all that." He moved toward the passenger door, holding it open for me. "Besides, how could I say no to this fierce machine?"

I shrugged my shoulders. "Well, I guess if you can afford it . . ." Who was I to judge? Maybe I'd be buying a new sports car too if I had the means.

"They had a great deal this weekend. Couldn't pass it up. Let me show you what she can do." Chris slipped into the driver's seat, leaned over and grabbed the back of my head, kissing me again. My lips parted, his tongue searching out mine. I melted into the leather, enveloped by the bucket seat, my body awakening with desire again.

"Maybe we should stay in?" I said. "I wouldn't mind skipping breakfast today."

"Uh uh uh." He shook his head, brushing his bangs out of his eyes. "We're going. My treat." He put the car into gear, and gunned it out of the driveway. "We're going to Bodega Bay, baby!"

I leaned my head back on the seat, letting the wind whip my hair, turning my face toward the warmth of the sun. This all felt like a dream. Why had I placed restrictions on myself, why hadn't I allowed myself to let go? Chris was good for me. He took the stress and tension away. Exactly what I needed.

All week I anticipated the weekend, when I could see Chris again. I hadn't meant to fall under his spell, but he was like an addiction, and seeing him gave me a much-needed high. Even when Corinne cancelled her Saturday lesson—hers and Kennedy's—I wasn't too upset. I'd have more time to spend with Chris.

Around ten that night, I lay spent on Chris's platform bed,

tangled in the silkiness of his navy sheets in the loft above the barn, amazed that I was finally in his arms. Chris lay on his side, even more handsome naked than I'd ever dared imagine. I'd been in a couple of relationships, but school and horses always came first, and I had no time for men. Besides, I always imagined Chris as *the one*. The candlelight flickered, casting soft shadows over the slanted attic ceiling. I reached out and played with the few blond hairs on his chest. I could see future Sunday nights becoming a reprieve before school.

Chris leaned over, his lips brushing mine. "You're such a kind soul. The one good thing in my life." He said this so quietly that I almost didn't hear him.

I laughed. "Oh, please." I nudged at his ribs, my palm splaying against his chest. "You've had a life full of wonderful things, starting with an amazing family."

"Ah. If you only knew . . ." He pulled his hand away, the spot on my hip where it had lain suddenly cold. Poor, poor Chris. Always thinking that he had had it so rough. The poor little rich boy. He'd never had to deal with money problems, unlike ninety-nine percent of the world. The cool breeze blew in through the open skylight, bringing with it the scent of eucalyptus.

Chris pursed his lips and exhaled. "I don't know if my mother and I will ever see eye to eye." He reached to the dresser and took a long pull of his beer. The candlelight reflected a dozen golden suns in the large dresser mirror.

"Of course you will. How can you even say that?" I laughed. "Come on, Chris. What could be so bad?"

Chris didn't look at me.

"You two go through this every couple of years, some misunderstanding comes up, but she always comes around."

"Not this time. She's set on me doing hunters, probably for the rest of my fucking life. I want to move on. Want to do my own thing. But *mother's* invested money into it. So now *mother* won't support me doing jumpers." Chris crossed his hands across his chest.

"She's talking all kinds of bullshit. Said she doesn't want me home for Thanksgiving. Of course my father won't stand up to her." Chris balled his fist, and punched a pillow. "This is the longest we've gone without talking. Why do you think I had to get this job? She says she's not going to pay for De Salle's upkeep anymore, and she's put my other two horses up for sale at that crappy sales barn."

Finally I understood. "You just have to give her time. She'll come around, especially once she sees how well you're doing in jumpers. Come on, Chris. You're her only son . . . her reason for living. All she ever talks about to anyone, anywhere, is you." And it was true. I knew from Dad that as a young woman, Chris's mother had been on the circuit for years, both on the East Coast and in California. She lived and breathed horses—and then once Chris was born, it was only about him. She had Chris showing in lead-line classes at five. Small pony hunters by eight. By eleven she purchased three top champion ponies so that he'd have every advantage. Even after he started college, he always had a string of at least three, frequently four horses. Most of them imported from Europe from top champion stallions. She could afford it. She came from money, and Chris's father was a venture capitalist, one of the first to invest in Microsoft. Even though Chris thought his father was henpecked, I'd seen him try to step in on many occasions, to say Chris needed to work for the horses. But his mother would laugh it off. Chris was hers to do with as she pleased, and no son of hers would work for a living. Until now. Now that he wanted to do his own thing.

Chris stared into the distance, the candlelight reflecting in his pupils. "Let's forget about it. I meant to talk to you about something else tonight. I've been thinking, wouldn't it be great if while you were at vet school I helped out with your clients? Maybe we could train together? Chris and Brynn: the unstoppable team."

Chris sat up now, the sheet falling around his hips. "Picture this." He waved his arms in a dramatic gesture. "We train out of Redwood, and we bring in a bunch of new students. With my name behind the barn, the place will be packed! Between my training, and your facilities—well, actually we'd have to build another barn, but that's okay. That's just details. We could easily add temporary stalls, say, take out an equity loan on the ranch. Your mom would go for that, don't you think? She's always liked me. If we brought forward a business plan? A proposal?" Chris beamed, his cheeks flushed. "You're good with numbers. We can sell the idea to her. I know we can. It'll be so fucking sweet!"

I stiffened. Through the open skylight, the black sky studded with shimmering stars lay above us. "I think you should talk to your mother," I said, twisting the silk sheet in my hands, then letting it fall loose again, flattening it across my belly. "You know, family is the only thing that lasts forever. And your mother will back you. She always has."

Chris sat back down on his heels, narrowing his eyes, pacing his breath. "You just need time to think about it. Sorry I dropped it on you so out of the blue, and you're still probably deciding what to do with the will money." He leaned down to get his underwear from the floor.

Will money? Holy shit. Chris thought I'd come into money, and had no idea the dire straits we were in. "No, no. It's not that—"

"Well, it's just an idea, and we can talk about things later. Let's grab something to eat. I'm starving." Chris pulled on his jeans and shirt and gave me a big smile. "Where do you want to go for dinner? My treat."

I had to hold back the urge to punch a pillow of my own. Our financial crisis was still a secret, so how the hell would he feel if he knew we had no money, and in the near future possibly no barn? No Redwood Grove Stables? Where might we be then?

15

The following week I sat listening to the 8:00 a.m. lecture on Equine Surgery and Lameness at the Davis School of Veterinary Medicine. Naturally I had chosen to specialize in equine medicine, and I was especially keen on this elective. Most of fourth year involved hands-on learning through the Veterinary Teaching Hospital, clinics, and working out in the field. I'd taken so many theoretical classes during the first three years that the handful of classes I had now seemed to be a breeze.

Many of my classmates complained about the early start time, but it wasn't getting to class early that was the problem: I was up by six, ran, showered, drank a double espresso, grabbed a high-protein breakfast—normally some power bar—and I was ready to roll by seven thirty. My apartment was only a five-minute drive from the vet-school buildings, good for days I was on call. No, it wasn't the early morning. It was that now, whenever I sat in class, I dreamt of riding Jett across rolling hills and pastures at Redwood Grove, and increasingly dreamt of the adrenaline rush of going over bright-colored jumps at a show. I wondered how I could make Chris's dream of us working together work.

Professor Dixon made her way across the floor at the front of the lecture hall, black-brown curls bouncing as she walked. How did she manage to always look so put together? Enthusiastic, young—for a professor anyway—and definitely engaging, she was my favorite.

I looked up at the board, typing frantically on my laptop, trying to catch up to what she'd been talking about, knowing I'd have to ask someone for help later. She spoke clearly, involving the class, energizing the sleepy room. She was like a spokesmodel for animal surgery. She made the material sound more exciting than climbing Mount Everest. I wished I shared her enthusiasm. Ever since I was eight or so I'd been watching minor procedures whenever one of the horses needed attending to, and I had enjoyed medicine. Enjoyed helping injured horses. "She's got guts," I once overheard Uncle Ian say to my dad after I had helped assist him in suturing an especially gruesome deep cut. I hadn't flinched, even though the flesh had ripped straight to the bone of the leg, the tissue shredded, difficult to stitch.

"She does—just not necessarily in the right place," Dad had responded.

He probably never realized I'd heard, and how deeply the disappointment in his voice had hurt me.

But now I wondered if maybe I'd made a mistake. Maybe I should have followed Dad's advice and spent time training with him. After all, he was the best rider I'd ever seen, and now I'd never have that chance again.

Professor Dixon walked across the front of the room, her lips moving, and I tried to focus. At least finally, this year we would have mostly hands-on experience. I'd have a chance to be around horses again.

"And with that, we'll see you at the clinic on Friday. Don't forget to look up the tutorial online." The class murmured, laptops shut, backpacks shuffled as students started to get up and leave, Professor Dixon breezed out of the hall.

"Hey, Chad." I tapped my classmate who sat in front of me on the shoulder. "Would you mind sending me your file with the notes on this? I think I missed a couple of pages." I gave him an apologetic look.

"No problem. Hey, you wanna go out with us Friday? We're headed to Maestro's for drinks. The gang wants to go dancing. We're thinking The Red Door at ten." His eyes sparkled in the lecture-hall lights, and I felt bad that I never returned his obvious affection. We had tried dating for a bit back in undergrad, but I just never felt that way about him.

"Wish I could," I said. "I have to head home Friday. Our barn has a show to go to at the end of October, and I need to make sure they're ready."

"Bummer. I hope you won't be missing out on all the class activities like you did last year."

As I walked out of the teaching pavilion I thought back to Chad's words. I wasn't missing out. I wasn't into drinking and partying. I hated the lack of control I felt with alcohol, and then the hangovers—the pounding headaches, the chills. Who needed that? And what of the wasted hours that I could have used for riding instead?

I lifted my face to the October sunshine. The intense summer heat had finally let up, and now it hovered around seventy-five degrees.

My phone vibrated in my pocket.

Derek's name popped up on my display. "Good morning, Derek. What's up?" I said, happy to hear from him. A touch of home.

"Something's going on, B. A trailer just pulled in. The driver says he's here to get Corinne's horses."

"What? That's not possible—" I thought back to my conversations with Corinne, and whether she'd mentioned a clinic.

"What do you want me to do?" Derek sounded panicked.

"Don't let him load them. I'll call you right back." I hung up and dialed Corinne's number. She didn't answer.

My phone chimed. A text message from Corinne:

Sorry. Moving horses today. We'll talk later.

I stared at the phone, blinking. Moving? Just a few weeks ago we'd all had such a great day. Kennedy. I'd be losing Kennedy. I stopped in the middle of the path, and students ran into me.

"Watch it!" someone yelled.

This explained why she and Kennedy had missed lessons. And all the recent questions about lesson times during the week, whether we were going to get a better wash rack installed, when would we get another groom.

I had to get home. I had to stop her. I hurried to my car, while dialing Corinne again. Voice mail.

"Corinne? It's Brynn. Not sure what's going on, but can we talk? I'm sure we can figure things out. Please, please call me. I'll be home this afternoon and would love to talk in person." I hung up, my voice shaking, my heart racing. I half ran to my car, then remembered Derek.

I dialed his number. "Derek. You can let the horses go."

Silence.

"Derek? You there?" I pulled my phone away to make sure the call hadn't dropped.

"Is she paid up?" came his quiet voice.

"She never falls behind."

"How are we going to deal, B?"

"Not sure. She's a reasonable woman. I'll talk to her," I said.

Derek didn't respond.

"Keep anyone you see calm. I'll be home by noon."

"I'll do what I can."

"Oh. And Derek?"

"Yeah?"

"If you see my mom, don't say anything."

I sped west along I-80, praying there were no cops on the road, pushing my little Honda as fast as it would go. Losing four horses from our training program would be devastating. I calculated in my head the income we earned each month, each dollar necessary for our survival.

"How could this be happening?" I said out loud. I had thought I was managing the clients well while still attending school. Of all the scenarios, I hadn't considered losing anyone.

Helena. Was she thinking of leaving too? Who else? My heart

raced. I realized I'd passed all the cars in the other lanes, and I looked down at the speedometer. I was doing almost ninety. I took my foot off the gas.

I had to talk to Corinne to find out what was going on.

As if on cue, the phone rang.

"Corinne," I answered, placing the call on speaker while trying to balance my cell on my knee. Now would be the time I'd likely be pulled over for speeding and talking on my phone.

"Brynn. I don't know what to say—"

"How about letting me know what happened? I thought everything was going great. You had some awesome shows this summer, and Dolce did so well in the last class you took him in."

"Things are fine. I just need more."

"What do you mean, *more?*" My voice came out high pitched and whiny.

"You're just not here often enough. Now, don't get me wrong, I know school is your priority, and while you're great, I need to be the priority. My kids and horses need to be the priority. I need you here one hundred percent."

I shook my head. "Corinne. I'm there for your Friday afternoon lessons, as well as Saturdays and Sundays. The horses are under excellent care the rest of the time."

"But *you're* not here. Your dad was always here. And I can't have our horses, our babies, with a substandard trainer on those days. No offense to Derek of course, but you know, he's just a groom."

"Derek's more than qualified," I interjected, feeling tears of frustration fill my eyes. How could she possibly talk about him that way? He treated her horses, and every horse, as if it were his own.

"His qualifications are not the point. My husband agrees."

"Your husband?" Now my voice had definitely risen two octaves. When had she ever listened to him? My eyes stung, my thoughts scrambled. "When it comes to horses, you've always done what you know is best," I said in a much softer tone.

"That's right, Brynn. And what's best for us is to leave and go to a better barn." Her voice was cold. "We've got the medal finals coming up, and I know you're a good trainer, but with Luke gone—"

"Corinne, I—"

"No. The decision's final. We have too much invested in this hobby—this sport. We want the best. You don't have the quality or professionalism we want. It's not personal, Brynn. It's just the truth."

I felt as if a horse had kicked me in the chest.

"Mom! Kennedy won't give me back my iPod!" The screaming rang out through my car.

"I've gotta go, Brynn. I'm driving, and I have a meeting at the girls' school. I'm already late. I'm head of the fund-raising committee again this year, and we have the Christmas gala coming up. Now with the move, I'm just swamped. We'll chat soon."

"I think we—"

"I have to go, Brynn. Hugs to your mother!"

Silence, then some teeny pop song filled the car.

I could barely see where I was going. The cars and lanes swam before me. Somehow I ended up in the far right lane. I scanned signs for the next exit. As soon as I got off the freeway I pulled onto the shoulder. Some asshole honked his horn behind me, and shook his hands at me as he drove past. I leaned my head on the steering wheel, placing my fists in between my knees to try to stop the shaking. I moved the transmission into park, staring blankly ahead. My eyes stung with unshed tears, my chest ready to explode. I tasted iron, drawing blood.

Didn't Corinne see all the sacrifices I made? How hard I busted my butt? After being with us for seven years, how could she leave?

It's not personal, she'd said. *Better barn. Lack of professionalism. We deserve the best.* Someone had been filling her head with nonsense. Corinne wouldn't have said that on her own—or would she? Maybe Corinne longed for the high-end fancy barn, the shiny tack trunks, lots of grooms, high bills. God knew she had tons of money. She had been the CEO of a startup that had been bought out by Oracle. Instead of going to work at a new company, she had decided to take care of the kids. She had traded her business suit for the thrill of horseback riding. She'd boasted at a dinner once that the family could now retire, though her husband still worked as a CFO at a biotech company.

"You can only be the best you can be." My dad's voice rang clear in my head. *"Clients come, clients go."*

"No! You're wrong!" I cried into the emptiness of the car. Sure, clients had left in the past, but never four horses at a time and never when we were completely upside down on our mortgage. A big raindrop fell on the windshield. Then another. Soon the sound of rain enveloped me.

I called Chris. I needed to talk to someone in the business, someone who knew what it was like to lose a client.

When Chris came on the line, I burst into telling him what had happened. A silence greeted me. "Chris?" I asked, but the line only crackled. "Chris?"

"Brynn, I'm sorry to hear this, but I'm in the middle of a lesson. Can I call you back?"

That was hardly the response I wanted or needed.

I whispered that that was fine.

"I'll call you later." Chris hung up, but not before I heard laughter in the background.

I put the car in drive and merged back onto the highway. I had to compose myself before I saw Derek. He was no doubt freaking out, and he'd be looking to me for support. Right now I had to figure out what to do with the business. Corinne leaving was like opening an artery and letting our ranch bleed to death.

By the time I pulled into Redwood Grove Stables, the sky had cleared and the place looked deserted. Water from large puddles splashed up as I drove through.

I glanced toward the house. Mom's old Volvo station wagon

wasn't in the driveway. I'd have some time to contemplate what I was going to tell her.

Derek came out of the barn as I got out of the car. He looked small as he stood hunched in his green parka. "What's going on?"

"She's leaving," I said, as I slammed the hatch of my Civic shut.

"I gathered that, but did you talk to her?"

"Yeah." I couldn't look him in the eye, but I felt his stare burn a hole in the back of my neck.

"And?" He prodded, catching up to me as I stormed toward the barn.

"She's gone. She wants more."

"More what?" His voice seemed to shake.

"Better trainers, more glitz, more attention." I couldn't keep the scorn out of my voice. I sighed, shaking my head. "I don't know, Derek." Then I realized that I sounded as doleful as he looked. I had to sound more confident, more sure of things.

"We're going to be fine." The barn, and especially the tack room on my right, looked empty with Corinne's trunks and tack gone. I pulled out my boots from my own tack trunk and sat to pull them on.

"So what's on the schedule?" I changed the topic.

"Schedule?" Derek looked up at me, as if he'd forgotten what else he had planned for the day.

"You know, the schedule." I gestured toward the whiteboard hanging up outside my office. "What's left?"

"Um. Helena's horses and ponies need to get schooled, then Mai's."

"Can you get Ness ready for me?" I asked.

"I was going to ride her."

"I've got it. I'm fine. I'll call Helena in the meantime."

Derek didn't move. What I wouldn't do to see that dimple in his left cheek.

"I'll talk to Helena, and we'll go from there," I said, my voice stern. "Let's just focus on the job at hand. Okay?" I stood up, wanting him to follow suit. Derek looked at me as if waiting for more assurances, more explanation, more something. I headed to the office, pulling my hair up into a bun. As I walked past Seraphim's and Dolce's empty stalls, then the two ponies' stalls, I had to swallow back a lump in my throat, a regret forming inside that I'd never had the opportunity to ride Sera while she was here.

Once in the office, I rubbed the back of my neck, hoping to relieve some tension. It didn't work. I might as well have been rubbing steel.

I picked up the phone, staring at it for a minute before dialing Helena's number.

"Helena. It's Brynn."

"Is it Effy?"

"No, no. Everything's fine. Ness is fine too." I paused, finding the right words. "I'm back in town."

"On a Wednesday?"

"I just spoke to Corinne." The line was silent. "Helena?"

"I'm here."

"I want to get to the point. You obviously know Corinne left."

"She told me she would. I didn't know when."

Helena's acknowledgement stung. Had everyone known but me?

"I'm hoping we can talk," I said.

"No need to. I'm not going anywhere, Brynn. I'm very happy with the training we get. I've been around the block a bit, and, I love Corinne, you know I do, but she does need more attention. She needs to experience things for herself. She's new to the horse world, to show jumping." She paused and cleared her voice. I clenched the phone more tightly. "I know you're awesome. I'm sure you can take us to where we want to go." Her voice cracked.

My eyes filled with tears, but I breathed in and willed them away. "I appreciate you saying that. It means the world to me. I promise I'll make it work."

"I know you will."

"I'm here if you want to come over." I swiveled the chair and looked out the window to my right. The clouds hung low and gray.

"It's all good, Brynn. I'll see you Friday."

"Most definitely." I hung up. Instead of feeling relief, I was more stressed. What if Helena was bluffing? No client wants to tell their trainer they're leaving. That was the industry: avoiding, lying, cheating. And I knew Helena was a wimp about confrontation. She might be too chicken to tell me the truth. Corinne was born to lead, and where she went, people followed.

I had to come up with some way to keep the remaining six clients and their eight horses—without them, there was no income, and with no income, the foreclosure would be upon us. Soon there wouldn't even be enough money to buy hay for the remaining horses.

How could I have been so naïve? How could I have thought that it would all work out until school ended? I needed to come up with an alternative solution.

That evening I stared into the empty fridge. What had Mom been living off of? I grabbed my keys and drove toward the small produce store in town. At the crossroad, the white stucco of the old mission church reflected in the moonlight. I pulled into the parking lot and glanced toward Dad's grave. I turned off the engine and sat in silence. I hadn't been here since the funeral.

A car pulled in next to mine. The priest that had performed the ceremony climbed out. He leaned over and peered into my car, waving. I half waved before starting the car and reversing as fast as I could out of the parking lot, my face burning hot. It was just as well. I wasn't ready to see Dad's grave yet.

Not until I knew how I'd keep my promise.

I woke covered in sweat. The red digits on my clock screamed 3:15 a.m. Subira snuggled next to me on the bed, and I petted her soft ear as I weighed my options. There weren't many. The training business had to make more money. Check. I was the only trainer. Check. We'd just lost our biggest client. A double check.

Option one: begging Corinne to come back. Almost as soon as I thought of the idea, I dismissed it. Given the conversation we'd had earlier today that was unlikely. Corinne had made up her mind.

Option two: more clients. But signing even one client with one horse wasn't easy, so how was I supposed to replace four horses in training? I thought back to all the shows Dad had gone to, all the evening calls he made to follow up with and please clients. He was always working to get and keep clients. I had never realized how hard that was. I had always assumed they just came to us.

Would the remaining clients trust my abilities as a trainer? Was that why Corinne had left? I reanalyzed our conversation. No. She said it wasn't my training.

Option three: bringing Chris on. He was a great rider and between the two of us, maybe we could do it. He'd called me back earlier, and had even offered to bring over Thai food for dinner, but I had been too exhausted to see him. Now I wondered if he would still be excited once he learned there wasn't enough money to finance the building of an extra barn.

I squeezed my eyes shut, willing sleep to come.

I sat up. Daybreak. Filtered light streamed in, like an iridescent film, onto the walls, the pictures, the trophies, the dresser, the lamp. Everything appeared sharp, defined, delineated.

I knew how I would save the business. It all made sense. I bounded out of bed, startling Subira. In my bathroom I splashed cold water on my face, then grabbed the first T-shirt and sweater from my dresser drawer. Hopping, I tugged on my jeans as I rushed down the hall toward the kitchen. I checked outside: Mom's old car was in the driveway.

The first light of dawn shone through the kitchen windows. Today held the sweet promise of change.

16

"What's that delicious smell?" Mom came into the kitchen, dressed in her white uniform, her running shoes squeaking on the floor.

I peered into the frying pan. "Oh. I don't know." I paused, folding the egg yolks carefully in with the whites. "I thought I'd whip up some of Dad's eggs—Montana style. Maybe a few berry pancakes on the side." I raised an eyebrow, hoping she would catch on to my playful mood.

She took in the chaos of the kitchen: the haphazardly strewn dishes, the dripping egg shells, green peppers, mushrooms, tomatoes, flour, and berries. "Are you cooking for thirty?"

It was an old joke between us. Whenever Dad had cooked, it was as if he expected a throng of teenagers and barn staff, ravenous, after early morning chores, ready for a hearty breakfast. This was a result of his childhood in Montana, his Irish Catholic upbringing, where horse ranches were full of eager bellies. He'd helped his mother cook as a young boy. With family and staff, it was a full-time job to feed the hungry Seymour clan.

Ever since I could stand on a chair next to the stove, I'd helped him in the kitchen. Dad's eyes had crinkled as he'd told stories while he whipped the egg whites for omelets and I mixed the pancake batter. He'd tell me it was our secret recipe, and that I couldn't reveal it to anyone under penalty of loss of riding privileges.

In the early days he'd speak of filling the house with children, but years passed, and I remained an only child. I never understood why they hadn't had more, and for years had felt guilty I wasn't enough for him. One morning, as I cracked eggs, Dad gave me a sidelong glance, then said, "You're all the daughter I ever wanted." That's all I had needed to hear.

We spent more time cooking than thinking about how much we were cooking. Then Mom would tease us, asking if we were putting on a town banquet. We'd take the leftovers down to the barn, to the kids eager to grab the pancakes, gobbling them up like donuts.

I held a piece of steaming pancake on a fork out to Mom. "Here. Have a taste."

She hesitated, then leaned in and took the bite. Chewing, she closed her eyes. "Mmmm. Better than ever." She'd gone back in time too.

We sat at the kitchen breakfast nook. Outside, the mist still clung to the center of the hills, like a soft towel swathing them after a steamy sauna. The pastures, golden during the dry months of summer, were now tinged with green.

We ate. We spoke about the rain. Mom didn't ask me what I was doing home on a Thursday. I didn't dare bring up Corinne.

Mom stood to get more coffee, drank it, then washed her mug in the sink. "I better get going to work. The new supervisor's a real piece of work. She yells if I'm even a few minutes late." Mom rubbed her back, and I was reminded how hard she worked, lifting heavy adults out of bed, changing their diapers, helping them into wheelchairs.

After she left, I said out loud, "I promise you, Mom, I'll make things up to you."

Subira's head lifted when she heard the scraping of my chair along the tiled kitchen floor, signaling that it was time to head to the barn, her fur reflecting the gold and copper of the morning sun. Old habits were tough to break. I filled a Tupperware container with some pancakes for Derek.

"Come on, Subira." I tapped my leg, encouraging her. I walked toward the barn with a lighter step than I'd had in months. Subira rambled along, sniffing everything in sight, checking out the field, then the stalls inside the barn, confirming everyone—and everything—was in their proper place. At twelve years old, it took twice as long to make the rounds, but she was still as thorough.

Derek stood in front of a row of buckets of grain, adding supplements. "Morning! I brought some breakfast down for you." I smiled, handing him the still-warm container. "I'm heading out to run some errands. I'll be back by early afternoon."

"I've got things covered," he said with his mouth full, eyeing the feed buckets he'd prepared.

I wondered if I should tell him my plan. But this was something that I had to do on my own. He'd know soon enough.

I drove toward the coast, winding my way among the green hills and valleys of the North Bay. Enormous gray rocks stuck out of fields of grass, as if prehistoric giants had played with blocks and had forgotten to pick them up. The air was pure, the sky a cobalt blue, but even with the terrific weather, I didn't think about rolling down my windows to enjoy the October day. My thoughts were filled with what I was going to say to Uncle Ian.

Ian Finlay was the reason I had wanted to become a vet in the first place. If my parents had been proud of my acceptance into the veterinary program at Davis, Uncle Ian had been doubly so. Uncle Ian had given me his battered copy of *All Creatures Great and Small* when I'd been accepted. He often told stories about how, as a young lad in Scotland, he'd actually known James Alfred Wight, before he turned to writing and called himself James Herriot. Who knew whether those stories held any truth, since Uncle Ian tended to embellish, but maybe that's where he picked up some of his trade secrets—even if he would have only been six years old or so.

Besides being an equine vet, Uncle Ian and Julia bred horses. He had long ago understood that to gain speed and agility over the ever increasingly difficult jump-offs, the European warmbloods would have to have more thoroughbred in them, and the popular jumping horses of the time in America, the thoroughbred, would need more warmblood in them. He had started one of the first warmblood jumper breeding programs on this side of the Atlantic. When questioned about his warmbloods, or told they were too heavy to be good jumping horses, he persevered, backcrossing thoroughbreds and warmbloods to get the ideal jumper.

He kept the best jumpers for breeding, and sold the rest to trusted friends or clients. He never sent off any of his prized young fillies or colts to the kind of overambitious trainers who'd cared more about their careers than the horses. "They'll just ride them into the ground by age ten," he'd say. "Give them a short career, then shoot them up with painkillers, those knobs. Maybe use them as broken-down school horses, or the few lucky ones might go into lay up. Why? When these horses can have a bonnie good career until they're eighteen?"

Granite pillars flanked the elegant iron gate at the entrance to the Finlay ranch. I gathered my strength as I got out of my car and walked toward their front porch. I had to do this. I had no other choice. I hoped Uncle Ian would understand.

Julia Finlay's face glowed when she opened the door for me. "Brynn! How wonderful to see you!" She came out onto the veranda and gave me the warmest hug.

"Aunt Julia. You look lovely, as always." Her blonde hair was styled in a fashionable, soft bob. Although worn with age, her skin remained smooth. She had on a purple silk shirt, and cream-colored pants, which suited her petite frame. Whether she was down at the barn helping with foaling, or out in her garden, she did it with grace.

"You're like the sun coming in and lighting up my day," she said, as she brushed a piece of my hair behind my ear. Funny, that's how

I always viewed her. Her soft hand smelled of roses and earth, and I wanted to bury my face in it, to have her tell me everything would be all right.

I smiled, but didn't know what to say. My throat closed up.

"Something is troubling you," she said, scrutinizing me. I looked at my paddock boots, not wanting her to see all the pain and worry I'd been carrying. She seemed to understand the silence. "Ian's in the back pasture, checking on the young ones." She gestured with a nod.

"Thanks, Aunty. I'll go look for him."

"Come back up to the house before you go for some lemonade and freshly baked banana bread."

"I will," I promised, as I headed down the veranda steps.

I rounded the corner of the house toward the pastures. Uncle Ian had a young filly haltered, trying to squint at her face. Her dark bushy tail rotated like a windmill as she attempted to squirm away.

"Need some help?" I asked as I climbed in between the boards of the fence to get to him.

"I want to peek at this wee one's eye. It's a bit swollen. Can you hold her while I look?"

I grabbed the lead rope and situated myself at the filly's side. She stood at about twelve and a half hands, a late foal.

"It's all right, little one. You're going to be just fine," I murmured into her ear. I ran my hand down from the top of the filly's head along the mane, making my way through the velvety fur, gripping her around her neck. She wiggled, then jumped, stepping on my toe. I flinched, but my boots bore most of the pressure, so all I felt was a dull ache. I held the halter tighter while Uncle Ian kept her head steady. He managed to open the swollen eyelid and shone the light in.

"How does it look?" I asked.

"Why don't you take a gander? It's good practice for you." He handed the instrument to me. I examined the large iris, searching for debris, pus, or cloudiness.

"I don't detect signs of moon-blindness," I said. "Looks like a case of conjunctivitis." I handed the ophthalmoscope back.

Uncle Ian squinted and studied her eye again. "I agree. What do you think it's from? What do you suggest we do next?"

"Well . . . it could be an allergic reaction to something, or something got into her eye: dirt, grass, a piece of shavings. I think we should flush it, apply an antibiotic ointment, and give her some Banamine to help with the swelling."

Uncle Ian nodded, smiling wide, his bushy eyebrows stretching across his forehead. While Uncle Ian worked on the filly, I ran through my prepared arguments so I would be ready when he questioned my decision.

"Now the Banamine . . ." I lifted her nose, and held the hard bones of her lower jaw steady while he squirted the paste in her mouth.

"Good girl," I said, then patted the teeny white snip on her nose. She looked like she had rubbed up against a freshly painted fence.

"Okay. Good to go. I'll check on her again tonight, reapply the ointment, and she should start feeling better tomorrow." He held on to her neck, while I took off the filly's halter. She ran off as soon as our hands let go, galloping and bucking over to her mother who grazed nearby.

"She's a bonnie one. She'll be like her mama. Maybe better." The mother had been a successful Grand Prix jumper for a few years out on the East Coast. Then she got navicular disease. The owners had wanted to sell her, but Ian caught wind and stepped in, bringing her here to be a broodmare.

"Not a bad retirement," I said, observing the mare.

We stood watching the filly prance around, her bay coat like a teddy bear's.

"Let's walk to my truck," Uncle Ian said, giving me a sidelong look.

"So," he said, as he put his glasses into his pocket, closing the top of the storage unit at the back of his vet truck. "What's of such dire importance that you had to see me today? Something wrong at school, Lassie?"

He led me to a bench at the side of the barn overlooking the pastures and hills, patting the seat for me to join him.

"This isn't easy for me, Uncle Ian." I hesitated. I clasped and unclasped my hands. "You know that I think of you as a second father, and now"—I swallowed hard—"with Dad gone . . ."

"Now, now. What's the matter, Lassie?"

I closed my eyes, gathering my thoughts. "As you know, it's fallen on me to run the barn and train the horses and clients."

"You have a lot on your plate now." He reached out and patted my knee.

I took a deep breath. "Corinne packed up and left with all four horses yesterday."

His eyebrows rose. "Where did she go?"

"Don't know yet. I'll find out soon enough. But if I had my guess, I'd say it was to Vivian Young's."

"What? The lass who used to work for your dad?"

"She's had her own business for a while now, down in San Anselmo. She has a ton of clients."

"Humph," Ian said. He leaned back against the bench and gazed out at the mare pasture below us.

"And the worst part is," I said, kicking at the dirt, "she left without warning. Texted me to say she was leaving."

"Ridiculous. Texting." He almost spat the word out.

"So, after a lot of thought . . ." I paused, laying out my plan in my mind one more time, "I've decided to quit school and—"

Uncle Ian jumped up. "You will do no such foolish thing! You listen to me, Brynn Seymour. This is something you've wanted since you were a wee lass. Davis is a top school, and it's a privilege to be in the program! What will your mother think? What about Dr. Dixon? I spoke to her just last week, and she told me that you're one of her most promising students, you are. You can't give up now. You've only got a half a year to go, the best part of the schooling." He paused, looking away. "I owe your mother and father that much."

"You know he was never a hundred percent behind my going to vet school . . ." My voice trailed. But as soon as I spoke the words, I realized how true they were.

"That's not true," he insisted. "He was proud. He was proud of your conviction, and your ability to follow through with pursuing your dreams. Don't ever forget that, Lassie." Then more gently, he added, "You just need to hang in a wee bit longer. There will be other clients. You'll see. If that Corinne woman doesn't respect your talent, then it's better she's gone anyway. You know your father would agree with that."

I stared at my feet for a while, trying to come up with a good response.

"The problem is, I have a feeling others will follow. I need to give the rest of my clients some assurance they're in good hands. In great hands. And frankly"—I peered up at him—"I think it's hypocritical of me to be running the barn while studying. The clients want someone who has their full focus on the barn. You know how tough this business is. I'm lucky they've held on as long as they have. They came to us for Dad. Not me."

"Dropping out of school is not an option." He shook his head, his fists clenched at his sides. "We'll think of something."

"There is no other way. I've considered everything," I said. "With Corinne gone, that's a loss of a third of our training income. You know that doesn't leave enough to get by on. The upkeep of the ranch is too much, and Mom and I, well . . ." I was glad he wasn't looking at me so he wouldn't see my embarrassment. "Dad left us in a lot of debt. I have to keep our clients and get more or we won't own Redwood Grove a few months from now."

Uncle Ian picked at a piece of grass. I buried my face in my hands. I wanted to be a kid again, playing free in the pastures, letting my dad handle all the problems.

"There, there, child." Uncle Ian's large hand patted my back. "Have you considered a leave of absence?"

"I'm not sure they'll allow that. And even if they did, I'm not sure I'll ever be able to go back."

"I'll look into all that—but you can't quit."

I heard a far-off neigh. I sat up straight, pressing my chin high, my shoulders back.

"I need your help, Uncle Ian. I've decided to ride in the Spruce Meadows Million Dollar Gold Cup."

His body shifted, his mouth opened, but I continued.

"I know you're going to say it's impossible. But it was always Daddy's dream to have us compete together there. He'd talked about it since I was going over my first cross rails."

"I remember."

"We can't achieve that dream now, but I can try to make it to the top on my own. That will bring me closer to his dream. And competing will be good publicity for me and our barn. It will prove to people that I'm a trainer worth hiring. If I win, I can keep the business going, support the ranch, make sure we don't default on the mortgage."

Silence filled the air.

"I'm going to need a trainer who will take me there."

Uncle Ian's gaze fixed on me.

"Will you help me find one?" I asked, then held my breath.

Uncle Ian took my hands, turning my palms face up. He stared at them for what seemed like an eternity.

"You have talent. There's no doubt about that. You'd make a skilled and capable vet, but I also understand why you must do this. I know you can achieve whatever you set your mind on, so if it's the Gold Cup you want, then you can get there. You have a magic about you that I've always seen, Lassie, and I know once you take charge of your destiny, once you believe in yourself, you'll make things happen."

"Thank you," I said. His eyes were moist with tears. "You don't know how much it means to me to have your support."

Uncle Ian looked away.

"On one condition: you have to promise to finish school. After you win."

"I don't know." But then I nodded. "I promise to try."

"So, a trainer then," he said, matter-of-factly, composing himself, scratching his head. "There's only one: Jason Lander. He's your man."

17

*J*ason Lander. Between Uncle Ian's endorsement and Google, I'd learned a lot about the peridot-eyed man I'd seen at my father's funeral. And though I hadn't met him, I remembered his penetrating stare the day he sat in the front pew at the funeral—as if he understood me, knew me. The picture I'd seen in that magazine at Chris's haunted me still—his ease with that horse in the meadow unmistakable, even in stillness. He was the youngest in history to have won the World Cup; at the age of seventeen they'd called him the show-jumping wonder boy. He'd followed it up with two more World Cup wins, but had stopped jumping three short years later. These days, he was more interested in yoga than jumping, but he had been featured in a few recent articles about his belief that horse riders who practice yoga have an advantage.

Jason was supposed to have been here at four thirty, but judging by the light, it was closer to five. He wasn't taking me seriously. Ian had convinced me that Jason was the right trainer: capable, honest, and affordable. They had a special bond, Ian said. He was like a son; they had instantly connected years back, and apparently he'd been the one to introduce Jason to my dad. It took Jason days to get back to Uncle Ian, and he had just arrived back in California from India.

I'd been riding Jett for nearly an hour, expecting Jason. I looked toward the entrance of the arena, and finally, there he stood. With the setting sun behind him, he seemed to fill the entrance with his presence. His features were concealed by the shadow of his Australian cowboy hat, but I could feel his stare. The reins slipped through my fingers, and I glanced down at Jett's mane, a sense of familiarity washing over me.

Jason walked through the arena, his footsteps muffled by the sand, his stride long and purposeful. His presence held authority and calm.

"I apologize for being late." Jason gave a slight nod. "Something took longer than I expected."

I slowed Jett to a walk and circled the arena, trying to consolidate my sudden fear that he wouldn't help us. I knew it was a long shot, with how little we could pay, and how we couldn't offer more than a part-time position. The frog-and-cricket symphony filled the silence, and I sensed Jason's eyes on me.

After circling the arena once more, I walked Jett toward Jason and stopped. His eyes bore into mine. "Jett's warmed up. Did you want me to take him over a few jumps?"

"I've been watching. From over there." He nodded toward the hill, the one with the oak tree.

"Oh," I said, trying to hide my surprise. "I've set up a course."

"That's all right."

I hesitated, but then slid out of the saddle, busying myself with securing the stirrups on each side so that they wouldn't hang—a safety precaution.

Jason pulled his hat off and ran a hand through unruly, brown hair. "How about we sit down and talk. This is an unusual circumstance, since I don't normally take on clients anymore. I've been busy with other things. I'd like to make sure we have the same goals, have an understanding."

I was already walking with Jett toward the gate, but his comment made me stop. Had I known he was watching maybe I would have ridden more properly. Maybe I could have jumped on my own, to show off Jett's potential. "Of course," I said. "Let's talk in the office."

~

In the office I sat in Dad's chair as Jason walked over to the wall of photos that, in essence, catalogued my dad's and my careers.

"Lovely," he smiled, tapping a framed photo of me on a pony. I blushed, as if Jason had gotten an intimate look into my life. I remembered that show. I'd won my first blue ribbon. "Spectacular property," he said. "Really spectacular." He peered through the coffee-colored wood blinds out toward the pastures. "You have something special here. I don't mean just in property value, I mean in the spirit of the place. You're so close to the city, yet you might as well be in the middle of nowhere."

"Yes, well, we think so." I needed to steer him away from talk of the land; I didn't need him guessing our troubles. "Uncle Ian highly recommends you as a trainer. I know you haven't taken on clients in years, so—" I cleared my throat again. "What have you been doing, umm, aside from yoga, that is?"

Jason turned, then smiled, walking slowly toward the chair on the opposite side of the desk. He was around thirty, maybe a bit younger. He pulled off his hat, and I noted his hair—much too long for a jumper rider—ran into longish sideburns.

"This and that." He continued to smile, rubbing a finger over the bridge of his slightly crooked nose. As he sat, his long legs stretched almost to the desk, and I sat more upright, tucking my own in under my chair. I wasn't used to sitting on this side of the desk interviewing people. I had sat in on a couple of client interviews, but never for hiring an employee.

I cleared my throat again, the air dry in my mouth. "Right." I pulled out a notepad so that I could take notes. It seemed like the right thing to do in an interview. "What can you tell me about your top influences in the sport? Your dreams and aspirations?"

"Isn't it a bit early for us to discuss our dreams?" The edges of his eyes crinkled, his lips turned up in a half smile.

God, what was I doing? He was a two-time World Cup winner

and I was asking him about his influences in the sport. It was he who was interviewing me more than anything. "Um, what I meant was . . ." I hesitated, tapping the pen on the notepad. I had to get to the point. "As you probably realize we're a small training stable. We're not a fancy barn, but Jett, the horse you saw out there, has more heart than any I've ever ridden. Any I've ever known, and I need you to help me train him—to train us, that is. I want you to take us to the Spruce Meadows Million Dollar Gold Cup."

Jason leaned back in his chair and let out a low whistle. "I think every rider dreams of winning the Gold Cup." His eyes narrowed as he stared at me.

"I'm not everyone." I rubbed the sweat off my hands on my britches. Here came the clincher. He'd either run or laugh again, and now was my chance to find out. "And I want you to do more than take us to the Gold Cup." I inhaled again. "We need to win."

Don't break eye contact. Don't let him see you falter.

Jason looked like he was deliberating his next chess move.

"Brynn." My name rolled off his tongue. He sat up straighter, his smile disappearing. "I got out of this business because I was tired of babysitting wealthy clients." He looked straight at me, tilting his head, his features suddenly softening. "But I love horses. Love their unbreakable spirit. They love unconditionally, and I believe in unconditional love—not the spur-of-the-moment or instant pass-in-the-night type of love. Horses trust completely, yet they also naturally sense danger. They flee from unpredictability and any sort of pretense." He paused. "Not unlike yourself, I'm sure."

I opened my mouth, a small sound escaping before I could stop myself.

Jason looked up at the pictures on the wall. "In my opinion, the horse has the purest spirit of all animals. If I help you compete, it's not to help you follow some materialistic dream. If I do this, it has to be for something bigger." He sat forward. "And I know I can help you and Jett get to the Gold Cup—Jett has more scope than you'd think—but you have to figure out what your real goal is. Outside of winning money, that is. That goal just doesn't work for me."

Horseshoes clip-clopped out in the barn. Derek was bringing the horses in from turnout.

I met Jason's gaze. "Well, I want to win. What else is there?"

"Well, let's see. Maybe to bring out Jett's potential. To bring out *your* potential. I'd do it, say, if you wanted to overcome personal fears. To help you achieve something that's been within your reach, but has escaped you. Or maybe if you wanted to follow your *own* dreams . . ."

I had to look away, to swallow, to breathe.

"You have to want it, to feel it, to taste it. For you. For Jett. For something bigger than yourself. That's what will get you your win. It's about the moment, Brynn, not the victory. If you focus only on winning for prestige, or making a name for yourself, or money, you risk breaking your horse's spirit, and in essence your own. It's got to be more than that."

I licked my lips, brushed some crumbs off my desk, and nodded. "I understand."

Jason's eyes rested on the empty bag of chips and the Toblerone bar on my desk.

"Hmmm. Well, I'll have to think about it. And of course, if we do this, there are rules. You'd have to follow them to a T."

I nodded again.

"There are four. Number one: nutrition. Key for you and key for your horse. You will feed Jett and yourself as I say. That means no junk and no alcohol. Number two: training happens only on the days I say it does. No over-jumping, no going behind my back to do extra just because you think you know more." He paused, and I nodded again. "Three, the training happens how and when I say it does. You can question, but in the end, my decision goes."

A horse neighed, then another. Feeding time. The ATV that Derek used to drive the hay around resounded through the barn. The air in the office suddenly seemed thick, and the temperature must have risen since we had come in. I broke eye contact and stared out the window. The sky had changed to a dark blue, with hints of carmine and gold.

"What's number four?"

"Yoga. You agree to do yoga with me at least four times a week, and it has to be before you ride."

I jerked my head up to see if he was serious, ready to laugh, but when I saw his eyes, I knew this was no joke. "You may want to watch us jump first," I finally said.

"I wouldn't have come here if I didn't think you and Jett had talent. I know his lineage, and I know Ian Finlay. I trust him." He leaned back in his chair again. "I've also seen you show at Young Riders at Spruce Meadows." His smile returned. "It's not just about the jumping, though. We need to work on something more than just the physical training. Don't get me wrong, the skills matter, but the extra height at the Gold Cup requires way more than that. And you and Jett were good back then, but you need to be better. And with your petite frame, it'll be tough. Not impossible, but tough. I mean, look at Margie Goldstein-Engle. She's what? Five foot four?" He eyed me from across the desk. "And from what I gather, you're not much taller."

My cheeks burned. He'd already sized me up.

"That's where the yoga comes in. To draw the potential out of both of you. I can help you, but you have to trust me. We have to work as a team."

The look in his eyes reminded me of that of a winning horse's. Filled with truth. Tenacity. Love.

When he stood to leave, my polo shirt clung to my back. I straightened my shoulders and reached out my hand, hoping he wouldn't feel it tremble. He shook it, holding my hand in his for a split second longer than necessary, bowing his head to me for a cursory moment. Then Jason grabbed his hat and coat and walked out of the office, leaving me to collapse in my chair.

ason's first day I scrubbed my face in the bathroom with a washcloth, rubbing until my cheeks and forehead were red. I clipped my already short nails, allowed the timer on the electric toothbrush to go for an extra round, flossed, and put my britches and polo shirt on. I grabbed my gray zip-up hoodie out of the closet. I would need warm layers today. I briefly considered makeup, then chastised myself. I never wore makeup to the barn, so why would I start now? Instead, I rubbed on my vanilla-flavored lip balm while on my way to the kitchen.

Mom stood with her back toward me, leaning against the sink looking out at the pastures, her drawn face reflected in the kitchen window. She held a cutting board full of vegetables. She was cooking. I couldn't remember the last time she had cooked. In response to my perplexed look she said, "I'm starting something in the slow cooker. It's that time of year. Thought we'd have something savory and rich to eat after my shift." She wiped at her nose with her sleeve, and I knew she'd been crying again.

"Mom, please don't . . ."

"It's just the onions. I hate chopping onions."

"That's the oldest excuse in the book." I wanted to hug her and tell her we were going to get through all of this. We stood, the sound of the knife—*scrinch, chop*—chopping against the cutting board. I reverted to the only thing I knew how to talk about. "I had a great ride on Jett, yesterday. I couldn't believe how strong and fluid he was. He cleared each jump without so much as a blink."

She didn't respond. I realized I was expecting Dad's reaction: beaming at me, hugging me, wanting every last detail. This was the last thing she wanted to hear.

As if she hadn't heard me, she reached for carrots from the fridge. "You're back to school what week? Right after the New Year?"

I tapped my fingers on the counter, went to bite at a cuticle, then tapped the counter again. I had to finally come clean. "Actually, Mom, we need to talk. Can we sit?"

Subira and I hurried down the path through the low-hanging clouds and fog. I don't know what I had expected, but Mom throwing the contents of the slow cooker onto the floor hadn't been on my list of predictable actions. To say she didn't take the news well was an understatement. I was mad at myself for not asking Uncle Ian to talk to her first. He would have been much better at convincing her. He would have made her see why this was necessary.

I couldn't make out anything beyond a few yards in front of me. By the time I got to the barn my hair and jacket were soaked, as if it had been raining.

"Hey, Derek," I said, stomping my feet at the entrance to the barn, trying to dislodge the mud from my boots. The horses were still in their stalls, rustling sounds filling the barn as the horses moved their hay around, searching for that perfect breakfast bite.

Derek had Ness, Payton's pony, in the tack-up stall.

Subira ran up to Derek, wagging her tail, giving a little whine to say hello to him. He leaned down to pet her. "Morning, B. How are you this fine morning?"

"Oh, you have no idea."

"What's going on?" He stood with one hand on his hip, his other holding a currycomb. Becoming his so-called boss was proving a difficult transition. I had always been the kid he had hung out with around the barn, the one he'd taught how to groom, the one with whom he'd joked and played games. How was I supposed to manage him when he knew all my moods and I couldn't hide anything from him?

I shook my head. I was overanalyzing. "Nothing much. Just a bit of a rough morning."

"The day hasn't even started." He rubbed at his goatee.

"It has for me." I looked at him more closely. "I meant to ask before, what is that thing growing on your face? Some sort of hedgehog? Trying to look more grown-up or something?"

"Whatever, girl. You don't know from style." He smiled, walking over to a mirror that hung in the alcove of the front entry doors.

I followed and leaned against the wall, watching him as he turned his face right and left to check out his goatee from both sides. I cleared my throat, then said, "Jason's starting today."

"I know. You told me before I left Sunday." Derek arched a brow, then walked back over to Ness, rubbing her with a currycomb in methodical circles.

Of course I had. "Well, we'll see how it goes, I guess." God, I hoped I'd made the right decision. "He should be here by ten, so I'm going to get caught up on some paperwork in the office. Can you have Jett ready for me then?"

The next couple of hours flew by. I figured out the schedule for the week, coordinating the horse training rides and lessons. Since we didn't have many clients left, I finished scheduling in under a half hour. Dust motes filled the air, so instead of working on the bills, I opened the blinds, dusted the pictures on the walls, wiped down my desk and the top of the filing cabinet, tossed my stash of Toblerone bars and Sour Patch Kids from the desk drawer, then finally got to the huge pile that I'd been ignoring for the last two weeks.

Opening each bill was like working on a rotting, maggot-infested wound—I'd seen enough of those on the neglected horses we'd been called out to in the Sacramento area via animal welfare. First the farrier bill, the vet bill, the hay bill, the grain bill, the one for shavings and the additional broken feed buckets, the electricity, the water, and of course, Derek's salary . . .

I closed my eyes for a moment and massaged my temples. Some of the bills were more than thirty days past due. I had already asked the vendors if I could pay next month. Now next month was here.

I pushed open the window in Dad's office—my office—inhaling the moist air, closing my eyes, letting it fill my lungs. I stood on tiptoe and stretched up my arms as far as I could reach, then moved into a downward-dog yoga pose, releasing the pressure from in between my shoulder blades, loving the extension in my lower back. I'd never really practiced yoga, only taken a class or two at college, but of the poses I remembered, this was my favorite.

"Looks like you're ready to rock and roll." Jason's voice startled me, and I practically fell forward on my head. He was holding a box, with two yoga mats slung across his shoulder.

I managed to right myself, though not as gracefully as I'd hoped. "You're early."

"Thought we'd get the day going. No use wasting any more precious time."

Jason placed the box down, turned on my desk lamp and turned off the overhead light. He rolled the mats out side by side facing the window, a little too close to each other for my liking. Then from the box, he pulled out a blue glazed pot filled with sand. Inside stood three candles. He lit them all, and placed the pot on the table next to the window. He eyed me up and down. "You don't plan on practicing in that?"

"I didn't think we'd be starting with yoga today," I said, running a hand down the front of my britches.

"Rule number four. Yoga. Did you already forget?"

"Can't we start tomorrow? I'm already dressed for riding."

"Are you challenging me?" Jason sighed, then squatted and started rolling up one of the mats. "I'm wasting my time," he muttered under his breath.

"No. God, no. I was just thinking it would be easier. But it's not a problem. I'll go get changed."

"I'll give you five minutes."

By the time I got back, Jason was sitting cross-legged, his thumbs and forefingers together, palms up on his knees, his back to me. He wore a tight gray shirt and red yoga pants, and a wide woven bracelet on each wrist. I tried not to disturb him as I pulled off my jacket and Danskos, and sat next to him on the other mat, wishing I was anywhere but here. This seemed completely unnatural, and, if I really thought about it, kind of crazy.

I could just imagine what Derek—and my dad—would think if they saw us here like this.

"Let's start with settling your mind. We'll do a bit of chanting, then we'll begin."

I let out a groan.

"Don't go dismissing it until you've given it a chance." In front of him sat an instrument I'd never seen before. Like a small keyboard. He played the keyboard with his right hand while pumping the back of the instrument with his left. It sounded a bit like an organ. "Just fake it 'til you make it. It's the easiest chant." He laughed, and closed his eyes and sang a tune in Sanskrit. *Lokah, Samastah, Sukhino, Bhavantu.* He repeated this over and over, and I had to admit, it had a bit of a soothing effect, though I never closed my eyes, and turned several times back toward the door to make sure Derek wasn't watching. I didn't sing along, but Jason didn't comment on that. When he finished, he told me with time it would come easier.

Then he placed his smartphone on the table and attached a cord to a small set of speakers. U2's "Beautiful Day" filled the office. We got into child's pose, and Jason started talking about how we needed to offer the practice to others in our lives, and how the best way to ride was to clear our minds of thought, and to be in the moment, just like horses were.

"They never think of the past or future," Jason said. "What happened in the past, stays in the past, and we can't predict the future, so the only thing we can control is now, and right now, the only thing you need to think of is simply, nothing."

We moved through some poses that made my thighs and arms shake. My hips and chest were especially tight. While in triangle pose, Jason came off his yoga mat and stood next to me, and I practically lost my balance right then. He placed a block in front of my shin, moved my hand to it, then placed his hand on my hip and adjusted it by pulling it to the left and up. His thighs pressed into mine from behind, pushing my whole body to the right.

"You need to stay in one line here, and keep your hips straight, as if there was a wall behind you."

I flinched, and tried not to jerk away, feeling heat in my face and wishing he'd move. What would Chris think about this? Jason slowly released me, and I glanced down, trying to keep my balance. He went back to his mat, and took the triangle pose himself. Then he asked for ardha chandrasana, or half-moon pose. Unlike me, he had no problems with the pose, and instead of getting into the full pose, I watched him instead, taking the chance to catch my breath.

When we finished, he bowed and said, "Om, Shanti, Shanti, Shanti."

I bowed in return. "So. Can we ride now?"

Jett stood groomed and tacked up in the cross ties. He pawed at the ground, as if anxious to start his training for the Gold Cup as well.

Jason walked up to Jett, and reached out his hand toward his muzzle. Jett mouthed Jason's palm, his lips searching for a treat. Jason moved methodically, calm and sure of himself. He ducked under the cross tie and stood next to Jett in the tack-up stall, one hand on Jett's neck. His fingers patted Jett while he scanned the tack. He ran his hand down the back of Jett's front leg and laid it on his hoof. Jett, expecting the next move, tried to pick up his foot, but Jason gently pushed it down. Jett complied. Once satisfied with whatever he was looking for, Jason asked Jett to lift his foot by gently squeezing the tendon that ran down the back of the canon bone toward the hoof. He examined Jett's shoes, running a finger along the edges, brushed some dirt with the brush on the back of the hoof pick off the bottom of the hoof, touched the frog, tapped the hoof, then placed it down. During this whole time Jason didn't say a word to me, only made low sounds that I couldn't decipher. But Jett listened, his ears moving back and forth like radar dishes.

"It's good to know what he looks like now," Jason said, "to know his conformation, to know where he stands at when he's normal, so that I have something to refer to if I'm ever trying to pinpoint an ailment."

I didn't respond, understanding but surprised, and impressed, at his thoroughness. It was how my dad would have approached a new horse in training.

"What type of bit do you ride him in?"

"I've been using an elevator bit," I said. "It helps me get control. He gets very excited when he sees the jumps, and I need to be able to slow him down. To bring him back."

"Hmmm. We'll switch that to a loose-ring snaffle bit today. It's a lot gentler. Derek? Can you bring me one? He looks to be a five and a quarter."

I hadn't even noticed Derek still waiting around. He looked at me for approval. A snaffle bit was one of the softest bits, and although I would normally approve, Dad and I had tried riding Jett in a snaffle, and quickly came to realize he took off with me after big jumps. I didn't have the strength to pull him back.

"I'm not sure I feel comfortable—" I started to say to Jason's back as he inspected Jett's hind leg.

Jason stood, turning toward me. He raised an eyebrow. "Remember? We were going to do it my way."

A flash of annoyance went through me. I tightened my fists at my sides and counted to ten before I said anything rash.

"Derek. Can you get that bit?" I didn't want to show any weakness, but I also didn't want to seem confrontational.

Jason undid the bridle, then took it off so that Derek could switch bits and put the halter on while we waited. He took stock of the saddle. "This saddle pad is no good. See here?" He placed his fingers between the hollow of the saddle pad and the saddle, right above Jett's withers.

"I've researched all kinds. This gel one is supposed to be the best."

"Maybe for other horses, but not for him. And besides, it's mostly a gimmick. It feels all cushy, but in reality it will slip, leaving no protection for Jett when you come down on his withers after a high jump." Jason placed his hand on Jett's back. "He's got unusual conformation. His withers are higher than most warmbloods', more like a thoroughbred's. We need to use a regular cotton pad and a thick fleece. It's lighter and breathes better, too."

I had to bite my lip. I wanted to tell him where he could shove that saddle pad. Dad and I had agreed on the perfect fit for Jett. I lifted a finger to my mouth to bite at my cuticles, but stopped myself, grabbing my riding gloves instead. They were good protection from myself.

"Did you want to ride him today?" I asked.

"No. I want to see you both go." Jason replaced Jett's bridle himself and readjusted the saddle.

"Then let's get going."

The drizzle had turned to rain, and Jason had to raise his voice so that I could hear him above the pounding on the metal roof. I preferred to ride outside, but today we didn't have a choice. At least we had a covered arena. Many barns in California didn't.

"We're going to start off with flatwork. I want to see you working him as if you were riding in a dressage show," Jason called to me as he took down some of the jump course I had set up in preparation of our lesson. Both Jett and I kept our ears cocked toward Jason, trying to hear him over the rain. After circling the arena a couple of times at a walk, I trotted, then cantered.

Jason had me bending Jett to the right and left, doing extended trot, collected trot, extended canter, and collected canter.

"Stop for a second," he called.

To show off, I stopped Jett instantly, his hind end almost sliding underneath like a Western reining horse. If Jason was impressed, he didn't show it.

"Your hand position is too low." Jason walked over to us. I halted at the center of the arena. He reached up and touched my hand to raise it up a good three inches. His hand lingered on mine, before he pulled it away. I looked away, feeling myself blush again. On the yoga mat was one thing, but off the mat it really felt too intimate.

"Better?" I said, placing my hands and arms at the height he had raised them to, trying to ignore the contact.

"That's a good angle," Jason said, barely touching my sleeve now. "What you want is a good lever on his mouth. Not too high, not too low. It's all about physics. You'll need to exert a lot less power on his mouth if you have the right contact, allowing him to come underneath you, giving you greater control. It's not about the severity of the bit, but how gently and persuasively you ask for him to listen to you. If you ask quietly, yet firmly, he'll give, and come back to you even at the biggest jumps. But you have to stop jerking on his mouth. The right angle will help."

"I never jerk on his mouth."

"You may not think you do, but the angle is way off. That's why he's tossing his head. You should be able to tell the difference now."

I started riding again, conscious of my hand position. He had me riding in circles and figure eights, and I had to admit—if not out loud—that although the higher hand position felt awkward, it was better in some ways, giving me finer contact with Jett's sensitive mouth, lifting him into a higher frame. As long as I could remember I'd always ridden with my hands where they had been, but now Jett came underneath me, responding to my cues as if I didn't even have to move a finger, with only my thoughts to guide him. After forty minutes of dressage-type movements, Jason had me canter over ground poles, each spaced one to two strides apart.

"All right then. That's a wrap for today."

I looked over at him confused. "What?" I called above the rain.

"That's a wrap for today!"

"We haven't even jumped yet!" The rain poured down around us.

"We'll do more work tomorrow." Jason picked up the jump poles, putting them away.

I walked Jett closer to Jason and stared down at him.

"I want to win the Cup this year." I glared, hoping I appeared more fierce than angry.

"I realize that. Let's take it nice and easy."

He turned and walked out of the arena.

I took a deep breath like we'd practiced that morning, but it didn't make a difference. Jett tossed his head, agitated, his body twisting, wound like a spring. He sensed my anger, and combined with the blowing rain and now a harsh wind, it made him anxious. I rode on, my hands gripping the reins, my legs too tight around Jett. Around the next corner Jett jumped several feet to the left. I felt like a rag doll, tossed, but I grabbed onto his mane to regain my seat. My heart rate shot up even higher. I glanced behind me to see what had spooked Jett. A hawk had landed on a nearby branch, watching us.

I reached down, touching Jett's neck. He had cooled out enough, and his breathing had settled. I hopped off, throwing a wool cooler blanket over him.

"Jason!" I called out as I walked back into the barn. He stood, his back to me, talking to Derek. Derek laughed at something. Subira leaned against Jason's leg while Jason scratched her head. *Traitor*, I thought, frowning at Subira.

"Great job, Brynn," Jason said as I neared. I narrowed my eyes. Derek moved to take Jett's reins from me, his laugh gone now, his smile disappearing as he noticed my expression.

"What the hell was that all about?" I enunciated each word carefully. "I'm not someone you need to teach the basics to. I did your yoga shit this morning, didn't I? We need to work on our jumping, not some stupid dressage moves. Don't forget, I've been doing this for years. My dad was one of the best trainers out there. He rode in World Cup qualifiers."

Jason leaned against the corner of the tack-up stall. His face was devoid of emotion, like the concrete walls of the stall. I sensed Derek found my outburst amusing, but lucky for him he didn't say anything as he continued to groom Jett.

"Tell me, Brynn, did your dad ever win?" Jason asked, bending over to pick up a rock.

I frowned at him. "Of course he won. What are you getting at?"

"What did he win, Brynn?" He turned the rock over in his fingers. Such a small rock handled so gently in his big hands.

"I don't know." I hesitated, thinking back to the pictures hanging on the wall of the office. "Shows. Grand Prix. Too many to remember." I pulled at the chinstrap of my helmet, unbuckling it.

"Too many to remember?" Only the sound of the rain on the roof echoed around us. Jett's tail stopped swishing. Derek paused his brushing and watched us.

"Yes. Too many to remember . . ." I paused then. *Asshole*. He got me. Dad may have won, but he'd never had the prestige of winning the World Cup, like Jason had. Dad was always second or third, never first when it mattered most.

Jason stayed quiet, turning the rock over and over in his fingers, inspecting it carefully. Derek unclipped Jett from the cross ties. The rain had slowed and the only sound in the barn now was the clip-clop of Jett's steel shoes over the concrete barn floor.

"Ayurvedic yoga is the science of life. Just like this rock here, it didn't come from thin air. It was formed by the wind, fire, and most importantly, the earth." Jason tossed the small rock into the plastic manure bin next to him.

"We need to work with both Jett and you, so that your mind, body, and spirit are in balance, one unit of thinking and being. The first shows are coming up soon, February at the latest, and it's already November. That doesn't give us much time." He looked at me expectantly.

"That's what I'm saying—" I started, but Jason cut in.

"You already know how to ride a course. I've seen the tapes and I watched you compete, remember?" He stood up straight, towering over me. He grabbed my elbow and led me toward the barn exit.

"We need to teach Jett he *can* jump higher. He also has to get comfortable doing it at a faster pace since he's a bit slow and clunky. For him, that means lots of flatwork, gymnastics, and low jumps. He needs to get his confidence up, his agility. Once that's in place, we'll be closer to the win."

"What about me?" We reached the end of the aisle, and he stood facing out at the sheet of pouring rain in front of us. We may as well have stood behind a waterfall.

"Your technique is good—not much to fix, just little things. And your instincts are fast and sure. What we most need to fix is what's up here." He tapped his temple lightly, to demonstrate. "You understand?"

"What's wrong with my head?" I asked, on edge again, ready to pounce.

"Nothing. It's beautiful." He smiled. I turned away in embarrassment. No one had ever called me beautiful. Cute. Nice. Friendly. But never beautiful.

"I'll see you tomorrow!" Jason pulled on his broad-rimmed hat and adjusted the collar of his dark oiled-canvas riding coat. Without another glance he stepped out into the rain, a brown and blue blur running across the parking lot.

19

On a cold, rainy December morning, I sat on the phone pacifying the hay farmer up in Oregon when Jason dashed into my office. He held his notepad, a conversation already on his lips. I pointed to the receiver. He nodded, but instead of turning around, he came to sit at the edge of my desk, his foot tapping as he wrote something on the pad. The room instantly seemed smaller.

The farmer asked if I was there.

I squirmed in my chair. "Right here, Wes," I said, nodding.

"Now listen here. We all go down on hard times, and I'm not gonna tell you that you ain't got a right to grieve and whatnot. Your dad was a good man and I liked him well." He drew in a breath. "But I need a payment for the hay Joe dropped off in September. Otherwise, I can't deliver no more. We got our own bills and we need to see you can pay before we ship."

I thanked God I didn't have the farmer on speakerphone. I didn't want Jason to be aware of our money problems. We needed the hay delivered this week.

"I'm sorry. I'll get that out as soon as I can," I said, trying to sound nondescript. "Yes. Uh-huh. That's right. That'll go out today." I tried to sound as professional as I could, attempting to get the farmer off the phone.

After another minute of listening to Wes's spiel, I laid the receiver down, took a steadying breath, and swiveled my chair to look at Jason. Jason still sat on my desk, his eyes narrowed in concentration as he flipped through the pages of his pad.

"Time to go over our options—our schedule." He tapped the pad with the end of his pen. "We need to decide the best shows for you to gain the most points in the fewest number of shows, while still qualifying you for the Cup. They require twenty points, and even though that's a hefty amount, all you have to do is get in the top four at the three shows to get that." He paused, and briefly eyed me before continuing, "I assume finances are to be considered, as we don't have an unlimited budget to send you to all the shows."

Did he guess I'd been speaking to the farmer about our outstanding bill? And that I'd lied? That the check wouldn't go out until after the first when I had more money in from the handful of boarders we still had. "Yes, that's right."

But Jason continued talking about our options. I glanced at the point system for the Gold Cup: each first place at a qualifier earned twenty, a second earned fifteen, a third place earned five, and each fourth earned four points.

"We can do it. That should be easy. All we need is one first place and we're in."

Jason looked skeptical, but the corner of his mouth lifted in a smile. "Good. Let's make it happen." He stood, but instead of walking away, he leaned in toward me, his hair falling into his face. His face was only a few inches away as he pointed out the West Coast League schedule. I breathed in his earthy smell while he talked.

"Do you agree?" he asked. His intensity overwhelmed me. The best place for me to be around Jason was when I was riding Jett—a good four feet higher than him. Not on a yoga mat less than a foot away, nor with his face in mine.

"What did you say?" I wanted to start this conversation over. Why hadn't he come at another time, when I wasn't distracted with the farmer?

"A show at Thermal in February, one at Del Mar in April, a

practice one at Spruce Meadows in July, then back to Spruce Meadows for the West Coast Gold Cup finals at the beginning of September. Three shows. And before that we need to sit down and review videos of the top riders. It always helps. Let's set something up for next week."

I said it was a great plan. He nodded, smiled, and walked out.

As soon as he was out of sight, with a shaky hand I wiped my face. "Please, don't let me be wrong," I said out loud. "Please, God, let us win."

A few days later, I pulled Jett's tack off, then grabbed a dandy brush and using quick, hard strokes around the girth and saddle area, brushed at the sweat. Dried sweat would itch and look unsightly, like the stains around the brim of a cowboy hat. But I had to hurry since I had a date with Chris in downtown Devon, our first real outing in a couple of weeks. I couldn't wait to see him. Time had gotten away from me while riding.

"A mark of a crappy horseman," Dad would have said. "Too wrapped up in himself to really care about the poor beast. And it's thanks to them they even get to compete." I used to get annoyed at him for following me around, double-checking that I'd groomed my ponies and horses properly, but of course he'd been right. He'd drilled into me the importance of horse care, a rider's number one priority. The rider always came second.

I used a soft body brush to smooth down Jett's hair until it reflected the light from the fluorescent bulbs above. I moved in a trance, having done this more than a thousand times in my life. Grooming horses was meditative for me, like brushing my teeth, or going through the motions of folding laundry. I picked out Jett's feet and pulled on his blanket for the night.

On my way out of the tack room, I grabbed a couple of carrots out of the bucket. "You want one?" I asked Jett as I undid his cross ties. Our routine was familiar to him since he was a foal, and he was eager to get at my pocket where the carrots were. I pulled one out, broke off a piece, and laid it out for him on my palm. He nuzzled my hand with the penetrating and tough muscles of his lips, then pulled the piece of carrot into his mouth, crunching it. I saved the other pieces until I had him in his stall. Jett nodded his head up and down, radiating joy. He knew he had pleased me and he was proud of himself. I was proud of him too. It turned out I'd had nothing to worry about for today's jumping lesson, our first time jumping higher. Jett had been perfect, rounding himself over every jump, picking up his feet, kicking up his hind legs. And jumping Grand Prix–level heights was more exhilarating than I ever remembered.

"Soon. Soon we'll get our chance," I said as I slid his stall door shut. Jett turned toward his pile of hay, swishing his tail. I practically ran through the barn checking on the horses, then turned the barn lights off and shut the heavy barn doors.

I jogged up the small hill toward the house. The air seemed extra crisp, tinged with dew, decaying leaves, and the acridity of the neighbor's burning wood. The holidays were around the corner and yet we still had no plans. How lonely it all seemed. The yellow lights shone from the large windows, and I half-expected gray smoke to curl up from the chimney, but who was I kidding? Neither Mom nor I had bothered to get wood for the fireplace.

The lights meant she was home, though. Frequently now I caught her cross-legged on the couch, writing in her notebooks. Sometimes I heard her up in the early hours of the morning. She'd been ignoring me, though. Punishing me for my decision. No matter how hard I tried not to let it bother me, I wished I had her support. Her backing. I was doing this for her. I was doing this for Dad. I was doing this for all of us.

At The Lodge, the locals' pick for an evening restaurant and bar, I scanned the parking lot for Chris's Porsche and didn't see it. Our reservation for the dining room would hold a few more minutes, one advantage in being a local. Even though it was called The Lodge, I doubted anyone had stayed overnight in the upstairs empty rooms in the last twenty years. It boasted about its reputation as a speakeasy in the 1930s, with photos of Jerri Feri, Frank Lanza, and Anthony Lima, local mobsters, garnishing the wood-paneled walls.

The place was bustling with Friday night activity.

Inside, I sat at the bar and ordered a glass of Chardonnay. A moment of guilt flitted, then disappeared. Jason had said no alcohol, but what he didn't know wouldn't hurt him. I took a slow sip and pulled out my cell from my purse to double-check the time. One voice mail from Chris.

"Brynn. Something came up, and I won't be able to make it. I feel terrible, and I'll make it up to you soon. Sorry, love. I can't get out of this—you know how it is, this crazy horse business. Call you later." His voice, like always, was smooth, sexy.

I took another sip of wine, and tried not to be disappointed. Tried not to allow the thought of Chris teaching pretty girls to fill my mind. This was the way our business worked, and I had to get used to it. I ordered an appetizer. When it arrived I reveled in the flavors of baked artichoke, tomato, glazed onion, and roasted garlic topped with crumbles of blue cheese. "As usual, Robert has outdone himself," I said to Zach, the bartender, pulling out my wallet, then hesitated as I tried to remember which credit card still had an available balance. I hoped my cheeks weren't turning red as I handed one to him. Luckily it went through.

Since it was still early I decided to take a drive through town.

I rarely had a chance to walk around the little cafes and shops that clustered Devon Creek's main street anymore. Even with the short winter days, the street was full of life. Devon Creek was a small community, but its shops rivaled those of Tiburon or Sausalito. I preferred coming here, though. Fewer tourists, more charm.

The old-fashioned iron lanterns cast yellow circles of light.

People milled around the storefronts and sidewalks, teenagers laughed, older couples strolled hand-in-hand. I parked my car, then walked along Devon Street, gazing at the local art displays in the numerous galleries. You could find something here for even the most discriminating art maven—everything from the franchised Thomas Kinkade to contemporary artists specializing in aluminum sculptures or paintings of nudes. I couldn't help smiling, overfilled with a sense of love for this small community.

"Brynn?" A deep voice behind me called. Jason. I cringed internally. I wasn't planning on seeing him tonight. The white of his T-shirt under his brown leather jacket contrasted against his olive skin.

"Hey," I said, attempting to be casual, and turned to the blown-glass display.

"I didn't recognize you with your hair down," Jason said. "Or with anything but britches or yoga pants on." One of his dark eyebrows lifted.

I smoothed the front of my dress, wishing it were a bit longer. My hem stopped halfway down my thighs, shorter than I normally wore, but I had wanted to entice Chris. I pulled my trench coat around me, spinning away from him, almost tripping in my high-heeled boots.

"I thought you were going out in San Francisco tonight," I said.

"My plans changed."

He stared at me. I had to look away. I had no idea why he unnerved me. He was just another guy. My trainer no less. "Out on a date?" I asked.

"Something like that," he said. "Getting to know the neighborhood. How about you?" He leaned against the entrance of the gallery, facing me. "Alone, walking the streets of Devon Creek. Is that safe?" He chuckled.

"I'm enjoying a quiet evening out. In fact, I was just heading over to Patterson's to get a cup of coffee."

"Mind if I join you?"

I wanted to be alone, but at the same time I had a million things I needed to talk to him about: Jett, the upcoming shows, the schedule. So why shouldn't he?

We walked toward Patterson's against a cold wind that had picked up. Jason moved a few inches closer. Outside Patterson's, people sat in clusters at the mosaic-topped tables beneath heat lamps. It was a favorite hangout in Devon Creek, the perfect après date-night dessert and coffee spot, and it made me uncomfortable to bring Jason here. It felt too intimate. But the idea of a hot cappuccino won out. As we neared, a pretty brunette glided through the glass doors, her head pulled back as she laughed at something someone said to her. A blond man followed, his arm around her, tugging her closer, his hair falling over his face as he nuzzled her neck.

I froze. Holy shit. Chris!

I jumped to my right, flattening myself against the wall. Jason stopped too, staring at me. His gaze followed mine to the couple outside Patterson's. I watched them make their way across the street, the blue of the woman's dress and heels resembling the color of Chris's new Porsche. The couple walked toward a silver SUV, with car seats in the back.

Not Chris.

Was I losing my mind? I rested my head back against the cool brick of the building.

"Someone you know?" Jason asked.

I didn't answer, too embarrassed by my behavior.

"Someone you don't want to know?"

I shook my head.

"It was no one," I said. "I . . . I . . ," I was an idiot.

Jason nodded his head. He didn't ask for an explanation.

Jason held the door for me as we entered Patterson's. The smell of waffle cones, ice cream, and espresso beans warmed me instantly.

We found a small table at the back of the shop. His knees angled toward the center of the room, not fitting under the small table, while I crossed my ankles, tugging my dress as far as I could over the goose bumps on my thighs.

"What would you like?" he asked.

"A cappuccino, please."

He let an older couple ahead of him in line. They were probably in their seventies but held hands, as if they were on their first date, their age-spotted hands adorned with simple gold wedding bands.

The honey-colored light cast a warm glow over the cafe. Jason brought our drinks over, his black tea and my cappuccino.

"So why are you doing this?" I said.

He gave me a confused stare. "What? Having tea?"

"No. Not the tea. The training. Why are you training me?" I asked. "You must have so many options, all probably paying way more than what I can."

"I was curious." He smiled.

A tiny scar near his right eye, a shade whiter than the rest of his face, melded with his laugh lines. "Oh, come on. That's not truly the case."

"You'd be surprised." He smiled again.

"I'd like it if you were honest with me," I said. He stirred honey into his tea, his spoon making a whirlpool in his cup.

"It's good for me to be here," he said. "My sister needs me."

"Your sister?"

"Her daughter. Eve." He tapped his fingers on the table. "She has AML. Acute myeloid leukemia."

My heart stuttered. Arrhythmia, I thought, the vet school training automatic. "I'm so sorry. How old is she?"

"Three." He peered into his large mug.

My throat clenched at the thought of a child so young, yet so sick.

"They're alone. Her husband's in the reserves. Got called up two years ago, and hasn't been home for two months straight since. My mother would normally help, but she passed away years ago, before Eve was even born." He seemed to flinch a bit, his eyes briefly scrunched. "Currently Eve's in the hospital, and Ashley, my sister, stays with her as much as possible. I relieve her so we take turns. She's gone through chemotherapy, radiation, blood transfusions, you name it."

"I'm sorry," I said again. I rested my fingers lightly on his. The touch seemed to startle him.

"She's my little sister, and Eve's my only niece. Plus, there's no one else."

I nodded.

"Ashley had a job, but with all the medical care Eve has needed, well even with family leave"—he paused, running a hand through his hair—"she got laid off. Was told they were restructuring, but I think that's all an excuse. She's trying to make it work just off of Tyler's salary, but"—his voice trailed—"you know how that goes." He ran his thumb along the edge of his cup. "Anyway, Ian calling was a blessing in disguise. Eve was diagnosed the same week I got Ian's call. She's been hospitalized since."

"I'm so sorry," I said again. I picked up the teaspoon and swirled it around in the thick foam, mixing in the dark chocolate flakes.

"What about your father?"

A shadow seemed to cross his face, and if he had flinched before, the look now held something much darker, more fierce.

"I haven't seen him since I was nine." Jason cleared his throat, took a sip of his tea, then his face went blank again. "What about you?" he asked. "Why are you doing this?"

"I already told you. I want to win."

"There's more to it than that."

What was I supposed to reveal? I had to support the ranch, I had to prove myself, I had to gain clients. I had made a promise to my Dad.

"I just have to," I said, taking a sip of my cappuccino, feeling the foam on my lip, and wiping it away with a napkin. Jason didn't take his eyes off me.

"What do you need to prove?"

"I just need to win. I need to get respect from people. To keep clients, to keep the money coming in."

"What about vet school? Isn't that your career goal?" Jason continued. "Must have been serious to leave right at the end. You don't strike me as a quitter."

I gave a half laugh, shaking my head. I was a quitter, always scared of failing. He had me pegged all wrong. "Career goal." I mulled over his question. No one but Dad had ever made me defend my choices—and I'd never had that conversation with him. "Yes. I guess it is my career goal, or I thought it was. But Redwood Grove, my mom, Jett—they all need me more than vet school does." Then quietly I said, thinking out loud: "Who knows, maybe I was supposed to ride Jett all along."

"Interesting." Jason leaned in, his forehead furrowed. "So you were meant to do this."

I gave a nervous laugh again. "I don't know. I'm meant to do this right now. Does that help? I mean I like the idea of everything that being a vet stands for. I like the security and stability it provides. But I have this"—I struggled to find the right word—"this need. A calling. I really need to be with Jett, to challenge myself, challenge him, to fulfill my father's dreams. I feel like his dreams have become my dreams." I shifted my weight.

"Or maybe they were always yours."

I glanced down at the table, at my hands, so much like Dad's. I had never spoken like this to anyone. Jason reached over and held the tips of my fingers in his, his touch feather-light, the point of contact so small, yet so comfortable. I pulled my fingers back, remembering Chris, wondering what he'd think if he'd seen us, how I'd feel if the situation was reversed.

Yet Chris and I had never been able to be like this, and with him, I always felt like there were big decisions to be made, or places to go, or things to do. We could never just be. Was that why I'd never told him anything like this before?

When I got home, I walked down to the barn to do my night check of the horses. Mom had left the small light above the kitchen sink on for me before heading to her night shift at the retirement home. Even though she was angry with me, I knew she cared. I knew her actions were fear-based. She had her own anger and resentment to work through. I knew all this, but none of it made it easier. I felt as if I'd lost two parents that fateful night.

I filled a glass with water and sat, sipping. I luxuriated in the memory of the evening. How strange it had all been. Waiting for Chris, then running into Jason. I thought of Jason's fingers on mine: warm, electric, familiar, then pushed the thought away, playing it up to some strange phenomenon of having a close working relationship together.

On the counter lay two letters. I skimmed the top one, from the UC Davis School of Veterinary Medicine. It was from Dr. Dixon saying that the director of admissions, under the recommendation of Dr. Finlay and the faculty, had agreed to a temporary leave of absence and, given space in the program, might allow me to finish off my schooling the following year. I breathed a sigh of relief, yet felt torn. Would I be able to go back? Would we be okay financially by then? I placed the letter down.

The accountant's name caught my eye on the second letter. Our barn account was overdrawn. I dropped the paper on the counter, sitting down, putting my head in my hands. How were we going to get through the rest of the winter and spring until I won some money? *If* I won money. My glass of water almost slipped from my hands.

I shook my head. I couldn't think that way. I had to win. I had to win something at all the shows, but most importantly, I had to win the Gold Cup. Otherwise everything Dad had worked for—everything *I* now worked for—would be gone.

20

$\mathcal{I}$ walked Jett out of the huge Grand Prix arena at Thermal. Helena and her daughter, Payton, were the only clients showing at the show, since Lani wasn't ready for the level of classes at Thermal, though Mai and Lani came to cheer the Redwood Grove Stable team on. Jason, Derek, and I had trailered Effy, Ness, and Jett. The mid-February sun had risen overhead in the too-blue sky, and the breeze that had almost blown our tent over the evening before had now died down, leaving the palm trees to stand at attention as if they were made of plastic. Even though the temperature was only in the low seventies, sweat poured in between my shoulder blades and my cream polo clung to my back.

"That was a fantastic round!" Jason said as I exited, patting Jett's neck.

"It felt fantastic," I said, drinking the air in gulps. "But, holy crap, the jumps were much farther apart than I expected. I thought we'd collapse partway through. We needed way more stamina than I thought." The euphoria of showing Jett was infinitely better than I'd remembered. Both the boring and grueling days of training had all been worth it.

"Here, B. Have some water." Derek handed me a cup.

My words rushed out. "It really came together, like we both sensed what the other was thinking. Jett paid attention to what I asked for, giving it to me before I even had to ask." I looked back at the arena, catching a glimpse of the next rider flying over the large Mount Rushmore jump. The horse knocked a rail, and the trainer next to me groaned, then yelled, "Get your speed up!" Riders and trainers stood around, most still in their britches and tall boots, burrito or sandwich in hand, gobbling their food in big bites while watching the show.

"It's what you've been working toward, Brynn," Jason said quietly. Something in the way he said it made me look down at him. His lips parted as if to say something else, his strong jaw line shadowed by a couple of days' worth of stubble. It had been three weeks since the night at Patterson's, and Jason and I had continued a very professional relationship, early morning yoga sessions followed by jumping lessons. Yet as he placed his hand on my boot, I could feel the heat of his hand even through the leather.

"I'm proud of you," Jason said.

I nodded, unsure of how to respond.

"Hey! Great round!"

I twisted in my saddle. Chris walked toward us from behind one of the hundreds of palm trees planted around the show grounds, his thumbs tucked into his breeches.

I cleared my throat, suddenly feeling as if I'd been caught, and I wondered if he had seen Jason put his hand on my boot. It was innocent enough, but I couldn't ignore Jason's touch, nor my response. "Chris, did you see it? Wasn't he absolutely amazing?" I leaned forward, patting Jett's sweaty neck.

"Only saw the last jump. Sorry." He cocked his head, giving me his apologetic smile.

"I can't get over how wonderful he was." I hopped down. "We might get that Cup after all. Won't we, buddy?" Jett neighed, as if in response. Derek and I laughed, then Derek took the reins. "That's why we're here, B. To show them what you've got."

I rubbed Jett's nose before Derek walked him back to his stall.

Chris eyed Jason. "Good job," Chris finally said, nodding, but his voice held an edge. The two hadn't seemed to warm to each other, and in fact, Chris had started to show up unannounced during my lessons with Jason. He'd bring me a large mocha, or lunch from Yakima's or fish tacos from Sausalito Taco Shop, which all seemed sweet, but I couldn't help but feel he was checking in on me.

"Any more classes today?" Chris asked, laying his arm across my shoulders.

"Done for now. We don't have that many horses." Helena and Payton had shown in the smaller classes earlier that morning.

"Right," Chris said, as if losing Corinne and her horses hadn't been my main concern and what I constantly brought up in our conversations over the last couple of months.

Jason acknowledged Chris but now shifted away.

"Your round on De Salle looked amazing." I changed the subject, taking off my helmet. "I stopped my warm-up to watch. You guys are on fire."

"Yeah, he was good. Probably the best I've ever had. But at this level, you need a string of De Salles. A minimum of three. Six would be ideal." He flicked some dust off his shoulder. "I'm working on it, though. Those investors I mentioned last week? Well, it just so happens they're here, and guess who just ran into them? Your one and only." He straightened, lifting his chin, flashing one eyebrow. "They're up for a meeting next week. Now we're talking about a syndicate. Really, I should have thought about that earlier—it's the only way to go."

"That's great," I said. "That's really, really great." And I tried to mean it. To be happy for him and not to let the fact that I only had one, unproven horse, bother me. It was true—to get to the top you really did need more than one horse, to deflect the risk of something going wrong. If Jett ever got injured, we'd be out of the running for the Cup. I sighed. No matter how happy I was for Chris, he would always be my competition, and how would we ever work around that? I glanced up at the scoreboard. "I think you're still in the lead, Chris."

"And you, little one, are not too far behind."

Sure enough, my name lit up on the scoreboard—Jett and I were in second place.

Jason studied the scoreboard, then me. "Nice round, kid. I'm going to go help Derek out. So I'll see you shortly to go over the plan for tomorrow's class?" He touched his hand to the small of my back, then quickly pulled it away.

I couldn't help but wish we were alone. I wanted to hear his honest thoughts, to analyze each and every jump, to strategize for next time. "With over fifty riders to go I'm not going to get my hopes up," I said.

Jason smiled. "You're learning not to be attached to the outcome."

Chris stepped closer to me, wrapping his arm around my waist. "Well, let's get some grub while we wait for the results. I'm starving."

I glanced up at Jason. "Well, actually, I've already made plans."

"Jason? Derek? No problem! They can join. We'll eat up at the VIP tent. I've got a table."

"You two go. I need to make a call anyway," Jason said.

"See? It's all good." Chris smiled that wide grin, then nuzzled my neck, whispering into my hair. "By the way, I'm sure you were stupendous. Sorry I missed most of your round."

Jason turned away, starting toward the barns while Chris held a hand on my elbow, leading me toward the VIP tent. I halted, turning back. "Hey, Jason!" I called after him. "Thank you!"

He tipped his hat, then he mouthed, "Sukhino Bhavantu." A shift in the wind kicked up desert sand, sending it into a small twister right in front of me. I covered my eyes with my hand, and by the time I looked up again, he was gone.

Fifty-three rides later, Derek and I stood at the gate. "And now, ladies and gentlemen, the results of our Sunset Five Thousand Grand Prix! First place: Chris Peterson on De Salle. Second place:

Roman Kuzara on I Should Be So Lucky. Third goes to Vivian Young on Love's First Trip. Fourth to Brynn Seymour on Victory by Heart. Fifth to Holly Davidoff . . ." I tuned out the rest, jumping up and down, throwing my arms around Derek. I could get used to hearing Jett's and my names over the loudspeakers.

"Where's Jason?" I asked Derek, scanning the crowd.

"Gone home. Said he had a family thing," Derek said as he fumbled for something in his pockets.

"Is it his niece? Did he say anything about his niece?" I ran after Derek, who was already walking ahead.

"No, didn't say anything. I drove him to the Palm Springs airport at lunch." Derek opened a tiny bottle of rum, no doubt from the hotel minibar, and lifted it in a toast. He took a long drink.

I pulled out my phone.

"Doubt you'll reach him now." Derek looked up at the sky. "He's probably in the air as we speak. Said his flight was at three." He handed me the bottle of rum. I shook my head.

"Did he say anything else?"

"You know Jason. Always quiet and absorbed in thought and all that. It's not like he's going to open up to me."

I wished I could be with Jason, to make sure he was all right.

"C'mon! Let's celebrate!" Derek said, putting his arm around me, pulling me along.

That was the last thing I wanted to do.

"You don't have a choice," Derek said, sensing my hesitation.

Dinner was at Hog's Breath Inn. Chris said he'd meet us there—he was getting a ride with Roman. Derek and I walked arm in arm through the lobby toward the taxi stand. Nearing the exit I noticed Vivian, alone, at the bar, in a sapphire strapless mini dress. I scanned the area for Corinne, or one of her other clients, but no one was around.

"Hold up a sec," I said to Derek, then crossed the lobby to the bar.

"Great ride today," Vivian said, as she took a sip of her martini.

"Thanks." I glanced down at the carpet. "You had an excellent round too."

"You know Love's First Trip is incredible, but Seraphim is my favorite. I can't wait to show her."

Bitch. I had to bite my tongue.

"She has a fierce spirit. But I like a good fighter, otherwise things get so boring." She rolled her eyes, then took another sip of her drink, wavering slightly on her stool.

Derek was outside the glass doors already, a cab door open. He waved at me to hurry up. "Well, I guess I'll see you—"

"I didn't know she was going to move to my barn."

I paused.

"I didn't steal Corinne. She came because she wanted to." Vivian's emerald eyes glittered in the low light. Even when she sat on a bar stool I was barely her height. "I wouldn't have done that to you."

Somewhere in the back of her eyes I noted loneliness, sadness. I nodded. My kinder side gave way. "We're going to Hog's Breath. Do you want to join?"

Vivian turned back to the bar, taking another sip of her martini.

I started to walk away.

"Why the hell not?" Vivian stood, grabbing her silver clutch off the bar. "I'll just cancel my plans," she said, pulling out her smartphone, typing as we walked. I had to wonder whether she really had any.

Roman, along with a couple of Chris's groupies named Star and Madison, and Ruth Stubbs, Helena, and Mai were already at Hog's Breath. Chris had saved me a seat and the waiter rushed to get an extra chair for Vivian.

"Hey, Derek, where's your boyfriend?" Roman asked.

"Back in San Fran. He's got a big case he's working on."

"You off the leash then?" A peel of laughter rang out.

"Hey, be careful! But, I am on vacay—and getting down tonight!"

I lifted an eyebrow. This was not the Derek I knew. I hadn't spent much time with him lately, too focused on myself, and made a mental note to find out what was going on with him and Bill.

After dinner and dessert, and what appeared to be his fourth vodka tonic, Chris announced that it was time to go dancing in downtown Palm Springs. Star and Madison made pouty faces, since they were both only eighteen and without fake IDs they'd never make it into a club. Leaving them behind was fine with me, although I would have been happier going back to the hotel too. We all piled into a cab and ten minutes later, bass was pumping in my ears at a nightclub.

Bleary-eyed, I stood off the dance floor, nursing my club soda. Derek found me, and leaned his elbows on the bar table next to me.

"I'm ready to head home," I said. "It's almost two. Do you want to split a cab with me?"

Derek's face fell. "I'm just getting warmed up." Sweat dripped from his long sideburns.

I looked away, watching Vivian on the dance floor. She had her arm around Roman and the two of them laughed about something.

"She's trouble," Derek said above the music.

I gave him a puzzled look.

"Mai just told me Corinne caught her rapping Sera."

The glass practically slipped from my hands. I kept my eyes on Vivian, grinding up against Roman.

"I don't believe it. Can't be true." I felt the steak I'd eaten turn in my stomach. Rapping horses was cause for disqualification in a show. I'd seen it done in old videos: the rider hits the horse's legs with a pole or stick while the horse is midair to encourage it to jump higher. The injury was rarely visible, as the legs weren't cut or wounded, but psychologically it was inhumane.

"Yeah, it is, B. Supposedly one of Vivian's ex-clients told Corinne they'd seen her do it—and not just to Sera but most of her high-level jumpers. And you know Corinne, she flipped out.

Vivian denied everything. Since it hadn't happened at a show, and technically since it wasn't illegal as a pre-show training technique, Corinne can't do a thing about it."

I didn't know how to respond and when another song started, Derek smiled at me and said, "I've got a bit more dancing to do." He clinked his glass to mine, then sashayed over to the dance floor, his cosmo high in the air.

I found Chris in the corner of the bar, thronged by a crowd. I pushed my way through. He barely glanced at me as he prepared for more shots. I contemplated going over to him, but decided against it since he'd probably try to convince me to stay.

In the privacy of the hotel room, I peeled off my clothes and stood in the shower, lifting my face, letting the water fall over my eyes and hair, enjoying the solitude. Tomorrow we'd drive home; I'd see Jason, and find out what happened with Eve. And then we'd start practicing for Del Mar, only two months away. Del Mar would be an indoor class with tighter turns and higher jumps. The competition would be much steeper than here and I had to get first or second or I wouldn't have enough points to qualify for the Spruce Meadows show. Today's fourth got me four points, but I had to get sixteen more to qualify. Sixteen more. And here I'd told Jason it wouldn't be a problem.

On a late Monday afternoon in March, I was finishing going over the bills and schedule for the next week. I leaned back in my chair, trying to refocus my eyes. Even though I'd won fourth place at Thermal, it was a $5,000 class, so my share of the winnings was only several hundred dollars. That didn't even cover our costs of gas for trailering, stall fees, or entry fees. Having Helena and Payton also show at Thermal, and pay us for hauling Effy and Ness and for my training fees, were the only things that had kept us above water.

A car door slammed and a high-pitched chatter in the parking lot outside the barn reached me. I walked out through the quiet barn and peered around the corner to check on things. I wasn't expecting anyone. Jason was at his small pickup truck holding a little girl's hand. Her back was to me, but I knew right away it had to be his niece, Eve. She barely reached above his knees. Her pink T-shirt was tucked into tiny green jeans and she stomped toward the barn in magenta cowboy boots. Her head was wrapped with a bandana.

"What brings you two out here?" I said, walking toward them.

"I *thought* you'd be working on your day off," Jason said, smiling.

I felt my face warm, so I turned my attention to the little girl.

"Hi, there. I'm Brynn." I extended my hand toward hers. When she looked at me, I inhaled sharply. She had the largest eyes I'd seen, but it was her irises that grabbed my attention. In her pale face with no eyelashes or eyebrows, her irises seemed to take up most of her almond-shaped eyes. Her gaze, steady and certain, focused on mine and never wavered as she took me in, as if she'd known this world for much longer than her three years.

"Hello. I'm Eve." She shook my hand fast, her fingers around mine in a strong grip. "You're the lady with the horses. Uncle Jason said I'd like you. When I grow up I want to be just like Uncle Jason. I want to ride horses and be a show jumper and go to the Olympics."

I had to laugh at how well she spoke, almost as if she was several years older. But I covered my mouth with my hand, trying to gain composure, putting a serious face on, and squatting down so that I was at her eye level. "Is that so? Well, I bet that if you set your mind to it you will get there." Then I leaned in and whispered, "And you're lucky. You have the best trainer ever." I winked at her. Her stare was serious, but she nodded, then scanned the empty paddocks. Her forehead creased. "Where are all the horses? Are they at home now?"

I followed her gaze. "Kind of. They're inside this big barn eating their supper. But we can go and see them, if you like."

Eve jumped up and down, wrapped her hand around Jason's, then reached for mine. "Yes, yes! Uncle Jason, can we go see them?"

"That's why we're here." Jason smiled at me. "Because I knew Brynn would love to show you all of the horses and especially Jett, her show jumper. And if you're really nice to her, she might even let you sit on him."

I threw Jason a questioning look, but I didn't hesitate long. "Well, it just so happens that Jett *loves* little kids, and you know what? I think he's been waiting for you to come ride him."

Eve squealed and gripped my hand more tightly.

As we walked to the barn, Jason nodded a thank-you.

When we got to Jett's stall and slid the door open, Jason held Eve back while I haltered Jett, pulling his head up from the hay. We showed Eve how to hold a carrot in her hand, palm flat, carrot lying on top, and Jett leaned down, gently mouthing her palm before crunching the carrot. As soon as his nose touched her hand she squealed, jerking her hand back, jumping up and down. "His nose is fuzzyyy!" She let out another squeal. But Jett didn't startle, just leaned his head down and let her pet him, his breath close to her nose, getting her scent. She touched him gingerly at first, but as she gained confidence, she moved her hand up in between his eyes.

"That's the softest thing you'll ever feel," I said, guiding her hand up and around his ear, letting her pet it.

"Oh my goodness! Oh my goodness! It's as soft as my rabbit!"

"You have a rabbit?"

"Peter Rabbit. He keeps me company in the hospital when I feel sick."

"Oh, what a good friend he is!" I replied, trying to sound positive. She'd just spent several months undergoing treatment, but she was in remission now, and Jason said that besides the eating disorder she developed in the hospital, she was doing well. They had to have an occupational therapist come reteach her how to eat, since for months she'd been fed via IV and tubes.

Once saddled and a proper helmet adjusted to her, we led Jett around the outdoor arena. I held him by a lead rope, while Jason wound his arm around Eve's teeny frame to hold her in place atop my saddle. And Jett, as if he knew he was in charge of this tiny child, hung his head low, and walked slowly, like an old schoolmaster, his gait rocking Eve back and forth. She held the pommel with both hands, her knuckles white, her eyebrows pulled together in concentration.

"Should we stop?" I asked.

"No, no, no! I want to ride more!"

And so we led her around for half an hour before Jason finally convinced her to dismount. At the end, she said goodnight to Jett, and Jason carried her to his truck. She laid her head against his shoulder, her lids heavy, closing. Jason buckled her into her car seat.

"I'll be one minute," he said to her. He kissed her cheek, and rolled down a window for her before shutting the door. She smiled, but her eyes closed completely and she seemed to already have fallen asleep.

He pulled me farther away from the truck.

While we walked, Jason spoke, "My father was a racehorse trainer down at the Santa Anita racetrack. My first memory is of him leading me around on a wild two-year-old racehorse." Jason stopped walking, his shoulders hunched. "The horse bucked me off, and I ate dirt and cried. My dad smacked me for being a wimp. My mother cried when I came home all bruised and beaten, but my dad told her to shut up. That's my first memory of my dad. And a horse." The same look I'd seen that night of coffee and tea at Patterson's crossed his face. Pain. Anger.

I wanted to say something, but was too shocked that this kind man, this man who'd been teaching me yoga, helping me open my mind, teaching me to jump, had these horrible memories from his childhood.

"He was a louse, a crook. Beat his horses. Beat his wife."

I placed my hand on his arm, squeezing it. "And his son?"

"And his son." Jason faced the sun, his chest expanding, his eyes closed. "I'm sorry. I shouldn't have laid that black memory on you."

"I'm glad you did," I said, laying my hand on his arm.

"Thank you for making Eve's most treasured wish come true."

Having seen Eve ride Jett, seeing their instant bond, seeing the joy on Eve's face was awe-inspiring.

Jason reached over, cupped my cheek with his palm, then leaned down and kissed the top of my head.

When Jason got in his car he rolled down his window and lifted his palm up, facing forward. The setting sun was in my eyes, but on the horizon I saw a little boy, beaten by his father, and I wondered at the darkness in the world.

21

*D*el Mar was like its name described. Of the sea. I'd always loved coming to shows here. Everything about it was idyllic: the hills, the winding streets with homes jutting out yet seamlessly merging with the landscape. And the ocean—stretching into the distance, roaring with energy. It did that too in Northern California, but here I could stick more than my toe into the water without getting frostbite.

But I wasn't here to enjoy the scenery. I was here to kick ass and to bring home a first place. I needed to prove that I wasn't afraid, that I could push forward and win. And what better place than at Del Mar's show grounds, one of the oldest and most prestigious equestrian competitions of the West Coast.

But the night of the Del Mar $100,000 Grand Prix, I wanted to crawl into a dark cave. Everything irritated me—including the overly loud Lady Gaga song played via the arena speakers. My muscles were tightropes. My skin itched. My mind raced. I'd had to train Helena's and Mai's daughters in the low pony hunter divisions earlier, and the stress of watching some of the unprepared riders had played havoc with my nerves. I'd fit in a yoga session earlier that afternoon, but I'd moved through the poses mechanically. I wasn't able to still my mind, my breath jagged and uneven, my asana practice stilted.

As Jason and I walked the course of the indoor arena, I fell into stride behind him, nodding my head as he talked, though the only thing running through my mind were thoughts of failure. I kept it all to myself. Jason would chastise me if he knew.

Jason stopped mid-stride, turned, and I almost ran into him. He crossed his arms, an expectant look on his face.

"Um, sorry. What did you say?" I stood embarrassed I'd missed another piece of important advice. Jason repeated himself, for the third time in less than ten minutes.

The stands on either side of the arena were full. VIP tables, dressed in dark cloth, lined the long side of the arena. Candles housed in glass lanterns fluttered pointlessly under the bright fluorescent lights at each table. International flags hung across the opposite side of the arena. I couldn't help noticing Corinne with a group from Vivian's barn. Envy flooded me, and I wished she was still with me.

"You're set?" Jason laid a hand on my shoulder.

"I think so." I nodded, showing more enthusiasm than I felt. In fact, I was petrified. My stomach was tight and my hands were cold, my heart clenching every time I thought of the round I'd have to ride. I'd never shown at this height, one-point-five meters and in an indoor arena. That was almost five feet, the top of the poles came up to my nose when I stood straight. The arena itself seemed as if it might burst with massive jumps, each more intricate and unique than the next. Purples, reds, blues, pinks. Flowers, columns, planks, boxes, a liverpool. The course itself was more difficult than any I'd ever ridden, with no lack of turns, rollbacks, and short lines.

"I don't think Enrique wants anyone to go clear," I muttered.

"He is one of the best," Jason admitted.

The course designer from hell, I added in my mind. And even though I'd seen jumps in Grand Prix close up a hundred times, it was always while walking the course with Dad, in preparation for him riding. I never experienced their grandeur, their immense height, as much as I did now.

On top of all the decisions and strategy, I had to worry about

Jett's stride, slightly shorter than an average horse's, which compli-cated our ride: I'd have to make him canter faster than normal, so that he could make the lines, yet carefully enough to get over the high jumps. The short space between jumps in the combinations would make it difficult to correct him before the next jumping ele-ment. So basically, if he refused a jump, we would have to start the whole triple combination over again. If he jumped in short, it could end in a disaster: Jett and I crashing.

"You'll be fine. Jett's really proving his potential, and just like I thought, has more scope than anyone gave him credit for," Jason said, peering at me.

I bit at a cuticle.

"Trust me," he said.

I nodded.

He held up his right hand, palm facing me.

I tilted my head in question.

"Have no fear," Jason said, still holding his hand up.

"It's the Abhaya Mudra—sign for have no fear," Jason said and then shook his head. "I still need to teach you so much . . ." But he smiled at me.

We walked toward the side exit as Chris and Vivian entered the arena kitty-corner from us. I smiled, then waved, but he didn't see me. I squinted against the bright lights reflecting off the sand. Spots floated in front of my eyes.

"Everything okay?" Jason asked, his eyes following mine toward Chris and Vivian.

"Fine, just fine." I screwed up my eyes. Why was he walking the course with Vivian? Why was she laughing, and why did her hand graze his arm just then?

"Whatever it is, you've got to let it go and concentrate on the course," Jason said, holding my elbow, turning me toward him. It took me a moment to look up at him.

"I'm fine," I said, my eyes drawn to Chris and Vivian again, her long legs easily keeping up with his stride.

"Let's warm up, Brynn," Jason's voice held an urgency which suddenly irritated me.

"I'll be there in a sec," I said, making a beeline toward Chris.

Vivian smiled, but noting the look on my face, lifted an eyebrow in question instead.

I grabbed Chris's arm. "Let's walk."

Chris hesitated, but then moved closer. "What's up?" He gave me a quick kiss, then brushed his long bangs off his forehead as he walked toward a set of jumps where Jason and I had been a few minutes before. Suddenly I had a deep desire to share Jason's advice with Chris, wanting to prove to myself that we could train together in the future, to collaborate, to strategize as a team. Otherwise, where did our future lead?

"Listen." I pointed to the scariest set of jumps in the ring. "That combination walks a short five strides to the oxer, followed by a bending line to the red and white skinny vertical. You're going to get caught if you don't get up enough speed before the in-and-out. That's a long one-stride, and the only way De Salle will jump it is if you're already coming in with a lot of pace."

Chris looked at the line I was talking about, pondering. "I'd rather keep steady then add a stride later."

"I know, I know. That's what I originally thought too, but Jason thinks you'll be caught at the in-and-out—"

Chris visibly tensed. "I think I'll be fine. De Salle has plenty of scope to pull that off." His lips drew into a tight line. "But thanks for the tip." He continued to walk the course, but increased his stride. I had to jog to catch up. Maybe I shouldn't have been surprised. He'd always thought himself a better rider. He'd always been the one to hand out the tips—or had he? I thought back to all the times we'd ridden together. Had he given me advice? Or had he kept things to himself? I slowed to a walk and let him go. Would we ever be able to work together if we were going after the same prize, or was Chris too competitive to collaborate? How had other rider couples done it?

I retraced my steps from jumps five to six, like Jason had told me to do. I noted the seventh jump was located in a spot where Jett would be going away from the in-gate. Not only that, but it was in the far corner of the arena. Having watched riders all week, I'd seen it was problematic. The horses didn't want to go at a fast enough speed into the corner. I'd even figured out why: the judge's booth was right there and a light flickered above the jump, casting looming shadows into the corner. But it was too late to do anything about it. The show was about to begin.

The loudspeaker above me buzzed to life. "Please clear the course. Our first rider is at the gate." I hadn't realized that I was the only one still walking the course. I walked one more line on my way out the side exit used by the jump crew, and said a little prayer.

Sitting atop Jett at the entrance of the indoor arena, I told myself I was ready for anything. I visualized each jump before heading in. When the time came, under the glare of the stadium lights, Jett and I rode in. The buzzer sounded and we cantered to the first jump, but the setup was all wrong, and we had a long distance, Jett having to stretch just to make it, but he did. We moved toward the next jump and for a moment I forgot where we were heading, scanning for the jump number, then remembering at the last second that we were supposed to do a turn and we lost some time. I tried letting go of my fear, the way Jason had said to, but I couldn't keep from analyzing each jump, controlling Jett, scanning the crowd, thinking of Vivian, Chris, their times, my position over the jumps. The announcer's loud voice annoyed me, the crowd seemed to be staring at their programs, or chatting to their friends. No one watched. The music crackled over the sound system. Details crowded my mind, and I seemed out of sync with Jett.

Jett rapped the last fence, the sound reverberating in the indoor arena. I peered back under my arm. The rail teetered, and I waited for the loud thump as it hit the ground, but it stayed up. The crowd cheered, and the announcer declared a clear round.

Back on the ground, Jason prepped me for the jump-off, the deciding round of the competition. Only fifteen of thirty-five riders remained. "OK. So you scraped by, got in just under the time allowed. But you almost knocked four rails. You got lucky that all of them stayed up. Brynn. Listen to me. To win the jump-off, you're going to have to clear your mind of everything."

"I know." I hung my head, rubbing my temples with my fingers. "I tried, Jason, but I just . . . I just couldn't." I turned away, too embarrassed not to have been able to follow his advice. He wiped his hands down the front of his jeans, passing me a water cup. I gulped the contents down in two swallows.

"Brynn. To get to Spruce Meadows you need to get a first or second place here. The competition's tough. Roman's been in the lead since the beginning of the season, and don't forget, they have four times as many shows under their belt—this is only your second one. You can't afford to lose."

I glared at Jason. "Not like that doesn't add just a bit of pressure."

"But I know you *can* do it. I wouldn't be here unless I believed in you. You just have to believe in Jett, believe in yourself." He wrapped his arm around my shoulders.

Just then, Chris rode by on De Salle. "Hey, stop putting moves on my woman!" he called, and although he said it in a joking manner, I heard an annoyance in his tone.

Jason stiffened next to me but didn't remove his arm from my shoulder right away.

"Don't worry about it. He's just being Chris," I said.

I felt the absence of Jason's arm, my body seemed heavier without it there.

"Vivian has three horses here, too," Jason said quietly.

"Three? That doesn't make sense."

"Love's First Trip, Edge of Night, and," he paused, searching my face, "and Seraphim."

"Sera's here?" I could feel all blood drain away. "She can't possibly be ready for a meter fifty class!" I scanned the area, as if expecting her to be right in front of me.

"Thought I should warn you before you saw for yourself."

We walked along in silence toward the indoor arena to watch the riders finish up their first round. I heard the crowd cheer for the rider, wondering if it was Vivian.

As Jett and I walked back into the arena for the jump-off, the crowd cheered. Chris stood on the sidelines watching. He waved when he saw me. He'd gone first, and although I hadn't seen his round, Jason had told me he'd gone clear, but was currently in second. I looked around for Vivian and Corinne, but they were nowhere in sight. As I circled the arena, Helena and Mai's Go Brynn sign waved at me from the stands.

I was the third rider of fifteen. The turns were sharper, the jumps higher. I felt like I was going to throw up. I tried to focus, but I couldn't get there—wherever *there* was.

I had no choice though. I had to finish this round, no matter how I scored.

"Let's do this, buddy." Jett's one ear turned toward me, the other stayed pointed straight ahead. He gave a small buck, as if in acknowledgement. I lifted my shoulders, squeezed with my calf, and we were off, following the only two sets of horse tracks in the sand before us. We went fast, but I still couldn't quiet my mind, couldn't align myself the way Jason had wanted me to, couldn't forget how scared I was of losing.

And then, at jump number four, the sunflower jump, everything melted away. It was only Jett and me. No crowd. No announcer. No judge. Just us—flying as one. And even before we finished, I knew we'd gone clear.

22

I clicked end on my cell phone. I had called Mom to tell her about my day, but all I got was her voice mail. I wanted to tell her the good news but not by leaving a message.

The boutique, hacienda-style hotel where we stayed in Del Mar overlooked the ocean, and I was lucky enough to have a view. The room was a surprise from Aunt Julia, and I only wished Mom could be here to see it.

"You need a good night's rest if you're going to win," Aunt Julia had said before I left for Del Mar. I was used to staying at the budget hotels near the freeway when I went to shows with Dad. I'd never experienced such luxury. I pulled the French doors wide open and walked onto the small balcony. The sun had already set, only a hint of red and purple reflected in the clouds above the horizon. A breeze brushed my bare arms, the silk of my dress dancing against my legs. I breathed in the heady smell of jasmine mixed with the mellow lavender blooming in earthen pots draped over the edge of the balcony.

I gazed up at the brightest star and thought back to Dad and the last show we were at together. We had just finished taking care of the horses, putting on blankets, refilling waters, picking out the stalls. The place was deserted, save for a few grooms checking on horses. Dad was relaxed after showing, and he leaned against an arena fence and stared up at the sapphire sky. He told me that the particles of energy that made up stars also made up all of us—all living things.

Each one of us had bits of stardust in our soul, and the good souls sparkled brighter than the rest. He took my hand and told me that my eyes were the gateway to my own star out in the universe.

"Which one is yours, Dad?" I whispered now. Nothing but the crashing waves below responded.

A barrage of noise came from the hallway, then knocking at my door. "Brynn!" Chris was at the door, ready for the West Coast League's annual banquet and awards ceremony.

I'd won second place in the Del Mar Classic, and the night seemed filled with possibilities. I couldn't help but skip toward the door. As I neared, the knocking turned to banging and laughter. Chris and two girls spilled into my room. Apparently the party had already started.

Irritation flooded me.

Chris poured champagne into a glass. "Have a drink!"

"Can we wait until dinner? I'm famished."

The girls, Star and Madison, were the same groupies that had latched on to our party at Thermal. Madison, the brunette, plopped unceremoniously onto the bed; Star, the blonde, looked through my things on the desk. I walked over, shut my laptop, and moved my notebook and purse aside. Star smiled, as if it was acceptable to rifle through other people's belongings.

"Oh, come on! You beat me and thirty-four other riders. Surely you can have a drink to celebrate." Chris held out the champagne flute toward me, golden liquid spilling over the side. He'd gotten fourth.

Is this what it was about? Me beating him tonight? Sighing, I accepted.

"To Brynn! An up-and-coming rider on her way to Spruce Meadows! And then the Gold Cup!" Chris raised the bottle above his head, then took a swig straight from it.

He pulled me into an embrace. His arm squeezed too tight, and I leaned my head away from his as he gripped my belly and hips against him. "Who would have thought you were so sly, not sharing your secrets," he whispered into my ear, then he laughed and winked. "So young, so gorgeous, so talented!" He leaned in and kissed my mouth. I pushed him away. I *had* tried to help him. Suddenly I wasn't sure I even wanted to spend the evening with him.

"Madison, Star, you have a lot to learn from Brynn here," he said to them. The girls giggled.

"Shall we go to dinner?" I picked up my purse.

"Yes ma'am! You heard Brynn. Girls, let's go!" Chris set the empty champagne bottle on the table, and I caught the glimpse he'd given Madison's pushed-up cleavage as she passed by him. I shut the balcony doors, holding back the urge to slam them.

On our way down to the banquet I scrutinized our reflections in the mirrors of the elevator. My face stern and drawn, the others giddy and drunk. I felt underdressed in my painted silk summer dress, light blue blending with amber and tea rose, hues of the Del Mar sky at sunset. I'd chosen to accessorize only with simple gold hoop earrings and the gold heart pendant from my dad. Now I regretted my choice.

Star and Madison wore couture black evening dresses that showed off way too much cleavage in the front and too much skin in the plunging low backs—the exact reason Chris had allowed them to come along, no doubt. Of course they were probably the newest spring designs, the way they screamed fancy labels and high price tags. Probably purchased on Rodeo Drive prior to coming to Del Mar. Diamonds sparkled at the girls' ears and throats, accentuating their slim necks and perfectly formed chins and cheekbones. Even though I was older than them, I felt young and incompetent, naïve and completely out of place.

We entered the foyer and headed toward the main dining room. A large banner, proclaiming the Del Mar Show Grounds, hung on the wall to the left. Tables were adorned with white cloth, silver candles flickering atop horse-shaped candelabra. Pewter horse-bit holders girdled the apricot-colored napkins. The restaurant boasted grand views of the Pacific framed by floor-to-ceiling windows, and I had to stop to take in the grandeur. I might as well have stepped into a palace somewhere in the south of France.

I looped my arm through Chris's, walking toward the host who eyed the giggling girls behind us. I wondered how long it would take to lose them. We followed the host's tuxedoed back to our table in the center of the room. To the left of the podium, awards and trophies graced a black-clothed table. Jason, Derek, and our barn's small group of clients weren't there yet.

The host pulled out a royal blue velvet chair for me. He proceeded to place the napkin in my lap, like a bullfighter, swift yet light.

"Time for a drink. Where's the bar?" Chris stood, before he'd even fully sat. His move jostled the table.

The host raised a brow, but gestured toward the back of the room. "The cash bar is right over there, sir. Wine is on the table."

Chris didn't even ask what I wanted as he walked away.

"Thank you," I said to the host. He nodded again, leaving me alone. Whether he pitied me or not, he didn't show, his face a mask of graciousness.

I ran my finger over the gold-embossed letters of my name on the card in front of me. Brynn Seymour. Brynn Seymour, second place winner of the $100,000 Del Mar Classic. Brynn Seymour, confused and lost. Brynn Seymour, here with a man who—what? What was the plan for us? What did I even want anymore?

Star and Madison lounged at the bar, long legs entwined in bar stools, sandal straps and tanned skin peeking out. At least five guys surrounded them now, drinking shots with Chris, angling to get close to the girls. I wished the bartender would card them, but I doubted he would, this being a private event.

The next half hour was the longest of my life. I was out of my comfort zone as people kept coming up to congratulate me, many of whom I'd never met. I wished Derek and Jason and Helena—or even Corinne—were here with me. I scanned the crowd, but no one from Redwood Grove Stables had arrived yet.

I poured myself a glass of wine from the bottle on the table, finishing it more quickly than I expected. I stood and walked over to the windows, a painted mural overlooking the ocean. The sky had turned a black garnet, my reflection staring back at me. My face seemed younger, calmer than the turmoil of emotions going on inside. I was surprised at the wide eyes staring back at me. This wasn't me, just some false representation of who I was.

I turned to survey the room one more time. Corinne stood across the room with Vivian's other clients. As if sensing my stare, she turned toward me, smiled and raised her glass in a small gesture. I smiled and nodded back, even as her stabbing words replayed themselves in my mind: *lack of professionalism, more experience, it's not personal.* I grabbed another glass of wine from a passing waiter's tray.

Katherine, the head of the West Coast League, tapped the microphone at the podium. "Everyone, please have a seat!" I glanced toward the bar. Not surprisingly Chris was still drinking, laughing louder than anyone else in the room.

I made my way back to the table. I hadn't had a chance to check who else was seated with us, trying to recall who the top eight riders in tonight's Grand Prix were. We were all seated together. Just as I sat down, Jason entered. I began to rise to wave him over, but noticed his arm around Mai, who looked stunning in a red satin gown. I fell back into my chair. Mai?

Jason wore a black tuxedo, his hair gelled back, the whiteness of the tuxedo shirt accentuating his skin. Our eyes locked for a second, but I looked away, down toward my napkin that had dropped to the floor. I couldn't help the sudden sharp pain driving through my chest. I had never pictured him with a woman, but why not?

I turned in my chair, staring at the podium, awaiting the guest speaker. Tonight, Rodrigo Pessoa, one of the most successful riders of all time, was scheduled to give a talk on his success through his "secret family formula."

Our family had obviously failed at success. Dad had worked hard and where did that get him? Some small barn, a few clients, and save for a few second and third placings, no big Grand Prix wins behind him.

Chris slid into his chair beside me.

"Welcome." I gave him a reproachful stare. He gave a lopsided one back, shrugging.

"Vivian," someone said. "Glad you could make it." The host pulled the chair out for Vivian, directly across the table from me.

"Hello, everyone." She nodded, as she sat elegantly in her chair, then acknowledged me. "I guess congratulations are in order."

A coldness crept over me. Vivian had won third, my first time ever beating her at a show. "Thank you," I said, raising my glass. "To all of us." I made eye contact with the rest of the people at the table.

Vivian gave a thin smile, and pointed at her glass. "It's bad luck to toast with an empty one."

"Here, here," Chris said, tapping his glass of scotch to the empty wineglass.

Roman, who'd won the class, was quick to answer. "Let me make this better for my two good friend riders." He leaned forward and filled Vivian's glass, kissed the back of her hand, bowed, then passed the bottle to Chris.

Vivian took a sip of her wine. "I have to say, your placing today is quite impressive. And I don't mean to burst your bubble or anything, but we all get those lucky breaks. You're going to have to be more careful next time. It looked like those rails barely stayed up."

The din around me seemed to fade as blood pumped in my ears, heat rising to my face. I placed my glass of wine down carefully, circling the rim of the smooth, cool glass, unable to lift my gaze.

Roman broke the silence around the table first. "Now, now, Vivian. Brynn did good riding today. She's been working hard, no?"

Everyone nodded except Chris, who seemed to be distracted by something in his drink, his ice cubes jingling as he swirled them. I finally looked up at Vivian. Her face looked tight, and when she smiled, her crow's-feet seemed to have disappeared, her forehead didn't budge. Botox, I thought. For some reason that gave me courage. We all have our failings. I couldn't let her best me.

I glanced around the group. "It's true. This may have been a lucky break for me. But I've earned enough points that we'll be heading to Spruce Meadows for the July qualifier, so I guess we'll see whether I can do it again. And then on to the Gold Cup, and well, then we can discuss who's riding on luck."

Roman and the rest of the group of riders laughed and cheered, raising their glasses, clinking them, slapping each other on the back. "Na zdrowie! Here's to good competition!" Roman said as he downed the remainder of his wine in one gulp.

"The secret to winning is that you must imagine the win even before you get there . . ." Rodrigo's speech started. I turned away from the group, my heart still racing, the same way it did right before a class. I tried to focus on Rodrigo, but his words faded in and out, while I took the silk of my dress and wound it tight around my finger.

I felt proud at not having looked at Jason, and mostly Mai, more than half a dozen times during the rest of the evening. I made excuses to myself that Derek, Helena, and her husband sat at that table too, and I had to check on them. Jason caught me once, nodded, then smiled. He appeared comfortable and relaxed, his legs stretched out as he leaned back in his chair.

I was presented with a check for $22,000, my portion of the winnings, by the head of the West Coast League show committee. This would buy us some time, pay for a few months of expenses for the ranch—maybe I'd even be able to stretch it through to the end of the summer.

As I walked up to receive it, Derek, Helena, Mai, and Jason

stood to clap. I blushed, lowering my head. A proud smile spread across Jason's face. Chris buried his face in his glass of scotch, or rum, or whatever he was drinking now. Vivian looked busy talking to Walt, the rider on her left.

When the last of the speeches finished, I hounded Chris. "Are you ready to go?"

"What? No way! We're all heading out to a party tonight. And you're not getting out of this one. You've got to loosen up, Brynn!" He winked, leaned in, and planted a kiss. "Live a little." His arm moved down my back, toward my waist. He leaned in, brushing my hair off my shoulder and away from my ear. "By the way, did I tell you you look stunning tonight?"

"Let me think? Nope. Don't remember that."

"Well, you do. You're the most beautiful girl here."

"You haven't said much to me all night."

"Haven't I? Well, I better make it up to you." His hand inched up my thigh under the heavy linen tablecloth.

I looked up, mortified, in time to see Mai whispering in Jason's ear, his head leaned toward her as he laughed at whatever she'd said. My chest tightened again, and I leaned in toward Chris and gave him a full open-mouthed kiss. When I pulled away, Chris looked more stunned than I'd ever seen him look, but his surprise was quickly overridden by a large grin.

I dabbed the corner of my mouth with a napkin, then said, "Why the hell not? I'm in. Let's get this party started."

23

*C*hris waited for me in the lobby while I ran to my room to drop off the check. I grabbed a sweater, and reapplied my lip gloss, puckering my lips in the mirror. I tried calling Mom again, but she still didn't answer. I dabbed a bit more perfume behind my ears, my body seeming to float as I ran down the stairs.

More than a dozen riders had already gathered in the lobby. Most I recognized, but no names registered. At a show I always knew the horses, but not the riders.

I ran up to Chris. "I hope I'm not holding things up."

"No worries. We're still waiting on a couple of people." He inspected me, holding me at arm's length. "Your legs look fantabulous!" He pulled me close, grabbing my ass, nibbling my ear.

Madison interrupted us. "Where's Star?"

"Little ladies room," Chris said, letting me go.

I groaned. "They're coming?"

"Of course! Everyone's invited. It's gonna be one helluva party!" Chris moved toward Roman and Vivian, telling a joke, causing the group to crack up.

Madison stared at me, a hint of victory on her face. Obviously she wasn't so in awe of my amazing showmanship and riding skills.

That's all I needed: Chris Peterson groupies trailing us.

Derek came to the lobby, and I asked if he was coming.

"I wouldn't miss this for the world, B!"

"What about Jason?"

Derek was already laughing with Roman and the others.

"What about Jason?" I asked again. "Isn't he coming?"

Derek pulled away from the group for a moment. "Nah. Says it's not his deal. Did you expect him to come, or something?"

He was right. What was I thinking? He was probably off with Mai.

A white stretch Escalade limo pulled into the hotel's circular drive.

"Ready to little bit of party?" Roman called to the group.

We all piled in. I sat between Chris and Roman, Derek sat with Star and Madison. The limo cruised through the small downtown area of Del Mar, stopping in front of a hole-in-the-wall bar. The place wasn't anything like the happening club Roman had gone on about.

"This is it?" I asked Chris, grabbing his arm before he headed in.

"Bar looks not so good," Roman said, red-faced. "Looks changed. Maybe new owner?" He pulled out his smartphone, comparing the number on the curb to the one on his phone.

"Well, ladies and gents, we might as well play a round of pool and grab some drinks! I know I'm in need of a refill," Chris said to the hesitant group still getting out of the limo.

"Not so sure—" I started, but he was already on his way in. I followed, passing through a cloud of cigarette smoke from the half dozen or so middle-aged men hanging out on the sidewalk in front of the entrance to the bar.

Roman's spirits returned once he spotted the pool tables. "Let's go! Two tables, two groups. Boys against girls!"

Since I was terrible at pool, I sat at a booth with Dana and Walt Fitzpatrick, a horse trainer couple I'd met earlier at dinner. They'd taken sixth and eighth places in the show. Soon I learned Dana and Walt ran a small training business in Wyoming. They'd been in the business for over thirty years, one of those couples that had figured out not only how to stay together, but how to work together, how to compete on the same circuit together. It *was* possible. Nice couple, married, no kids, working their butts off to make ends meet. They still showed in Grand Prix, though they said it was getting harder and harder. Their dream, just like everyone else's, was to compete in the Gold Cup.

"How about a drink?" Walt asked.

"One margarita for me." I held up my finger, a little bit in defeat. This wasn't the evening I'd had in mind.

Walt signaled the waitress over. The waitress-slash-bartender, a remnant from the eighties, strode over. She blew up her teased bangs, which had seen one too many bottles of bleach, eyeing the laughing group at the pool tables through her turquoise-lined eyes. She took our order but made it clear we weren't welcome, and had no business intruding on her space.

"How did it feel today, Brynn?" Walt asked.

"Besides it being the best experience I've ever had?" I smiled at the memory of going clear. "I keep thinking I might wake up tomorrow and find out it never happened. I can't imagine what it would be like to win first place."

Across the bar, the group roared with laughter. We all turned in time to catch Chris helping Star out with a shot, leaning over her, his arm on hers as he guided her cue. I stared, ready to go intervene, but the waitress returned with our drinks, blocking my view.

I sat back, grabbing my margarita glass.

"You did good," Dana said. "You've had quite the year. And you should be proud. Keeping your father's business going and all. It's not something everyone can do. Plus I overheard at the banquet one of your old clients misses you—or her daughter does, anyway."

"What?" I spilled a bit of my drink on my dress.

"I don't know the woman, but her name was something like Catherine, or Cory."

"Corinne?"

"That might have been it." Dana looked over at Walt. "Walt? You remember? Anyway, the mother hushed the daughter up, but

ANNE CLERMONT

the girl went on how she missed the trail rides, and having fun at your folks' place. The point is, you've done well. And jumping like that today, showing everyone up like that. It was good." Dana smiled.

"I think it will all sink in tomorrow." My head reeled. Did Kennedy miss the ranch? Did she miss me? I licked a bit of salt off the edge of the margarita glass, then took a sip.

"Well, pinch yourself. You did it." Dana lifted her glass to me. "And some ain't too pleased."

"What do you mean?"

"What do I mean?" She laughed. "Girl! Wake up! You've got a lot to learn. Most of the good ol' boys here have been at this game since before you were born. You think they wanna be shown up by some twenty-three-year-old? And a girl at that?" Dana sucked on the olive from her martini. "Hey, I'm not ashamed to admit it. They're not the only ones. Frankly, I know I'm jealous."

"Plenty of girls show now. Look at Vivian," I said.

"Yup. That is true. Doesn't mean the boys like it. You've just gotta learn how to play the game."

I followed her gaze to where Derek and Roman were high-fiving. Vivian leaned back against the wall, eyes narrowed, a cue in her hand, tapping her foot, staring at Chris and Star.

"I have to say, *he's* managed all right given the rumors flying around about him," Walt said.

"Rumors? Ha! If only," Dana said. "I happen to know there's a lot of truth in them."

I practically choked on my margarita. After everything that had happened in the last few months, I'd practically forgotten the warning Vivian had given me as I left Chris's apartment.

Dana continued, "My girlfriend rides with the mayor's wife, the one he screwed." Then seeing the look on my face, she said, "Oh dear. You didn't know?"

Walt cleared his throat. "Well, I'm sure she's heard."

All eyes turned to me, and I focused on my margarita glass.

"You *have* to know by now. How he went off with Alison to New York? They'd had a short affair. She bought him all kinds of toys and high-end clothes and shoes and a couple of weeks later she found him with a young girl, barely of age, back at the barn."

I felt my fingers grow cold, the glass practically slipping through them.

"Oh dear. You *didn't* know. Yeah. She got just a bit pissed." Dana gave a laugh. Not an unkind one, but as if she were laughing at a kid. "That's an understatement. What a stupid move on his part. Alison had a chat with her husband who met Chris at the barn and the next thing you know, Chris was hightailing it back to California to his mommy. Well, all that's in the past now. He's likely learned his lesson. What's most important is *your* future." Dana squinted at me, leaning forward, taking a hold of my hand. "And all you have to do is prove it wasn't just luck."

Through a fog I heard myself say, "It wasn't luck." I stated it as a fact, though my head reeled with the fact that Chris had an affair with a girl, correction, a *woman*. A mayor's wife. He wasn't here because of the argument with his mother, nor because he thought we'd make a good team. It was because he had been chased out of town.

"Here's to skill! And to Brynn!" Dana raised her glass in a toast.

"To Brynn!" Walt said, raising his. I raised mine, but my arm felt deflated and weak. I clinked my glass to theirs, then took the longest swig I'd ever had, letting the mellow sensation fill me.

The Escalade wound through the narrow roads of the Del Mar hills.

"Next party, you see, will be better," Roman said, laughing. "No more bad bars, yes?"

"Sounds good, Roman. Sounds good," I said, gazing out the window, ignoring Madison's red panties staring me in the face as she made out in the back of the limo with one of the riders. Lights from lower Del Mar twinkled like stars below.

When we pulled up to the gates of a mansion up in the hills, the rows of neatly lined cars edged the curving driveway like beads on the edge of a purse. Cadillac, Lotus, Mercedes, Ferrari, Mercedes CLK, Porsche, BMW X6, Lexus . . . a luxury car showcase. Any one of those cars would pay for two years' worth of hay at the ranch. I considered staying in the limo, letting Chris go on his own, but the way he held my hand in the limo, and the way he brushed my hair aside and grazed my shoulder with his fingertips, so gently, with such affection, I couldn't believe for a moment that any of the rumors were true. My head swam with alcohol, and even though I knew I should confront him about what I'd heard, I knew I wouldn't be able to form a decent thought in this state. I told myself I'd deal with it in the light of day.

A young valet held out his hand to help me from the limo. The sweet scent of pot wafted toward me from the group of valet boys standing farther away. As we all walked up the wide marble stairway toward the glass carved doors, I held on tight to the cold marble handrail, more wobbly on my high heels than when we had left the hotel, my head spinning from all the drinks I'd had. A fleeting sense of guilt washed over me, remembering Jason's rule, and my promise to him, but then the front doors came into view.

"Wow, this is incredible," I said to Chris. Music and laughter drifted toward us from inside.

"Now this is sick. About time. I practically fell asleep back in that hearse." Derek ran to catch up to Roman and Vivian.

I leaned against the balustrade, surveying the view while Chris and Roman rang the doorbell. The Pacific Ocean, now only a patch of darkness in the distance, joined the black sky—save for the scattered drifting boats flickering like fireflies.

A man with short-cropped blond hair who looked like he was in his late twenties had his arm around a girl at least six inches taller than him. Her body belonged on the cover of *Sports Illustrated*. She wore a strapless mini dress; a butterfly tattoo appeared to take flight on her shoulder. The man embraced Roman, slapping him on the back. "Roman! Mój kolega!"

They exchanged some words. Then he saw the rest of us. "Friends of Roman's, friends of mine. Pool in back. Drinks in kitchen. Come, come, friends. Night still not old!"

The few of us hesitant ones followed like a small group of children about to start first grade, hanging back, holding on to each other. Dana's and Walt's eyes were wide, their mouths agape. I was impressed, but they were doubly so—bet they didn't get too much of this scene back in Wyoming.

I could barely see into the room through the hundreds of people crowded into the lower level. A grand staircase stretched before us to the second story. A huge room opened on the left, ceilings at least thirty feet high. The lights were turned down, the music up. A group of young girls danced on a makeshift stage, their skin shimmering like ripples on a mountain lake at sunset, reflecting the incandescent and black lights. Their colorful shorts and bikini tops were adorned with beads and gems, scarcely covering their sparkling skin. Fog encircled them like a cloud.

I heard Star's loud piercing voice. "Chris, ready to dance?"

"Where's Madison?"

Star shrugged, and I didn't answer. I wasn't here to babysit. If she was old enough to go out, then she should be old enough to take care of herself.

But Star looked around, then pointed to the dance floor. "She's already dancing."

"Good. Brynn, let's go!" Chris grabbed my arm. "But first, a shot!" Out of nowhere shot glasses appeared and someone lit the liquor on fire. Chris placed his palm over it, and extinguished the fire inside the small glass. "Drink!" I hesitated, but as he took his palm off, I swung the green liquid to the back of my throat. "Absinthe," I heard him say when I scrunched my face up at the sweet licorice flavor and the burn of alcohol. I enjoyed it for a moment until

Jason's stern face floated before me, his arms crossed in front of his chest.

"Oh, stop judging me," I said to the illusion. "You're probably out with Mai somewhere, doing God-knows-what."

The beat from the large speakers filled me to the core, the bass rocking my insides, vibrating through me, making me drift higher in my haze than I'd ever felt. This was definitely the biggest dance party I'd ever been to. And the most beautiful bodies and faces I'd seen in one place. To my left a male couple ground against each other. To my right dancers twirled, crouched, legs and arms moving faster than the strobe light, and I caught glimpses of silhouettes, like cutout paper shadows.

I followed Chris through the thick crowd, bodies jamming us closer, perfume mixed with sweat. We found a small spot to dance, and suddenly we were the only ones in the room. I finally had Chris to myself. I let myself go. We danced for minutes, or hours, but I still had plenty of energy, and I didn't want it to ever end.

Chris leaned in and said something, but I only saw his lips move.

"What?" I yelled.

"Need another drink?"

"Yes!" I said, laughing, leaning on him. He looked so sexy with his black button-down shirt and navy blue slacks. His blond hair fell in unruly clumps, and I brushed it off his forehead.

"I'll be right back!" he yelled toward me.

I nodded, allowing the beat of the music to carry me. I closed my eyes, permitting my body to move in ways I never knew it could. I felt free. Free from judgments, the haters, the piercing eyes, always questioning, asking, wanting. No Derek, no Jason, no Mom, no clients.

I felt joy. Like I was finally accepted. Chris was here, and we were on our way up. My body didn't even belong to me anymore, as if I knew how to dance, when I'd always sworn I couldn't. "Set me free," the dance song said, and I let go, my eyes moist from the tears of joy I finally felt I could cry.

~

One song blended into the next. Then another. I danced in a trance, my arms waving, my legs moving. I glanced up expectantly for Chris, desperately in need of a glass of water. I stretched tall, but my tall was shorter than most of the crowd. I couldn't see Chris's blond hair anywhere. Someone pushed me from behind and suddenly I felt like a prodded animal in a cage. The heat, the crowd, the siren from the song now made my stomach clench. The sound screeched in my ears, the vibrations too strong, my eardrums ready to burst. Where the hell was he?

A drink sprayed my arm, spilling across my dress. I wiped at it, getting syrupy stickiness on my hands. I raised my arm to block the strobe lights from my eyes. Someone brushed at the silky fabric, but I pushed the hand away. I shoved through the dancing crowd toward the back of the house.

Every height and size of man seemed to swarm the bar. Except Chris. I thrust the sudden flutter of my heart aside, telling myself I was fine.

The back wall of the house opened to a stone-covered patio. An outdoor kitchen and barbecue gleamed under the moon, and a fire pit threw orange and red flames into the sky. Chill music greeted me as I stepped across the stone patio, and I welcomed the coolness of the air. I folded my arms around my chest, my fingers sticky against the spilled cocktail. I stumbled over a patch of grass as I made my way to the emerald-green pool below. I scanned the crowd for familiar faces, and saw none. I moved to the poolside lounge chairs, and sat, my head spinning.

I leaned my head back against the cushion, gazing up at the sky. I closed my eyes, but that only made the world spin faster, out of control. I opened my eyes again to see drunk partygoers jump into the pool.

"Beautiful night, isn't it?" A deep, mellow voice pulled me out of my daze.

"Uh-huh."

"Almost as beautiful as you," the voice continued.

A man in his midfifties sat on the lounge chair facing me.

"Am I supposed to fall for that? Swoon? Blush?" I asked. "I don't think I have to tell you how cliché that sounds."

"Well I can tell you this. Everyone around here is fake. Fake tits, fake teeth, fake smiles. But you"—he waved a hand up and down—"you're the most real thing I've seen all night."

"Thanks."

"Here, you wanna do a line?" He pulled a gold case from his pocket.

"No thanks, uh . . ." I squinted, trying to remember if he'd given me a name.

"Steve." He reached his hand to shake mine.

"Steve. No thanks, Steve." I closed my eyes again. He was old enough to be my dad. I thought of my morning sessions with Jason and the serenity of the cool air filling my lungs during sun salutation. Getting up at six would be impossible tomorrow; now I knew why his no-alcohol rule was so important.

Water droplets splashed my arm as someone jumped in the pool. I looked up at the couple playing in the pool. I raised my eyes higher to the other side. My heart sped up. Chris! I sat up to wave, but then . . .

He leaned down. He was kissing a woman. His hand up the slit of her dress. Moving. Searching. Her toned legs wrapped around his waist. I clasped my hand over my mouth, blinking, wishing the image away.

Vivian.

I stumbled up, just as Vivian's eyes made contact with mine. I could have sworn there was a spark of victory in them.

"Hey, need some help?" Steve asked as I tripped over his feet.

"I'm fine." I walked as fast as I could up the winding path to the house. Inside, the crowd hadn't thinned, and making my way to the front door felt like moving through quicksand. I spotted the exit, but I couldn't get to it. The dark room, the lights, the strong scent of sweat. Nausea percolated. I placed my hand over my mouth, grabbing onto a column, swallowing the sour taste of vomit. As soon as it subsided, I rushed to the front door. I stepped out and breathed in the fresh air. Slowly, the nausea passed, and I walked carefully down the stairs. Fog had rolled in off the ocean. I clung to the marble handrail, my hand slipping along the cool stone. The moisture in the air clung to my eyelashes.

"Where's the limo?" I yelled toward the stoned group of valets.

"What limo?" one of them asked.

"The big white one. We came in a huge group."

"Don't know, lady. Maybe ask one of your friends?" the boy said. I think he was trying to be helpful, but I waved him away.

I walked down the circular driveway toward the street. The limo was nowhere in sight. I dug around in my clutch for my cell, checking and rechecking the small compartment, but the smooth familiar shape of my smartphone wasn't there. "Shit!" I yelled out loud. I must have dropped it, either back in the limo, or at the party somewhere.

I stumbled again. In frustration I pulled at the thin straps of my heels, yanking them off, letting them twirl in my fingers. The cool, wet concrete of the street soothed my burning feet. I walked along the curving hills for a while, but soon realized I'd spent the last of my money at that dive bar and hadn't brought any credit cards.

"Unbelievable," I said to myself. I sat down on the curb, hanging my head in my arms, willing the world to stop spinning. I had never drunk this much before.

I wrapped the thin silk of my dress around my legs as best as I could. I imagined Jason appearing. He'd find me, pull me into his strong arms, then take me home and tuck me into bed.

But he wouldn't be caught at a place like this. I wondered where he was now. In bed with Mai?

Headlights swept across the road as a car turned into the driveway. I stood expectantly, but they weren't the limo's. A few more cars drove in and out. I moved behind a column, ashamed to be sitting at the bottom of the driveway. I'd just rest my head against the column, close my eyes, wait. The limo was bound to be here soon.

24

My dad had taught me to never stand directly behind a horse because I might get kicked. Herbivores can spend as long as ten hours per day grazing and since they need to be on constant lookout for predators, their eyes are on the sides of their heads. It allows for an almost perfect three-hundred-and-sixty-degree view—except directly behind them.

I woke up at dawn in front of the mansion and stared out at the view ahead of me—the hills dotted with homes, the blue of the ocean below—and I remembered Dad's lesson. I hadn't seen what was directly behind me—Chris behaving like the idiot-cheater-asshole he was.

The sky brightened with the rising sun. I figured it must be around six thirty. I'd been so blind. So stupid.

I stood up, brushed the leaves and dirt from my dress, and walked up the driveway. A few cars were still in the driveway. I climbed the stairs to the front doors, wiping at my teeth with my finger, praying to God I didn't look as terrible as I felt, and knocked quietly on the etched glass. No one answered. I wasn't sure what I was expecting, but I also didn't feel right about my two other options. One: ring the doorbell and wake the host who had probably gone to bed late; or two: walk into someone's house without an invitation and possibly get mistaken for a burglar.

The door swung open.

Roman's friend stood on the other side, hair neatly combed.

He wore a red-and-white jogging suit and neon yellow-and-black running shoes. He seemed as fresh as if he had spent the day at a relaxing spa drinking a secret-formula cleanse juice. He eyed me up and down.

"Oh, dear," he said, clucking his tongue. "You look like you slept in bush."

"You have no idea," I mumbled.

"Party over," he said, scrutinizing me, "or going still on, depending on who you are . . ." His eyebrow lifted above deep-set gray eyes.

"I, um, well, you see, I was here with my friend Roman last night." I crossed my arms in front of my chest.

"Roman? Tak! My good friend! You are looking for him? I don't know where is he. Who you are?"

"Brynn."

"Brynn. Boy name, no?" He eyed me up and down again, his face perplexed.

"But where my manners are, no? Come in, Brynn." He rolled the r as he said my name, and pulled the heavy glass and steel door wide open.

"I'm actually looking for a phone. I was supposed to get a ride home with my friends, but it looks like I missed it."

"Tak, tak! Come in moja grószka."

I had no idea what that meant, but at this point I didn't care. I held my clutch and heels tight against my chest, wishing I had a cover-up or better yet, my sweater that I'd lost somewhere the night before.

The place should have been designated a disaster area, but was still as impressive as the night before. People lay on every surface available: floor, chairs, couches, their limbs contorted every which way. I stepped over beer bottles, glasses, and cigarette butts. Gold-framed mirrors lined the wall of the large dancing room.

He took me to the kitchen, the doors still open to the patio outside. "Sit, okay?" he said, pointing to a tall bar stool at the edge of an island. I plopped down, too weak to argue, happy to take my feet off the gummed-up floor. The cabinetry, in a deep cherry mahogany, extended along the top wall and below the counter in a semicircle.

"Juice?" he said, turning away. Sure enough, there was green juice in the blender. I put my hand up to my mouth and laughed. I laughed until tears spilled over. The laughter felt good, like a cleansing of its own kind.

"No juice?" he asked, eyeing me. "I have not coffee, juice only." He arched his eyebrow in question, still waiting for my answer.

"Juice would be fine. Thanks." I said, wiping under my eyes, wondering if my mascara had smudged. I wasn't used to wearing any. My head throbbed, likely from dehydration as much as from alcohol. The back of my throat burned. The juice tasted surprisingly good; even though it was green, it tasted of strawberries and mangoes and like the good green earth back home. I finished my glass, and stared into the bottom.

"Can I use your phone?" I said, but reconsidered. Who would I call? Chris? Jason? My mother? "Or better yet, do you think you could call a cab? I need to get h—um, to my hotel."

"You don't want to stay? I have nice shower upstairs. Clean clothes," he clucked again, "would fit you . . ." He nodded approvingly. "You stay. We have nice pool."

"I've seen your pool. Thanks." Memories of Chris with his hand up Vivian's dress went through my head. "I really need to get back."

"I drive you."

"No, really. That's okay." I shook my head, standing up and placing the glass in the sink. "I just need a cab."

"No. I drive. Come, come. Friend of Roman friend of me."

Aleksy turned out to be all right. He drove me back to the hotel in his red Ferrari, and didn't even hit on me. Well, maybe his hand rested on my knee at a stoplight once. I gently removed it, and he didn't try again. He waited for me to enter the lobby as if we'd been on a date. I turned and waved goodbye, and he waved back, his bright teeth flashing through the passenger window.

He leaned into the passenger seat. "I come watch your show next week!"

I smiled and turned away, not giving him another thought, nor bothering to tell him my next show wasn't for over a month.

After going through an ID check, I retrieved a new key card from the front desk and slogged to the room. I closed the door and leaned against it, my head pounding more than it had an hour ago. I scanned the room. My shoes and riding boots were lined up against the wall, my laptop sat neatly piled on top of my notepad. The sheets on the bed were turned down, and a little piece of gold-wrapped chocolate on the pillow beckoned me. How strange to see a made bed first thing in the morning. A wave of shame washed over me. How could I have broken Jason's rule of no drinking and partying?

I threw my shoes and purse down, peeling off the ruined dress as I walked to the bathroom. I drew a hot bath, and threw in some scented oils left on the side of the Jacuzzi tub. I had an hour to be at the show to help pack, and needed to make myself feel somewhat human before seeing Jason.

On the way back to the show grounds I thought about what I'd say to Chris. I wanted closure. I wanted to tell him where to go, but of course he conveniently made himself scarce. I walked past trailers, staff busy breaking down awnings, taking down drapes, and packing horse supplies into boxes.

When I got to Chris's tent, orange hay ties, coffee cups, and empty grain bags greeted me. The sod that had been so meticulously laid down the day prior to the show had turned brown, the grass crushed in the mud, ready to be tossed in the dumpster.

I stood in front of the empty stalls, white vinyl, stained with mud and manure, stretched across a rickety metal frame, a red stamp designating it as number 34B. A skeleton of the fancy decor that had been there just the day before.

My fists clenched and unclenched at my sides. He'd left without so much as a goodbye. I leaned down, and found a fourth-place yellow show ribbon, Chris's name scribbled on the back. I bit at my cuticles, drawing blood, then yelled "No!"

A passing Mexican groom stared at me from under his hoodie, then hurried away.

I turned on my heel and walked back to our stalls.

"How many times have I told you how important that rule was to me?"

I leaned my head down, rebraiding my hair. The bath, the two liters of water, two cups of coffee, and of course the green juice at Aleksy's house hadn't taken the smell of alcohol from my breath.

"Dammit, Brynn, it really doesn't seem like you want to win. Sometimes it feels like you think this is just a joke." I'd never seen him lose his temper before.

"I know. I know it's not a joke. I'm really sorry. I don't know what happened. It was a shitty night. I made poor choices." Mai's hand on Jason's arm flashed before my eyes, making me see red again, reminding me of the jealousy that had led me to go out with Chris. I wished I had stayed in the hotel room instead.

"You could have called me," Jason said.

"Were you in?"

A look of surprise crossed Jason's face, then the hardness crept into his jaw again. "Yes, Brynn. I was in. Did you expect something else?"

"No. I just thought. I saw you with Mai, and I thought—"

Jason stopped and laughed, then shook his head. "I ran into Mai in the lobby on the way to the reception last night. I escorted her into the banquet hall, but we didn't go together. And we sure as heck didn't leave together. Though I did see you leave with Chris and the rest of them."

I hung my head, feeling shame, and the incessant pounding of my head and heart.

"You know, Brynn, sometimes you act so grown-up, and at other times I feel like I'm dealing with a child. You want to go out and party? Ignore my rules? That's fine. But I'm not going to stand by and watch."

I grabbed his arm as he turned to leave. "Please. It was a mistake."

Jason paused, straightened his shoulders back and closed his eyes. "You're right. I'm overreacting." He sat on a bale of hay, and placed his face in his hands. "I've seen this before, though, and I'm sensitive to it. I've been down that road, and trust me when I tell you, it gets ugly quick."

He was quiet for a moment and I gave him a nod of understanding.

He continued, "When I won the first World Cup, I had trained hard, worked for years to get there. Thanks to Ian, no less. He found me at the racetrack at the age of eleven, when I was just a kid try-ing to make some extra money to help pay for the cockroach-filled apartment above a gas station we had to move to after our house got repossessed. Ian was treating a horse at the racetrack at the stable I was working at, mucking stalls. He'd known my dad, and our history, from seeing him around the track. He pitied me, I guess, took me under his wing and got me my first job at a jumping stable. That's how I met your dad. Through Ian." Jason looked at me now, his eyes holding mine. "Your dad gave me some of the best lessons of my life. He was the real deal. A true horseman."

I sat next to him, shocked at this news, trying to wrack my brain, trying to remember if my dad had ever mentioned Jason, but I would have been less than ten years old then. "Your dad came down to teach clinics sometimes, or to show, and whenever he was in South-ern California, Ian would take me to see him. I took lessons with whomever I could the rest of the time, having to stay close to LA, to my mother, who got sick with cancer. I got other people's horses to ride, and soon people noticed I had talent. I got lucky. But by the second time I won the World Cup, I let it all go to my head. I was riding on fumes, riding on pure luck. Within months of the second win, the prestige, the clinics, the stardom, all got to my head, and the booze, drugs, parties, and girls were easy to come by. I became unrecognizable even to myself." Jason stood, and looked at me for a long moment. I debated hugging him, but didn't feel it was right. He said, "I'm headed to the office to check out."

I stood. "What happened? What got you back on track?"

"My mother died. I had promised Ashley I'd come take care of her for the weekend, promised I'd be there. Ashley had a friend's wedding to go to, so she left, thinking I would be there. But I forgot. I got high at a party, slept through the day, went to another, and by the time I remembered, I found my mother lying in a pool of vomit and urine in her kitchen. She'd knocked her head, then choked on her own vomit. She was at the end stage of her life, and needed constant care—and I had promised to be there."

I stared at him, opened my mouth to say I'm sorry, but Jason only nodded. Then turned and walked away.

Surveying all the equipment and horse supplies that needed to go home made my head pound louder. Suddenly it seemed as if the earth swayed, and I had to grab the edge of the stall to keep from falling. I closed my eyes, knowing it was just the hangover and lack of sleep, though really, a lot of it had to do with Chris the night before and now Jason. I'd never seen him even remotely upset.

Derek showed up late, his cap pulled low, his sunglasses perched on his nose, looking like I felt. He had gotten back to the hotel in the limo with the rest of the group. When I asked him why he hadn't looked for me, he said they all had, but he'd assumed I'd gone home with Chris, since he was nowhere to be found either. I couldn't blame him for making that assumption. That's what should have happened. I didn't tell him what I'd seen at the pool, unable to relive the scene just yet.

"Damn, B. I'm not used to that anymore." He moved like a broken-down horse. Then, as if noticing his surroundings for the first time, he said, "Where's Jason?"

"Office. Checking out." I made my way to the end of our short row of stalls, noticing all the stuff that still needed organizing and packing. I asked Derek if he had any ibuprofen.

"Nope, but a Bloody Mary sounds good." He groaned, plopping onto one of the lounge chairs, head between his knees.

"You've got ten minutes. Get it together, because I need your help." I threw a polo wrap at his head. His response, a pitiful moan, escaped as he stretched out on the chair, his feet up on the patio table, his cap over his eyes.

My first task was to lug the large container filled with horse shampoos, conditioners, body sprays, liniments, lotions, and ointments. Almost tripping, I peered over the edge of the container. A dandy brush lay amongst the litter on the ground. Balancing the container on my knee I leaned down to pick it up when a shadow darkened my path. My eyes moved up a pair of designer jeans. The nausea that had subsided earlier overcame me again.

Vivian.

"Chris went home," she said, her hand on her hip.

"I know." I shifted the container, trying to get around her.

"You should have watched him more carefully."

I paused, closing my eyes, wishing she'd leave. I opened the side compartment door of the trailer and slid the container in. Vivian leaned against the side of the trailer. "It's not my fault, you know. He wanted to be with me."

I inhaled through my nose, counting, trying to remember the pranayama techniques Jason had taught me. Prana: life force. Yama: extension of breath. Being able to find energy and the spirit or soul.

"Is that all you came to tell me? Because I've got to load this trailer." For the first time ever I noticed how dry the skin on her arms was. Dry and flaky, reminding me of the snakeskin in the glass cabinet at the nature center on the coast that our teachers would take us to when I was in grade school.

Vivian straightened. "I don't trailer my own horses anymore. It's so much easier to have other people handle all that. Of course, it *is* an added expense."

"What do you want, Vivian? You've got Corinne, Kennedy, Seraphim, Best of Luck, and the others. You've got Chris. What else?"

A vein throbbed at the side of her temple. "I tried to be your friend. I offered my help and you didn't bother calling. You know, some people might take that personally."

I was hot yet chilled and clammy, my whole body trembling. "What do you want?" I asked again. "I've got nothing left."

Vivian eyed me, wrapping her braid around her finger. "I think it's too late for anything now, but you might consider dropping out of the running for the Gold Cup. You won't ever get there. You'll always lose. You'll always be a loser." She paused, leaning in toward me, her breath hot on my cheek. "Just like your father."

My hand whipped out before I even had a chance to control myself, hitting her across her cheek. The sharp sound split the air, startling me.

Vivian brought her hand up to the blooming patch, her green eyes wide, her lips open in a wide O.

I stood taller. "Don't you ever talk about Luke Seymour like that again."

A flicker of fear went through her eyes, but quickly disappeared. "You watch yourself, Brynn."

I stepped toward her, feeling more powerful than I ever had, wanting to take her on. My fists clamped at my side, ready. I took another step, but then someone grabbed my arm.

"Brynn, don't." Jason wrapped his hand around my wrist and moved in between Vivian and me.

"You should leave," Jason said, his back blocking my view of Vivian. "Now." Forceful, yet quiet. There'd be no arguing with him.

"Nice of you to step in, but this is between us," Vivian said, "and we're not done."

"Oh, you're done." Jason turned toward me, wrapping his arm around me.

Vivian eyed us, then stormed away.

25

*I*t took me a while to process Jason's story, and somehow his honesty made me even more determined to win. The following week I begged Jason to forgive me. Told him I'd acted like a fool, and I'd take his rules seriously, that he could trust me. He said he understood, and if there was anything to gain from yoga, it was that we were constantly evolving, learning, and hopefully improving.

Back at home the walls of my bedroom were the same mossy green they'd been for the last ten years. My vet school textbooks lay disorganized on my dresser and in my reading nook. The kitchen was empty, and the sitting room still ached for laughter and conversation. I was reminded that my place was here, at Redwood Grove, with Mom.

Outside, the fields had again dried and yellowed, and Chris's absence left no hole in my life. It was as if it had never happened. Not that I should have been surprised. Our relationship had never defined who I was. And if anything, now I could zero in on the Gold Cup. Not some stupid notion of romance.

The day we loaded the trailer for the drive to Spruce Meadows, I tried to block the torrent of thoughts of last year, the nostalgia I'd felt. Dad standing with the hills and sky behind him, like a hero from some old Clint Eastwood movie. This time, instead of three horses, we only loaded one: Jett. None of our clients had horses experienced enough to jump even in one of the smallest jumping classes at Spruce Meadows. But Helena, Mai, and their daughters and even Stuart said they'd be there to watch.

An unwarranted tremble rocked me as Jett walked into the trailer. I shook my head, knowing my mind was playing tricks, awakening memories of loading Seraphim. Derek came and wrapped his arm around my shoulders, and my eyes moistened at his touch, all the emotion I'd been trying to hold inside taking hold of me. I walked into the trailer to see Jett. I wrapped my arms around him. "It'll be all right," I whispered. "We'll be fine. I promise."

Jett snuffed and whirred against my arm, then lifted his nose and blew warm breath into my hair. We *would* be fine, he and I. We'd make it. I'd make sure of it.

Outside, I glanced up at the house, just like I had last summer, and wondered if Mom would come down to say goodbye, but I hadn't seen her Volvo in the driveway all day. She was probably avoiding this moment. She hadn't wanted us to go last summer and me leaving now would open up too many wounds.

"Let's just wait a minute," I said to Derek and Jason. I didn't have to explain what I was waiting for, and they were kind enough not to ask.

Derek busied himself with sweeping up the drive and Jason said he forgot something in his truck. We waited fifteen minutes but she never came.

"We have to go now," Jason said, coming up behind me.

I readjusted my ponytail, buying time, then nodded.

Jason and Derek didn't say much as we got in the truck, and we remained quiet for most of the drive. In Oregon, I kept my eyes peeled for where the accident had happened, but as we passed, there was nothing. Not even a glitch in the landscape to mark where a life had ended. I closed my eyes and rested my head against the window, listening to a Canadian indie band that Jason had turned on.

Jason drove. Derek sat in the back with his cap pulled over his face, the seatbelt tucked under his armpit, his legs stretched across the backseat. I stared out at the passing landscape, the truck stops, the farms, the trees getting denser the farther north we drove. It had been over a month since the show at Del Mar, and even though I felt good about the round we'd jumped, I knew that it *might* have been just luck. I rubbed my shoulders. My body ached and I hadn't had a good night's sleep in months. I'd accumulated a total of nineteen points so far and I needed one more point to qualify for the Gold Cup. This was my last show before the Gold Cup; I couldn't screw up.

The competition would be the toughest to date. All the other riders had major advantages over me: some had multiple horses to ride, giving them more chances to win, and all had competed in more shows than me. They'd had time to earn their horse's trust and hone their cues, to learn how each reacts under different circumstances.

I swallowed hard as I thought back to Vivian at Del Mar. I glanced over at Jason. "Do you think what Vivian said was true?"

Jason turned down the volume, throwing me a quick glance. "About what?"

I hesitated. I'd held it in for so long now but had to know what Jason thought. "Back at Del Mar. About my father."

Jason didn't respond, and I peered out the window, drawing my knees to my chest, wrapping my arms around them. "That he didn't have what it takes. That I'm just like him?"

Jason laughed, a deep, resonant laugh. "Did you actually listen to that heartless excuse for a woman?"

"It is true, though, isn't it? Dad never won. He always got close to winning, but he never won first. Not when it mattered." I studied Jason. His eyes were fixed on the road. He glanced in his rearview mirror, lifting himself to check on Derek. I looked back too. Derek's mouth hung open, drool trickling down from the corner of his mouth.

"Remember when we talked about the second lesson I needed to teach you, working on your mind, not just jumping?" Jason said. I nodded. "The asana practice is helping with that, helping you clear your mind, but you might be ready to understand how this ties in with your riding." Jason paused for a moment, as if trying to collect his thoughts.

"Your dad was a great trainer. I always respected him—"

"But?"

"To win, you need to be comfortable with the void. You have to be able to get in the arena and let everything in your mind go."

"What? Lose control?"

"It's not about losing control, it's about *giving* up control. There is a difference. You can't control a hundred percent of what the horse will do, what the weather's like, the footing, the crowd, whether a photographer will step out and snap his flash right as you're going over an oxer. But you can give up what you're thinking about. Trust the horse to be your partner, to let him sense what you're thinking before you're even aware you're thinking it. Becoming one with the horse, instead of worrying about how you look, what the crowd thinks, whether they'll judge you if you make a mistake. You have to let all of that go and ride as fast as you can. Let the horse go, without always checking him."

It was so different from what my dad had always taught. Or was it? I was conflicted, not sure whose word I was supposed to trust. Was everything Dad had taught me wrong? "But I have to give him cues, don't I?"

"You will—by letting yourself enter that void. You'll send signals to Jett, and he'll understand what you're thinking even before you do. In the first round, you can get by with your regular ride. But in a jump-off—there's no time for that. You have to be comfortable with a very different type of ride. Gallop, and trust your horse to make decisions too. The sport is so competitive now. You have to be single-minded about achieving maximum speed in minimum time. Trust Jett to do his job of keeping the fences up—yours is to get him to a good enough distance. Then trust. Don't worry what other people have done or will do in their round. You focus on your next jump."

I stared out the window, trying to process what he'd said.

"It's risky, there's no doubt about that," Jason said. "You have to be comfortable with that risk—to trust Jett one hundred percent—but that's why most riders fail to win. They can't let go. They don't trust enough."

A sadness overcame me, my eyes blurred, and suddenly I was unsure if all the grueling training we'd done—the early mornings, the late nights—was enough.

Even though I'd only missed one summer of showing in Calgary, the changes that had taken place shocked me. The land surrounding the show park had not been impermeable to sprawling suburbia. Cookie cutter homes and strip malls had taken over farmlands, and part of me mourned the former countryside. Over a quarter of a century had passed since the Southern family held the first tournament in 1976, back when vast open space and farmlands surrounded the newly formed center. Thirty years later, Spruce Meadows had established itself as a premier venue, recognized as the largest annual international sporting event held in Canada.

Derek read the newsletter with facts about Spruce Meadows, fascinated. "Did you know the shows attract crowds greater than at any Canadian football game—annual attendance is almost a half a million fans!"

How many would be here this weekend? The thought terrified me.

Once Jett and our supplies were unloaded, I walked along the wide asphalt pathway toward the International Ring. The path wound among landscaped lawns and flower beds, past arenas, filled with sparkling white sand, flowers, and evergreen shrubs under bright jumps. Benches and iron lampposts, decorated with banners and planters that spilled over with orange and pink and fuchsia flowers, lined the walkways. Fathers clasped sticky toddler hands, children licked their ice-cream cones, teenagers giggled as they walked clad in shorts and tank tops, young riders ambled in britches and polo shirts as a sign of honor and fraternity—even if they weren't show-ing here, they meant to. One day.

Horseshoes clipped and clopped on the pavement as grooms walked horses by, coats brushed to perfection gleaming in the sun. Horses with arched necks, excitement in the eye, each telling their own story. This was Disneyland for horse people.

Above the empty International Ring, I sat on a steel bench in the grandstands, propping my chin in my hands. Only a handful of people milled about, preparing for Saturday's show. I scanned the ring. From up high, the arena resembled a squashed pentagon. The ring was surrounded by grandstands on three sides, the fourth and fifth edged with three glass-faced buildings. Each building boasted indoor and outdoor viewing levels, where sat many of the horse owners, corporate sponsors, and others with money.

The footing wasn't the typical white sand but lush, blue-green grass. I walked down the steps toward the field, found an entrance, and wandered into the middle of the field. I spun around, letting my arms out like wings. The edges of the field appeared far away. Sud-denly I felt overwhelmed by the enormity of the ring. My thoughts turned to images of knocking every rail, crashing into a jump—failing. A cloud passed above me, then cleared. I shook my head, clearing the dark thought. We'd know soon enough.

On Saturday, the day of the North American show, the sun beat down on Spruce Meadows. It had stormed the night before, and I fretted over the grass footing. My first round, and all the others so far, had gone well, with no horses slipping. The crew worked dili-gently to replace the divots in front and after the jumps, the grass holding up after the downpour.

Only six riders made it into the second round, including me and Jett. In the warm-up, we'd done only a handful of jumps; Jett could tire easily in this heat. I rode Jett up the hill toward the International Ring after my warm-up for the jump-off. Jason walked alongside, informing me that he'd heard someone say it was thirty-two degrees Celsius. I didn't know what that translated to in Fahrenheit, only that in my tall boots, white britches, button-down dress shirt, and red jacket—topped off with my black leather riding gloves and my hair up in a hairnet underneath my black helmet—I might as well have been about to ride off to battle demons in hell while wearing armor.

Derek greeted us at the entrance to the arena, his face the color of the British House's red roof. "God almighty, I think it's nearing ninety. Give me San Francisco fog over this any day," he said, wiping the sweat off his forehead with the edge of his T-shirt.

I took a sip of water, too nervous to drink more, my shirt clinging to my skin like a wet sheet beneath my jacket.

"It's just one class," Jason said, tapping his fingers on the railing of the arena.

I'd never seen him more anxious.

"I got that," I said, staring ahead at the massive jumps.

"Just ride like we talked about, and don't worry about the result. Think about the ride. The moment. This is your chance to explore your and Jett's potential, his scope. To see what you two are made of."

"I need that point to get to the Gold Cup."

"You're in," Jason said, scrutinizing me as if I should know. "There are only six in the jump-off, so worst-case scenario you get sixth, and that gives you the last point. You're going to the Gold Cup no matter what."

Right. I inhaled the smell of cut grass, its pattern resembling a freshly vacuumed Berber rug. I had to squint to see the jumps at the other end of the arena. They seemed about a mile away. The announcer's voice boomed over the loudspeakers, first in English, then a woman spoke in French.

"There must be over fifty thousand people here," I said. A haze coated everything I looked at, like a film over my eyes.

"Are you feeling shy?" Jason asked. He smiled, raising his brow at me.

"I appreciate the humor." Sarcasm layered my voice, but even though I chided, I wanted to run, to hide, to go back home. I wanted to ride Jett through the Nicasio Valley hills, with no one but the hawks and deer to keep us company. I asked Derek for my phone for the tenth time that day, praying that my mom would text or call, telling me she was there, up in the grandstands, ready to watch. There were no new notifications. I handed the phone back to Derek, wondering why I even bothered.

Vivian was at the halfway point now. My stomach turned watching her struggle as she rode Seraphim, her white britches glaring against Seraphim's rust coat. Sera's tail swished up and down, round and round, jerking high over every jump. I squinted. Vivian rode with too much spur, pushing her forward, yet yanking on Seraphim's mouth to slow her, trying to gain control as they thundered past us toward the last combination, the whites of Seraphim's eyes, her nostrils flared as she whipped her tail ferociously.

My hands trembled. I wanted to gallop Jett into the arena and yank the reins out of that woman's hands. Seraphim needed more rein, less control. "That horse belongs with us," I said through gritted teeth, clamping my slippery hands over Jett's reins.

"It's okay, B. Let it go," Derek said.

My name echoed across the grandstands. A soothing song played in the background, and I wished they'd play something more upbeat. The gate swung open, and a woman nodded for me to go in.

"Wait! Is Uncle Ian here?" I asked, turning to Jason. His flight was delayed, and he'd texted that he was close, but I hadn't seen him yet.

Derek's eyes lifted to the stands above the clock tower entrance we stood in. "He's here. Right above us. He's videotaping. And Helena and Mai and their girls and Stuart are all there too. They've all come to cheer you on." That news helped calm me. My own Team Brynn.

Jason gave me the Abhaya Mudra, and led us to the gate.

Jett didn't need to be told to go forward. He was ready. We cantered in, a beautiful canter as if I were riding a rocking horse. I ignored the scowl that Vivian shot me as she passed on her way out. The crowd cheered. The music changed to an old Shania Twain song. As I cantered past the grandstands, laughter drifted toward me from a sponsor's party. My anxiousness dissipated, my senses keen, clear, sharp, relishing every particle of air in my nose, tasting the smell of every blossom. I focused on the jumps, as if stalking my prey, staring each jump down, calculating, counting, planning.

"We love Brynn!" A girl waved a Go Brynn Seymour sign. It was the chubby girl who had been at Woodside—the one Vivian had insulted. I nodded at her, then trotted toward the mirrored skyscraper jump, the one that Jason worried about most. I stopped, giving Jett a chance to inspect it. He sniffed it, seemingly satisfied. I pushed Jett forward into a canter, his hooves thundering over the ground. The crowd cheered louder, the anticipation mounting. The buzzer sounded. I had forty-five seconds after the buzzer to start my round.

So we rode.

And it was breathtaking. Each jump better than the next. Jett was magnetic beneath me, as if each jump was meant only for us. I counted strides, followed Jason's plan. The air swooshed past me, the brilliant jumps magnified a thousand times under the blue Alberta sky. Everything appeared as if it was in high definition, the haze gone. I blinked, and the double oxer materialized directly ahead, the mirrored towers reflecting the white clouds. A drop of sweat dripped into my eye.

I squeezed my eyes shut, then reopened them. The clarity vanished. I wanted to rub the sweat out, but I couldn't reach up, needing to keep a hold of Jett. We were galloping too fast. And that's when I knew we were in trouble. I heard the crowd again. *Get in the void, Brynn!* But I couldn't find the blank space. Please God, I murmured, blinking. Then again. But I had slowed too much, having both pulled on the reins and concurrently spurred. I did what Vivian had done. I had to get Jett's engine up. He wouldn't get over otherwise.

I spurred harder, and yelled. "Get up!" But he couldn't gallop faster. I hadn't given him the chance. "Get up!" I yelled again, reaching behind to use my crop. But I was too late. The jump rushed at us. I had milliseconds.

First I saw the silver poles. I leaned forward over Jett's neck to make sure my center of gravity shifted to give him as much chance as possible to get over, to help propel him, like military cavalry soldiers had done in battlefields, where jumping ditches and obstacles was a matter of life or death.

As I fell, I recalled the past eight months, all in one frame. I would lose. I'd known I would lose way back when Jason first sat in my office. I would get close, oh so close to the coveted blue ribbon, but I'd never win. I would always take second. Or third. Or fourth.

Just like Dad.

Vivian was right.

A loud thud—Jett's hind legs caught. I wanted to yell, but my voice caught midair. The world tumbled and my head came somewhere on the other side of the jump. Jett's cry, an eerie sound, pierced my soul, then the resounding crash as all six rails of the jump fell, the heavy mirrored standards crashing down with them, assailing my ears. I squeezed my eyes shut, afraid to open them again.

I tried to roll like every rider is taught to, but my leg wasn't coming loose, my foot caught in the stirrup. I yanked harder. It twisted, but it wouldn't come out. Everything happened too fast. I panicked, knowing I was in the worst place possible. I wasn't sure what to do. Then I remembered Dad's voice, *"Relax. Let go."* The same as Jason's message.

I breathed in, releasing, letting go, and we came down, Jett on top of me, my leg torqued.

Everything went black.

$\mathscr{I}$ tried to sit as I came to, but a jolt of pain shot up my leg to my tailbone. Wincing, I fell on my side, grabbing for my knees, but each tiny move sent me into agonizing pain, electrical shocks running up every nerve. No air came. My chest burned. I felt like a fish out of water, gasping, clutching at my throat.

Jason's face materialized, his eyes wide, his hand gently caressing my cheek. "Brynn!"

I stared at him, wide-eyed, as he came in and out of focus, trying to communicate that I couldn't breathe.

"You're winded. Relax. It'll come."

I closed my eyes while Jason massaged my back. My muscles loosened, like a brace releasing from around my burning chest. I sucked heavenly air into my lungs. I drank it in, then I rolled to my knees.

"Jett?" I tried to call out, but no sound came.

"He seems all right. He's right over there." Jason gestured as he helped me sit up.

Jett stood less than twenty feet from me, head raised at attention, the saddle turned, reins dragging on the ground. Someone approached him. I wiped the mud out of my eyes, then wiped at my face, checking my hands for blood. But the wetness I'd felt was only mud mixed with thick blades of grass.

"Stay down," Jason said, his hand on my shoulder. I obeyed,

closing my eyes. The sun blazed hot on my face, the grass brought cool, damp relief. Paramedics loomed over me, kneeling and peering from every side. Someone unbuckled my helmet.

"Can you breathe?"

"Can you see the light?"

I thrust my hands over my face to block them out, rolling onto my side, trying to sit up again.

"I'm all right," I said, my breath coming fine now.

"Please stay down," one of the paramedics said.

"I'm fine," I said, giving him a hard stare. He paused, but Jason held his hand up, and the paramedic backed off.

"Brynn, you should wait a minute," Jason started, but I pushed his arm away. "Stuart is here, he's a doctor, you should let him check you out."

"I'm fine," I said.

He hesitated, then took hold of my elbow to help me stand, but I shrugged it off. As soon as I was on my feet, the crowd cheered. I was unsure of how to respond, my body burning more with shame than heat. I took a step, the pain in my hip and leg shot up to my spine. I stumbled, then quickly righted myself.

"Let's get a stretcher," Stuart said.

I shot him a dirty look.

"At least get in the golf cart," Jason whispered.

"Don't make a bigger fool out of me." I wouldn't allow myself to be carried off, so I pressed on.

"The only foolish thing here would be to let you walk," Jason hissed in my ear.

"I want my horse," I said, walking toward Jett. Out of the corner of my eye I made out Vivian and Chris standing near the gate. Vivian smiled as she reached for Chris's arm. Chris seemed like he might have been worried about me, but maybe he was only squinting to see more clearly. I turned away.

I wanted to wipe the stupid grin off Vivian's face, but I had to wipe the dirt off my white britches first. I leaned down, but it was pointless. My britches were stained with mud and grass. I straightened, and the world spun. Jason grabbed my arm, but I pushed him away and walked over to Jett. One of the crew members held his reins while others rebuilt the jump. I scanned the knocked-down pillars, exhaling in relief. The mirrors were only aluminum.

I took Jett's reins, reaching up to rub him behind his ears. Jett lowered his head, like he believed he'd been at fault—oh, how wrong he was. Little lines above his eyes crinkled, his eyes deep, liquid, and mournful.

"I'm so sorry. I'm so, so sorry for screwing that jump up, buddy," I whispered in his ear, clutching the reins. He breathed out, making that whirr sound I loved.

I walked us both, with as much dignity as I could, toward the gate.

Following the paramedic's advice, Jason brought me to the mobile first-aid stand to get checked out further. Stuart, our own medical doctor, followed my every move. I tried to hide the jabbing pain in my hip and leg, biting my cheek to distract myself as I sat down. But after he checked my pupil response, took my blood pressure, measured my temperature, and peered in my ears, I'd had enough. "What's next? A bacterial swab for strep throat?"

No one laughed.

"Brynn, you may know a lot about riding, and I take yours and Derek's advice when I take lessons, but I know about medicine. So just let me do my job." Stuart no longer looked the relaxed trail rider, the guy who bounced around on his solid draft mare. He wore the kind of look that told you to shut up and do as you're told.

As soon as Stuart gave the okay I pushed myself off the chair, desperate to leave the makeshift medic stand. "I've got a horse to check on."

Jason frowned, staring down at me, a sheen of sweat on his brow.

"Don't give me that shit, Jason," I said. "I'd like to see you as a patient."

He paused, his forehead relaxed, and then he laughed, taking his hat off. "Okay. You've got me." He fanned himself with his hat. "At least you haven't lost your feisty spirit."

It took a long time to walk across the expansive Spruce Meadows grounds to the barns, especially since I refused a ride in a golf cart. Jason kept the slower pace with me.

People recognized me from my earlier crash, or maybe it was from the mud and grass stains on my britches. Some said hello. Some ignored me, too shy to acknowledge who I was. A few stopped to ask if I was all right. Jason told them I was fine, only shaken. I kept my eyes down, unable to smile or speak.

The cool air inside the barn brought relief from the heat, but as soon as I spotted that ominous black leather medical bag lying in the aisle, and Derek holding Jett in the cross ties, my stomach knotted.

"Ian's just checking him over, Brynn," Jason said, as if he'd heard the dark thoughts cross my mind.

Derek peered up at me, his face ashen, his forehead creased. I halted. Was he as pissed at me as I was at myself? Did he blame me for hurting Jett? I would if I were him.

"Is he going to be all right?" I cautiously stepped forward, moving behind Uncle Ian who stood, his back to me, as he leaned down examining Jett's hind leg.

"Not sure yet. He's a wee bit sore, you know, so it's hard to say what's going on." His voice came out muffled.

"Is he off?" I would never forgive myself.

Uncle Ian didn't answer, still running a hand down Jett's leg.

"Derek?" I looked at him, hoping he'd answer me.

"Yeah. He's off." Derek didn't meet my eyes. He held Jett's halter with both hands, staring straight ahead.

"Goddammit!" I yelled.

"Calm down." Jason rested a hand on my arm, looking around to see if anyone had heard my outburst.

I folded my hand into a fist, biting down on it before I exploded, and said something I would later regret.

Uncle Ian stood to fetch a hoof tester from his bag. "He may be fine in a few days, Lassie."

"What do you think is wrong?" I could barely breathe now. "Let me look at him." I tried to push myself past Uncle Ian, but he stopped me.

"It's too hard to tell at this point, Lassie. I've got to run some diagnostics. Let's just take it an hour at a time, all right?" He turned back toward Jett. But then, as if he remembered something, he turned toward me. "Why don't you head back to the hotel room and rest? You took quite a tumble."

"I'm *fine*." I walked up to Jett, and Derek moved aside. I rubbed the white star in between Jett's eyes, just the way he liked. Tiny white hairs rubbed off on my fingers and mixed with the black of the rest of his face. He dropped his head almost to my waist.

"What aren't you telling me?" I asked Uncle Ian.

"Brynn. Lassie. I'm telling you everything I know right now. It's too hard to tell. Too early. Why don't you head back to the hotel room?"

"I'm fine," I said, my voice rising. I knew I should calm myself, but I couldn't.

"I've known you longer than you've known yourself, and what you need is to take a break," Uncle Ian said.

"Yeah, thanks, *Ian*. I know how long you've known me, and my mom and my dad, and just how smart you are. But you don't need to tell me what to do anymore. I'm a grown woman now, and I don't need people bossing me around. I wish you would all stop treating me like a kid!"

The barn fell silent. Even Jett jerked his head up to stare at me. Derek and Jason gaped at me.

"What?"

Derek and Jason retreated.

I stormed away from the three of them, kicking a manure bucket on the way out, spilling its contents all over the aisle. I wanted to scream, and I didn't give a shit what they thought. I was tired of being treated like I knew nothing and they knew best. I'd proven I could run a business and still compete in some of the best competitions in North America.

What the hell else did they want from me?

I bolted to the truck, cutting through the back fields to the parking lot, fuming, blood roaring in my ears. I ignored the pain searing from my thigh up into the small of my back. I stepped on a rock, almost twisting my ankle. I kicked it as hard as I could, but it didn't go far, skipping only a foot or two in front of me. I kicked at it again, this time missing completely.

"Son of a bitch!" I cried out. I'd made it out to the gravel trailer parking lot where we'd left the truck that morning, glad it was empty, and no one saw me take my anger out on the rocks. I got in, slamming the heavy driver's door closed, resting my forehead on the steering wheel. For an instant I worried about Derek and Jason, and how they'd get back to the hotel, then dismissed the guilty thought. They could find their own ride.

I drove over eighty miles per hour on the back roads toward our hotel. At a red light I searched for a Ministry song on my phone, blaring it as loud as my ears could handle. The truck's speakers reverberated through the base of my spine, pulsing through my fingertips, my brain crushed by the sound, desperate for the music to replace my every thought. I changed lanes, cutting someone off. A horn blared. I hadn't meant to, and normally I would have waved an apology, but not this time.

By the time I pulled up to the hotel, Ministry and Rage Against the Machine had my adrenaline pumping even harder. I yanked the ticket stub from the valet.

"Keys?" he asked, timidly.

I fished the keys out of my pocket, then threw them at him.

I stormed toward the elevators, ignoring the friendly smiles on the staff and the tourists. What the hell did they have to feel so happy about? Oh, right. Their full bank accounts and easy lives.

Helena and Payton waved at me from across the lobby. "Brynn!" Helena wore a sun hat and carried a buttercup-colored beach bag. Payton wore a breezy cover-up over her polka-dotted bikini. I surveyed the lobby, wondering if I could sneak behind the grand pillar to my left, or maybe a plant. Even a fat tourist would do. But no such luck. Helena and Payton were almost upon me.

"Brynn! I didn't think you saw me."

"I didn't," I said, looking away.

"I was hoping we could chat," Helena said, breathless from running toward me. Her hand squeezed my upper arm. I cringed. My arm hurt from the fall, plus I didn't want her tenderness and sympathy. Helena: Always nice, always full of the right, kind words, always found a way to lift my spirits. But I didn't want my spirits lifted. Her patience, her kindness, and her perfection annoyed me.

"Now's not a great time." I squinted toward the elevators, hoping she would take the hint.

"Oh, this really won't take long, and I need to talk to you as soon as possible."

"How about tomorrow?"

"No. I'd rather it was today, it's really important." Her hand tightened like a tourniquet around my arm.

"All right then." I succumbed, feeling like her prisoner.

"Great. Payton? Can you give us fifteen minutes?" Her daughter, earbuds in, texted on her phone.

Payton glanced up. "What am I supposed to do?" she whined.

"I don't know, Payton. *Find* something," Helena's voice was uncharacteristically harsh. Payton's chin dropped as she clamped her glossy lips into a line. Then she scuffed her feet across the granite floor toward the pool.

"There's a quiet space in the lounge," Helena said to me, nodding toward the room to our right.

27

*H*elena sat at a semicircular booth in the lounge. The blue and yellow zigzags on the purple carpet in front of me made my head spin as I struggled into the booth, the coral of Helena's shorts screaming against the red velvet booth almost making things worse.

"Brynn." She laid her hand on my arm again. I winced, and this time she noticed, removing her hand quickly. "I'm sorry about your fall. I shouldn't have grabbed your arm, poor thing!"

"I'll be fine," I grumbled.

"How is Jett? His fall looked rough."

"He's getting checked out now."

"I sure hope he's okay," she said, adjusting her loosely braided hair.

Silence fell around us, with only the distant piano music drifting in from the lobby, now muffled by the velvet upholstery, the carpet, and the painted ceilings of the lounge.

"I'm leaving."

My gaze shifted toward Helena. A calm fell over me, my ears suddenly plugged. I glanced at her lips, shaped into a perfectly curved bow.

"I'm leaving," she repeated as if I wasn't capable of understanding.

I scrutinized the waves of her hair, her thin arched eyebrows, her upturned nose. Then her words sunk in: she was leaving me as a trainer.

She leaned on her forearms toward me. "I signed the papers with Vivian this afternoon."

I couldn't breathe, feeling worse than when the wind was knocked out of me earlier. My eyes stung.

"What?" I didn't even sound human. I tried standing, but my thighs slammed into the table's edge, knocking me down. I grimaced from the pain.

"It's only that . . . Payton's friends are there, and it's not that you're not a great trainer, it's that . . . well . . ." She paused, searching her words.

I wanted, no, *needed* to hear them. "If it's not that, then what?" I croaked.

She didn't respond, making circles with her fingers on the smooth acrylic top of the table.

"Is it because of my fall today? Helena, is that why?" It came as barely a whisper. I sought out her eyes, but now she avoided mine.

"No, no. Of course not." She clasped her hands together, keeping her gaze down. I wanted to throw up. I pinched my burning nose, preventing what was surely coming next. But I wouldn't allow any tears to fall.

"You can't leave," I said, my voice low, pathetic even in my own ears.

"I'm sorry, Brynn. Vivian made a really great offer we couldn't refuse. She's a bit closer to where we live, and she's cheaper. She has more services, plus Payton will be with Kennedy again, and they're so close, best friends really. It's been tough on them too," she paused, glancing briefly at me again. "So you see, it's just better for us this way."

I glared at her, trying to contain my anger. Vivian was going to *lose* money, just to get every one of my clients.

"Brynn, sweetie, I'm so sorry. I promise, I'll always be there if you need me. I care for you, your mom, your dad. You'll always be a part of our family." Her hand extended toward me, her four-carat diamond flashing in the incandescent light.

I managed to shimmy out from beneath the table without hurting myself. "You're no fucking different than any of the others." I stood over her. Petite, sweet Helena. Then I turned, on my heel, wanting to run as fast and as hard as I could, as far away from everything as possible.

Instead, I walked as casually as I could toward the elevator, wondering how much worse things could get.

28

I stood in my stirrups while Jett galloped. I whipped off my helmet, tossing it as we raced around the Spruce Meadows International Arena. The crowd cheered, everyone jumped up, stomping their feet, calling my name. "Gonna Fly Now" by Bill Conti blared over the speakers.

Jason and Derek hugged, Mom waved to me, Dad smiled, his head tilted down, proud, yet not wanting to show too much emotion.

"What do you say, Jim, is it time to get that morning workout in?" Two announcers bantered jovially. Then a trainer's whistle jolted me.

"I like to start my clients off with thirty minutes of cardio on the treadmill or an elliptical machine, then . . ."

I slammed the alarm clock. The room was full of shadows, bits of light filtering in, falling at unfamiliar angles around me. I wasn't at home.

Hotel outside Calgary.

In an instant, memories flooded my mind. The dream hadn't been real. I wasn't winning anything. I was the one who'd lost. I was the loser.

I'd lost the class. I'd lost my clients.

Helena.

I had only four clients left: not enough income to cover even half of our overhead.

I'd retrieved a message from Uncle Ian sometime in the middle of the night, right before drinking my second or third or fourth glass of wine. Jett had injured his hind left stifle. Uncle Ian still wasn't sure whether it was only soft-tissue damage, a strain on the muscles, or worse, a torn ligament or fracture. He'd done an initial ultrasound scan, but we wouldn't know definitively until the swelling had subsided, and he would ultrasound it again. Jett could recover quickly, or could be on stall rest for as long as six months.

I sat up, acid from my stomach rising, burning my throat.

I imagined Seth Armstrong, his beady eyes staring at me while he matter-of-factly explained that we didn't have any money, that the bank was going to repossess the ranch, our house.

I saw Mom as she packed her boxes, putting on that cool facade, trying to be strong. I imagined Jett taken away from us as payment for the mortgage, standing somewhere at auction, or, God forbid, being sold to some inept rider who wouldn't take him to his potential. He'd stand in a barn, or out in a field somewhere, getting soft and fat and too old to jump, his feet festering with thrush. I'd heard the horror stories. Those estate auctioneers never had any experience selling horses. They got what they could, trying to get anything they could for the horse, unable to see the real value in a show jumper like Jett.

An empty bottle of wine stood to my left, the glass lay flat next to it, a crimson stain spreading across the maple nightstand. All I wanted was to huddle under the blankets. I shifted to stand but decided against it. My body felt like it had been mauled, everything burning, screaming in pain.

I remembered yelling at Uncle Ian, at Jason and Derek, and then of course Helena. My face burned with shame. I pulled the sheet even higher.

A soft knock on the door broke the silence in the room.

In my drunkenness I had forgotten to put out the privacy sign.

"No room service!" I called.

The knock came again.

"No, thank you!" I yelled louder.

"Brynn. It's Jason."

Shit. I didn't want to see him. Or anyone, for that matter. I pulled the covers over my head, hoping he'd go away.

"Brynn. Open the door." There was a pause, then his imploring voice, "Please?"

I hesitated, but then gathered my strength, and stumbled out of bed. I tugged my old Young Riders T-shirt lower.

I opened the door. Jason stood twirling his hat. He peered down at my bare legs and feet. I curled my toes, suddenly embarrassed at my appearance. He looked up, his eyes gazing deep into mine. I could almost taste his desire. And as much as I hadn't wanted to see him, I also needed him—I'd needed him since that day at Patterson's. He grounded me like only being around Jett, horses, nature, could. But there was more.

Heat rose through me, opening me.

He took one large step toward me, and as his arms encircled me, I rested my head on his chest. I barely reached his shoulder. The hotel room door clicked shut behind him, leaving us in silence.

I inhaled, my chin trembling against him. He smelled of maleness, horses, the earth. I ran my hand up his hard chest, the cotton of his shirt in contrast soft. Jason pressed his hand against my hair, then moved the weight of it slowly off my back, letting it fall to one side, moving his fingers through it, then pressing his palm against the back of my head. I rested, my ear against his heart, listening to it beat.

Jason pressed my head closer to him. "Dear, dear Brynn," he mumbled into my hair.

And we stood there in silence, with fingers of light weaving through at the bottom of the dark, drawn shades.

29

*D*ays or weeks passed since I'd come home from Calgary, but I stayed away from the barn, slept in late, and ignored all phone calls, e-mails, and text messages. Most were from Jason or Derek. Jett was fine. The injury had only been soft tissue damage and a slight strain. He needed rest, but Uncle Ian was sure he'd only require a couple of weeks off.

As for Jason, nothing ever happened that day at the hotel. Not because I wouldn't have wanted it to, but he'd come to comfort me, and I had nothing to offer in return. Every time I thought back to the fall, how I'd reacted at the barn, how I'd yelled, a heat crept up to the tips of my hair follicles and I knew that Jason deserved some-one better. Someone who listened to him, who learned from him, someone who didn't waste his time.

A basket of flowers caught my eye, the setting sun deepening the kaleidoscope of colors. Corinne had sent a get-well card and the arrangement of pink roses, orange tiger lilies, purple irises, and gold asters. I'd wanted to toss them, but Mom had been attending to them, and displayed the arrangement on the side table of the sitting room, my favorite room in the house. I set aside the Barbara King-solver novel, of which I hadn't managed to read a word. My land, the horses—they'd all be gone soon. My oath to Dad broken.

The white curtains billowed in the gentle breeze as the fresh summer air filled the room. I sat with my feet tucked beneath me, the dark leather soft and worn against my bare feet. I didn't turn on any lights. I felt rather than heard Mom enter. I ignored her, hoping she would leave me with my thoughts. I still couldn't forgive her for not coming to Spruce Meadows to watch me ride.

"Hi." Mom's voice wavered. She walked quietly across the room. How did she manage to keep the wooden floor from creaking beneath her footsteps? I had never been able to do that. She paused at the flower arrangement, picked off a few dry leaves, and pulled out the drooping stems, then sat down next to me. "I know this is a tough time, and I really want you to know that I'm here for you. I think you did—you *are*—doing a wonderful job, and I'm so proud of you . . ." She worried the bottom of her shirt. "What you've done to help me—to help the ranch—I know it wasn't easy. I know I haven't been of any help. In fact I've opposed everything you're doing."

She pulled at her earlobe, her gaze at her feet now. "And I want you to know that it wasn't your fault . . . what happened at Spruce Meadows, what happened on the freeway. Accidents happen. Everyone falls. We try, we stumble, sometimes literally." She smiled, and I guessed that was her way of trying to lighten the mood.

I didn't smile back.

"It's part of life, to have problems and challenges, to deal with them, then to learn and move on. We'll never have no problems. Only new ones. New challenges. I'm learning that now."

I stared out through the tall windows. The tick of the old clock measured the passing time. She seemed as if she'd aged five years in the last one, her skin translucent, smudges of gray under her eyes, the lines in the corners of her eyes deeper. But she was still poised. Gracious. Her lips, even without lipstick or gloss, held a reminder of the ruby color of her youth. I looked away, not wanting to feel anything, too tired to allow any more guilt or responsibility to weigh me down. Outside, the hills were nothing more than a silhouette against the setting sun, the sky transformed into a pastel drawing, shades of pink and mauve mixed with blue.

"So, if you want to talk . . ." Her voice trailed off, her face, turned toward the window, a reflection of mine. "God, Brynn. When I watched your round on TV and I saw you fall—" The emotion in her voice overcame her. She gave out a sob, but composed herself quickly. "I just don't know what I'd do if I lost you too . . ." She leaned against me, resting her hand on my head. She ran it down the length of my hair, tentatively at first, then with more certainty. "You're my baby. I need you."

I squeezed her hand, wishing I could be stronger for her. Wishing I could be strong enough, capable enough to win.

The sun went down, the last of its rays receding in less than a minute, leaving nothing but darkness in its wake. I didn't know how to talk to her or what to say. But I did feel a quietness having her next to me. We were connected, mother and daughter, connected through blood, through Dad.

The shadows disappeared. The temperature dropped. Mom stood, pulling the windows shut, one by one. She paused to drape a blanket over my feet. "Those boys have been working really hard down at the barn. You might want to check in with them." I flinched, but it didn't matter. Jason and Derek were fine without me. I'd just cause more problems. "Don't stay up too late, darling." She leaned down, her lips brushing the top of my hair, then she slipped out of the room as unobtrusively as she had come, leaving me in the near-darkness of the evening.

The next morning I woke to the pitter-patter of rain. I couldn't remember the last time it had rained in the summer. The rain washed the dust off the window, promising to wash the dust off the land. I sat at the edge of my bed and stared at my feet on the hardwood floor. They'd been idle long enough.

I trudged to the barn for the first time in two weeks. But when I got there, I continued past the entrance, down the trail through the gate into the gold pastures, my pace picking up. Just a speck of sun would surely brighten the drops on the leaves of the California oak trees and on the blades of grass under my feet, but I wanted to feel the rain.

Tears began to fall, and as soon as they stung my eyes I felt relief. I wrapped my arms around myself, holding my pain in, as I had been doing for over a year now. But the tears continued to well up and spill over, warm on my cheeks, mixing with the cool droplets.

I spread my arms out wide, like I had when I was a kid, running around the field with airplane wings at my sides. An ache moved through me, as if it had been coiled up for too long. I forced myself to keep my arms out, to allow the energy to stretch through me, letting it go.

At the bottom of the field, I ducked under the fence. A dark Jersey cow and her calf stood in front of me. Afraid to startle them, I hesitated. They didn't move. As if she sensed my pain, the cow bellowed out a soft sound, continuing to chew her cud. Her mellow eyes were black and moist. Billowy white clouds emerged from her large nostrils into the morning air. The calf leaned into its mom's flank, nuzzling against her, seeking protection. Rain beaded, then fell off their black fur as if they wore raincoats.

I pushed forward through the tall yellow grass, my jeans soaking up the freshly fallen rain through to my skin. Instead of feeling cold, I welcomed the sensation. My skin bumped, rubbing against the denim of my jeans, but it made me feel alive, and I needed to feel alive. I'd felt dead for so long.

Near the edge of the redwood forest, a rainbow appeared. It started down in the valley and stretched toward the ocean. The hues of the rainbow glinted, scintillating, like phosphorescent play in the gray sky. The rain stopped, and a ray of light broke through the clouds to the valley. I turned my face toward the sun, closing my eyes, letting the brightness redden the thin skin of my eyelids.

The land lay before me, fresh and alive and new. I wiped at my nose with the back of my hand.

"Thank you," I whispered. I had a sudden need to see Jett, to touch the muscles under his silky coat, to smell him, to hear his breath.

I stumbled in the mud and dead grass full of thistles and foxtails, keeping the top of the hill in sight. I watched as three jays attacked the hawk that lived at the edge of our property. They dove at him, biting, and instead of fighting back he flew harder and faster than he had before. The jays were relentless but the hawk didn't use aggression, instead continuing on his flight path. I panted up the hill, my breath shallow and quick.

I walked into the office, hoping to find an extra jacket. My wet jeans clung to my legs, my shoes squished across the floor. I peeled off my wet sweatshirt, turning on the light.

Jason sat at my desk, his head in his hands, his fingers braided into his thick hair.

"Jason?" I'd never seen him this burdened, dejected. I wasn't sure if I wanted to enter. I wanted to hold on to the transforming moment I'd experienced in the valley, not wanting to lose its magic.

Jason didn't move. I walked closer. "Jason? What happened?" His stillness unnerved me.

He raised his head, pushing the collar of his fisherman's sweater up around him, reddened eyes staring back at me. "It's Eve. The leukemia's back. And worse than that, we were told she has a ten percent survival rate. The only options were to let her go, or to try a bone-marrow transplant. Of course we opted for a transplant. I was a close enough match, I had seventy-five percent of the twelve markers they look for, so I ended up being the donor."

"Jason! Oh, my God! Why didn't you tell me?"

Jason didn't even look up at me, and I felt stupid. Maybe he had tried; I'd never answered my phone.

He continued, "But it's not good. Her body seems to be rejecting it, though the doctors say it's still early. It can take weeks for her body to adjust and to take to it. She's weak. Her white blood cell count is very low."

I caught my breath, and moved to kneel by his side. Little Eve. I cradled his face in my hands, remembering the day she visited the barn, her elation at riding Jett. "You have to keep faith. You have to believe she's strong enough to fight." His cheeks were icy against my palms. His lashes clumped, his olive skin darkened with unshaved stubble.

"I just don't know how to do it anymore. I don't know how to be brave for her." His sorrow was my own. And here he'd been riding Jett, helping with the horses, teaching Derek, all while I'd been wallowing in bed. The strength I'd captured in the meadow gave me courage, and I knew I didn't need to flee anymore.

As Jason and I walked down the UCSF Children's Hospital, I placed my hand into the crook of his elbow, as if it were the most natural place for it to rest. Clorox and disease permeated the air, reminding me of the last time I'd been at a hospital, the night of Dad's death. I shook my head, forcing each foot to fall in front of the other.

Butterfly, meadow, and barnyard animal murals tried to mask the heartache lurking behind each closed door of the pediatric bone-marrow transplant wing. Jason paused before we reached her room, placing a hand on top of mine. "Are you sure?"

I nodded. We had to scrub up in an anteroom before going in.

"Right now she pretty much doesn't have an immune system, so everyone has to scrub before going in. Even the nurses and doctors." Jason handed me a face mask. "She's in a lot of pain, and one of the side effects she's experiencing is that her mouth is full of ulcers. They have her pumped full of pain medicines, but her body is rejecting a lot of them. They call it playing the whac-a-mole game. Pain is up, she gets a med. Then she's nauseous, they give her something for that, which makes her not sleep, so they give her a sleep aid . . . well, you've gone to vet school, you get the point. Luckily she's been sleeping most of the last three days."

I pulled my mask on, adjusting it to fit over my nose and mouth. Jason pushed the wide door open and I felt the air push out toward me instead of in, and I realized the positive pressure helped maintain a sterile environment. The room was brighter than I'd expected, one wall pink, the remainder blue. Eve had a room to herself, but under the window there was a second bed where Ashley and Jason took turns sleeping. One of them was always with Eve, every hour of every day, and yet during his time away from the hospital he had still helped at the barn—at my barn. The mask seemed tighter, and the disposable gown made me even hotter than I was.

In the bed closest to the door a shadow of a girl lay atop a colorful pillow. The bright pink pajamas accentuated just how pale she was, her skull, round and smooth, the skin almost translucent under the fluorescent lights. Next to her lay a worn Peter Rabbit plush toy, about half her size. Above her bed, a huge pin board spelled out her name in a sparkly red foam. Pictures of Eve and Ashley, Eve and Jason, Eve and her dad, her dad in his uniform—a desert landscape in the background—and hand-drawn cards filled out the collage. And there was the picture of her on Jett, pinned to a bulletin board.

A barrage of machines stood beeping and flashing next to her bed, an IV drip attached to her arm. I wasn't frightened—I'd seen similar ones at the vet hospital, though I was surprised at just how many there were. I counted ten IV lines.

Ashley sat at the edge of the bed, her back to us. Jason introduced us, though she barely glanced at me, her charcoal eyes darting back to Eve's face, as if to confirm she hadn't disappeared. Regarding the two siblings side by side I could see the resemblance, though she was as petite as he was tall.

A doctor came in, short and squat, pushing his small glasses back onto his nose. He looked to Ashley. "Mrs. Lane?" Above his mask, his eyes crinkled into a smile.

Ashley didn't move.

"We have *some* good news." The doctor shifted on his feet, as if he'd been standing too long.

Ashley turned to me. "Brynn? Would you mind?" She nodded toward Eve's hand, lifting it gingerly toward me.

I opened my mouth, not sure what to say, only to breathe out an "of course." I moved next to the bed, taking Ashley's place, trying not to disturb Eve. Eve kept her eyes closed and seemed so frail that I worried my touch might break her tiny bones. Ashley placed Eve's hand in mine. Cool and dainty, it was an emulation of what a child's hand should feel like, of what it had felt like just a few months ago. There were no dimples where the knuckles were, no pudgy fingers, only the ivory, featherweight clear skin overlaying her silver veins and bones. I cradled Eve's hand in mine, swallowing back the lump in my throat. Eve's face looked puffier than it had the day she'd ridden Jett at Redwood Grove. The photo of the girl on Jett, who'd laughed and squealed when Jett nuzzled her and blew into her ear, bore no resemblance to this one.

Jason and Ashley stood with the doctor near the door, out of earshot. Ashley's long black hair draped over her thin arms. Her shoulders slouched in her navy T-shirt, and her bony knees beneath her khaki shorts looked like they would buckle. Her face pinched in worry as she listened to the doctor.

When the doctor left, Ashley clutched Jason's arm, resembling a child herself. "Jason, I don't know if I can handle this. How much longer do we have to sit around waiting? I can't watch her suffer anymore." Her eyes welled up with tears as she glanced at Eve. She seemed desperate. Small. I turned away, listening to the beeping of the monitor, brushing Eve's hand with mine, adjusting the cuff of her PJs, trying to keep my own tears at bay.

I'd been so selfish. It wasn't just me suffering. Everyone around me suffered too. And Jason and Derek had picked up my slack. I'd been such a fool—and now I only had six weeks left to get my shit together, to get Jett and myself back into shape. I had a show to win.

30

*T*he next six weeks flew by filled with early-morning yoga sessions followed by riding Jett on the flat, and in the late afternoon jumping and gymnastic sessions for Jett and me. I turned into bed by nine practically every night, only managing to read a handful of pages of either *Anne Kursinski's Riding and Jumping* or the *Yoga Sutra of Patanjali* books Jason had given me. Jason's yoga mat stood next to mine in the corner behind my desk, and by the time I'd stumble into the office at six every morning, he'd already have the windows open, a new playlist on, and had been meditating for a good thirty minutes. Some days we'd practice outside. On others, when the fog was too thick, we stayed inside. Within two weeks I was beating him to the mat. The first day he saw me there, he paused, surprised, one eyebrow raised. But then he cleared his throat and acted as if it was nothing unusual. I couldn't help feeling proud. When I opened my eyes and glanced at him, I saw his mouth turned up in a smile as he meditated, and I felt like I'd just gotten the biggest reward in the world.

We would start with asana practice, some days solar flows, some days lunar, but we always ended with breath work. The Savasanas lying on our backs were awkward at first, and I had no idea how to completely relax, but a couple of weeks in, instead of focusing on Jason lying next to me, or thinking about all the things I needed to do, or worrying about whether we'd win, everything started falling away.

After our asana practice, it was Jett's turn. Jason taught me how to stretch Jett's front and back legs, how to massage his back; he even showed me some acupressure points. Now it only took me a moment to get Jett to groan when I got the right spot. Jett's stifle only had a minor injury, and between the time off while I had lain around in bed, and Uncle Ian's ultrasound machine, he seemed as if he'd never taken an unsound step.

In the mornings we worked on flat work, nothing too difficult, always stopping just before Jett became tired. In fact, Jason wanted us to stop just when Jett wanted more. In the afternoons, we either practiced gymnastics or hill work—riding up and down the hills in the back. "This will help his endurance over the long course in that International Ring, and it's the best way to build muscle in his shoulders and hind quarters," Jason said.

We jumped him at the Gold Cup level a maximum of two times per week. One morning I walked outside on Jett to find Jason in his leather chaps atop Pea number one's twenty-eight-year-old mare. I laughed.

"Is she even rideable?" I asked, eyeing her swayed back.

"Of course. She runs around in pasture every day, doesn't she? She'll be just fine. Won't you, old mare?" Jason leaned down and patted her neck. She was a seventeen-hand draft horse, and seemed to perk up with Jason on her back. "She's got plenty of life left in her. Maybe no dressage Grand Prix's in her near future, but some trail rides will spark her back up. You watch. She needs a bit more excitement in her life than being groomed every Tuesday."

When I opened my tack trunk the day we packed the trailer for the Gold Cup at Spruce Meadows, a large package lay on top of my saddle pads. I scanned the barn for Derek or Jason, to see if one of them had left the gift, but the barn was empty. As soon as I saw the writing on the card, I knew who it was from. The perfectly slanted letters, the capital B, oval and round, the long and curved y, each n precise. I slipped my finger under the seal, tearing the envelope open.

Darling,

I believe in you. I always have. I'm sorry I haven't supported your riding career. I was wrong, and I'm sorry to have pushed you away from it. This is your passion, and you can't let anyone, especially me, stand in the way.

I know you and Jett are meant to jump together. Never forget it. Have faith in yourself. Have faith in him. Have faith in me.

I'm sending you off with a small token and some of my favorite quotes from Ovid's Metamorphoses.

And even as she fled, she charmed him. The wind blew
her garments and her hair streamed loose. So flew the god
and the nymph —he on the wings of love and she on those
of fear.

Fear has been the catalyst of much that is wrong in my life, and not surprisingly in my writing. I realize that now, and I am ashamed that I've been in hiding. That I haven't supported you. I never wanted it to be so.

Never fear, my darling. You were meant for this.

Love,

Mom

P.S. I'm truly sorry I don't get to hug you goodbye, but you know . . . work.

I clutched the letter to my heart, my eyes welling with tears. I pulled the ribbon off, tearing the wrapping paper. Inside the box lay a brand-new oiled leather bridle with an engraved brass plate, the script similar to my mom's handwriting: Victory by Heart.

Over a day and a half, Jason, Derek, and I made our way back to Spruce Meadows, this time to compete in the Gold Cup. We took turns driving; Jason was resting in the small tack room of the trailer, which housed the sleeping bunk.

The doctors had told Jason and Ashley that Eve was a fighter and that she'd turned a corner. In the weeks since I had visited, Eve's white blood cell count was up, her mouth ulcers had began to clear, and she was more awake and alert than she had been in months. Ashley's husband, Tyler, arrived the previous week on a month's leave from Afghanistan, and the family of three was back together—if only temporarily. Ashley seemed to gain strength and encouraged Jason to go to Spruce Meadows.

It was September second, with Calgary weather forecasted to reach into the seventies. Thank God. There'd been a year when Dad had competed during Labor Day weekend in the snow. Rain was bad enough on that grass field, but snow?

"Not much longer," I said to Derek as I glanced down at the GPS. "Maybe two and a half hours."

"Hope Jason's getting a good nap," Derek said, adjusting the side mirror of the truck with the power buttons.

I took a sip of the now-lukewarm coffee.

"He's probably meditating," Derek said.

I gave Derek a stern look. "Hey, come on. You know all of that has been good for me." I tossed a chocolate-glazed Timbit in my mouth.

"Don't hog 'em all!" Derek grabbed for the box.

"What? You want one?" I laughed, dangling the box of donut holes toward him, pulling one out, popping it in my mouth. I closed my eyes, exaggerating my delight, though it did melt in my mouth in pure sugary bliss.

"You better give 'em up, Brynn, if you know what's good for you." He gave me his best Clint Eastwood impression, his eyebrows coming together in a V, his eyes narrowed. "I'll tell Jason you're eating donut holes . . ."

"You wouldn't dare!" I punched his shoulder. "Here. Before you go off the road." I passed him the box. We'd stopped at the donut shop an hour back, and luckily Jason hadn't seen me indulge my craving, but something about those things made me hunger for them every time we drove through Alberta.

"What about you? You barely slept." A furrow lined his forehead.

"I'm fine. Wish you guys would stop worrying. I couldn't sleep if I tried."

"I don't mind if you doze off for a bit."

I glanced at the monitor to check on Jett. He fidgeted, his head bopping up and down, leaning his body to the right, pulling on his tie. I held my breath, digging my fingernails into my palm. Then Jett relaxed, and I rested my head back against the seat, listening to Derek chatter on, wishing I knew what the future held not just for me, but for all of us.

As soon as we parked I was out the door and inside the trailer, needing to check on Jett, to talk to him, and to make sure he was all right. As I walked up the ramp, Jett turned his head to look at me, his eyes mellow. He stomped his foot, as if telling me he was done with the drive. I laughed. "Me too, buddy. Me too." I leaned my head against his face, his eyelashes brushing against my cheek. "Let's check out the grounds, and ride by the International Ring, huh?" Jett whirred, and I snuggled against his velvety neck. "You always knew, didn't you?"

After giving Jett a schooling ride in one of the warm-up arenas, I decided to ride him around the Spruce Meadows show grounds. Only volunteers and show staff hurried about in preparation of the show, Jett's shoes echoing in the silence of the night.

"We're supposed to have a record-setting number of visitors," one of the show staff said. "Over eighty thousand expected on Saturday alone."

My head reeled at the thought of all those people watching me ride, but I was ready. As I passed a lamppost with a Spruce Meadows Gold Cup flag fluttering in the wind, I reached up and let my fingers brush against it. I would jump, and I would win. Back at the barn, I handed Jett's reins to Derek and told him I was headed to the tournament office, then turned back and gave him a big hug.

"This is *it*. It's finally happening," I said.

"Are you surprised? Cause I'm not. I always knew this day would come." Derek squeezed me a bit tighter to him, and I had to pull away so as not to get too emotional.

On my way to the show office I ordered a cup of coffee at Time Faults, the only restaurant still open. "Actually make that an herbal tea with lemon, please," I said. The moon hung above the regal facade of British House, full and round as I walked across the grounds, the path lit by cast-iron lamps. The temperature had plummeted, and I cursed that I'd forgotten my sweatshirt. I hugged my show binder to my chest, sipping my tea. Near the tournament office, I heard quick steps behind me. I glanced back and recognized the figure, tall and lean, dark hair spilling around her shoulders. I swore under my breath, then kept walking, focusing on the moonlit path in front. I wouldn't let her get to me this time.

After I signed in at the show office, back at the barn, only a few incandescent bulbs shone above the horse stalls. My boots barely made a sound on the asphalt of the aisleway. I inhaled the spicy scent of cedar shavings, hay, horses, and ammonia. I paused, smiling. I was finally here. As I reached Jett's stall I noticed his door was ajar. My heart stopped. I ran the last few steps, already knowing he wasn't there.

"Jett?" I peered into the empty stall. His hay tossed, his grain bucket on its side.

"Brynn?" Derek called from down the aisle.

I ran toward him. Derek, Jason, and Uncle Ian surrounded Jett. Uncle Ian's damned black bag stood in the middle of the aisle.

"What's going on?" My voice rose in panic, matching the sudden rise in my blood pressure.

"Well, I came to check on him, and I didn't like the way he was

standing in his stall, not putting any weight on his hind leg . . ."
Derek avoided my eyes.

"But I just rode him! He was fine!"

"He probably *is* fine. Right, Dr. Finlay?" Derek's eyes only briefly
made contact with mine. I glanced at Jason, his vein throbbed in his
temple, his broad shoulders slumped.

"Let's not get in a panic here. Let's figure out what the problem
might be. Aye?" Uncle Ian said. He began to unclip the cross ties
from Jett's halter. "Derek. Can you jog him for me outside?"

"Yessir."

As we stood outside the barns waiting for Derek to jog Jett, I
wasn't so sure I would be winning anything. I imagined Jason's arms
holding me tight, but he kept his distance. So I stood alone, the
wind off the Rockies blowing right through me.

*D*erek jogged Jett head on toward us. Uncle Ian and I squatted, heels and toes firmly planted on the concrete walkway, scrutinizing Jett's pace, his evenness as he trotted. The floodlights around us made it bright enough to see by. Derek ran, leading Jett, a myriad of shadows stretching and merging on the ground on either side of them.

"He looks off," Uncle Ian said, mumbling under his breath.

"Again," I said just as Uncle Ian said, "Enough."

Uncle Ian peered over the top of his frameless glasses at me. He blew out air from his cheeks. "There's no point in jogging him one more time." He rested both hands on my shoulders.

"I just want to make sure," I said.

"There's no point," he repeated. "Plus we don't want anyone seeing us out here, guessing something's wrong."

He was right, of course. Every horse would be checked for lameness before the show—the FEI division horses would be jogged Thursday morning. We had about sixty hours to get Jett sound before their jog. It was getting late, past dinnertime, and even though all the horses had been fed, grooms would be returning for night check, with some settling in to the tack room or empty stalls.

"Is it from the stifle injury?"

"Not sure yet."

"He hasn't shown any signs of lameness." All the weeks we'd spent preparing, riding, and he'd been completely fine.

"Brynn, Lassie." He pinched his nose with two fingers, then looked up at me. "It's still early, and I haven't had a chance to run all of the diagnostics." And I couldn't be sure but I thought I saw his eyes fill, and it hit me: this was almost as stressful on him as it was for me.

"I have to ride Saturday," I pleaded, as if he could change the unknown outcome of Jett's lameness.

"I know, Lassie. I know." He ran his fingers through his white hair, then picked up his black bag.

As I walked back to the barn I thought I saw someone fall into the shadows.

Jason and I ate at Time Faults. The quaint pub stood lit up, the front deck empty. Picnic tables with closed umbrellas and an outdoor bar normally welcomed customers, but it was Monday night before a large show, and the crowd was thin. We sat inside. A handful of people huddled at the wooden bar and long rectangular tables. A baseball game rattled on above them. The cheerful decor included historical photos of riders, a moose head, and old Alberta license plates. I stared out the back window at the chain-link fence surrounding the barns, which were off-limits to the public.

I picked at the spicy chicken wings, but even with all the hot sauce, they were flavorless. I took a sip of the fountain water from a paper cup. It too had a funny taste. I wiped my mouth with my napkin, glancing up at Jason. He hadn't said a thing, barely eating his veggie burger. The silence between us stretched on, a Barenaked Ladies song drifting from speakers high up on the wall.

"I'm going to stay with him tonight," I said, staring at the handful of grooms and what looked to be horse owners or investors also eating a late dinner.

"It won't make a difference, Brynn. It's not like he's colicking." Jason's words came slow, as if worried he'd offend me. Of course he was right. A colicking horse had to be watched twenty-four-seven— but what could I do for Jett?

I stared down at the water cup in front of me, tearing away at the paper rim, unrolling the edge with my fingers. My cuticles had started healing, pink skin masking the terror I'd waged against myself during those weeks where I barely left my bedroom.

"I can't stand around and do nothing." I wasn't sure if I expected Jason to understand, but I had to do this. I needed to stay with Jett, to check on him in the middle of the night, to feel for any heat in his tendons and hoof.

"You need to get back to the hotel, have a good night's sleep. We've just finished driving over thirty hours—"

"You won't change my mind." I stood, tossed my plate into the trash, and marched toward the security gates of the barns.

Jason sat in a lawn chair to my left, his long legs stretched in front, crossed at the ankle, his hat pulled low over his forehead. By midnight all the noises of the evening shift had died down. The grooms had performed their night check over two hours ago. Jason somehow managed to look comfortable, as if he wasn't annoyed at having to spend the night in a barn. I'd argued, of course, but he wouldn't hear of leaving me alone. He'd rustled up two nylon chairs from some grooms, found a couple of clean horse blankets in the back of our trailer, and wrapped one carefully around my shoulders.

"Have you ever talked about it?" Jason's voice was low now.

"Talked about what?" I pulled the blanket tighter around my shoulders, the temperature having dropped to the midforties.

"Your father's death. The day he died."

I sucked in my breath. No one had ever bothered to ask me before. "No."

"Did you seek counseling?"

"No," I said again, curtly. Seeing him flinch, I softened my voice. "I didn't need to." I pulled my hand up to my mouth to bite my cuticles.

Jason leaned forward, placing his warm hand over mine, gently stopping me. His own fingernails were neat and round, the whites perfect half moons along the finger's edge, trimmed, and even though he had strong hands, they were soft and supple.

"Maybe it would have been a good idea." He propped his hands in a prayer gesture under his chin, watching me carefully.

"Maybe." I stared out the barn exit doors at the bright lights still on outside the barn. A security guard walked back and forth, maybe keeping himself awake by moving.

"You know, Brynn, sometimes we try to be tougher than we really are. I know how brave you are, but it's okay to let go sometimes."

I pulled away from him. He was too close to me. His body was electric, his masculine scent spiced and warm.

"It's been over a year. Maybe it would have helped if you had."

"Maybe. But I didn't have time to figure that out, remember? I had a business to run, school to attend, my mother to take care of. Who cared what *I* was going through?"

His hand returned to mine, squeezing it. He leaned in closer. "Would you like to talk about it now?"

I wouldn't look at him. "No." The hollow silence of the barn surrounded us. The small bulbs above the stalls were off now, with only a handful of small emergency lights still on. "What am I supposed to tell you?" I examined the stall doors across the aisle from me, the deep scratches, the chipped paint. "How I felt so scared that I thought my heart would stop beating? How it took everything in my body not to turn and run with Cervantes and Seraphim? How at the same time I was riveted in place, like my feet were encased in cement and how I had to tell them to move, one in front of the other, to run to him?"

"That helps."

I stared out at the black night. The security guard hadn't walked by in a while. "I didn't know what to do, Jason. I just knelt there, cradling his head, brushing the hair off his face, trying CPR, and I was so desperate for the ambulance to come, but it seemed to take forever, and when I finally heard the sirens, I kept pumping on his chest, and breathing air into him, watching his lungs expand with my breath, praying someone would get there in time, that maybe if they shocked his heart it would start up again. When they finally got there, I just remember this young guy, he seemed like he was barely out of high school, his eyes wide, just staring, you know? I thought, what is wrong with him? Why is he just standing there? Why isn't he grabbing the equipment he needs? Everyone was so slow, and I wanted them to hurry the hell up, because I knew we were out of time. And I watched them surround Dad, calling out orders as they hooked up the defibrillator, and I stood, hugging Jett. And it was Jett that gave me the courage to make it through that night—"

Jason pulled me closer. "It's going to be all right. You did the best you could, Brynn. You did good."

"What does it matter if I didn't save him? I should have checked the latch. I should have stopped him from going into the trailer. It was all wrong. The whole day seemed wrong. I had this bad feeling . . . it all started with that damned earthquake."

Jason knelt in front of me. "You know, in Sanskrit there is no word for guilt. There's just no such thing. You have to move past whatever hurt you, and make peace with having hurt those around you." He stroked my hair. "And I should know." Jason's hand moved up and down my back. Slow. Warm. Still, even in movement.

"It takes a long time to understand, but when you get it, it becomes obvious." Jason reached his hand toward mine, and I knelt on the horse blanket beside him.

"When I found my mother in her apartment . . ." Jason played with the beads on his bracelet, then finally found this voice again. "The days and weeks that followed I cut myself off from every-thing. I went to a really dark place, unable to ride, unable to see my sister, unable to live. I wanted to drink myself to death, to numb the guilt and the pain that came with it. The typical pattern of self-destruction.

"I'm not unusual or different from anyone else that this has happened to. It's been studied by yogis in history for thousands of years. So my sister showed up with her friend one day, an intervention of sorts, and her friend, this yogi guru, left a book for me to read. It was about healing the mind, healing the spirit. And it seemed to make sense. I started reading it, and the more I read the more my head cleared, so I looked up local classes then joined. What I learned was that we are all fundamentally divine. We're all good. We make mistakes. Every single one of us. It takes practice, but with time we can forgive ourselves. Especially if we believe that we're a part of a greater good—of God, the Holy Spirit, the Universe, Buddha, whatever you wish to call it. We can change. We can better ourselves. And all we have to do is act with the best intentions."

The best of intentions. The words circled around me, wispy, ethereal. I laid my head in his lap and even though I wasn't sure I understood, I knew one thing: I could have lain there, listening to him, with his hands running through my hair, forever.

Spending the night in the barn left me cramped. By 5:30 a.m., Uncle Ian was back. I held my breath as he again examined Jett while Derek jogged him, running beside Jett, trying to extend his stride so that we all could get a better look.

"He's still a bit off," Uncle Ian said.

"I don't think it's his stifle," I said, watching him move. "It's not consistent with that. It may be in his hoof."

Uncle Ian pushed his glasses up, and nodded. "I agree."

Derek brought Jett closer to us, and I asked Uncle Ian for his hoof-testers, big metal prongs, a larger version of metal pincers. I lifted Jett's left front foot, gripping it between my knees, letting the hoof rest on my bent thighs. Derek kept a tight hold of Jett's halter. Jett shook his head impatiently up and down.

Uncle Ian leaned over and felt the hoof. "You know, Brynn," he said, then smiled. "I think you're right."

"You seeing what I'm seeing?" I asked. "Stone bruise?" When we pressed the metal prongs against the bottom of Jett's hoof, Jett yanked at his foot, trying to take it back. But there was no heat, like there would be with an abscess.

Uncle Ian looked up at me and smiled, and a wave of gratitude filled me. But almost immediately my heart sank. "What about the lameness testing?"

"We may be fine before then. If not, I'll talk to the vet, explain the situation, and they may let us retest on Friday. First, let's get him moving, get his blood circulating without putting too much pressure on that foot. I'm going to shockwave it. It's not usually carried out on the hooves, but it can't hurt. When I'm done, Derek, can you apply a poultice?"

"Sure thing, Doc," Derek said.

I walked over to Jason, and as if he'd read my mind Jason answered the question I was going to ask. "Jett will be fine if we don't ride for the next couple of days. He's fit enough. Those hills and all those gymnastics sessions have built up his condition and stamina."

"But he needs practice, and we need to get him into the ring."

"He's practiced enough. He knows his stuff, and so do you. He'll be fine as long as we can get him in the ring by Friday."

"Two days. That's all we've got," I said. "And we can't even give him anything for the pain after tomorrow . . ." My voice trailed. It was illegal to give horses painkillers before a show. "But there's nothing we can do, so let's take it as it comes," I said to no one in particular.

Derek gave me a strange look, and Jason smiled.

Exhausted from spending the night in the cold barn, I walked back to the truck. I desperately needed a hot shower to ease my cramped muscles. Just as I neared the parking lot, I spotted Vivian and Chris getting out of a green Mustang. Chris noticed me first. Our eyes met for a split second, and he dropped his arm from around Vivian.

I turned my head, and walked the other way.

32

*I*n the late evening I drove back from the hotel to the show grounds, stopping in at Time Faults. A tea for me, a coffee for Derek. Derek stood, tack hanging on a hook, the bridle taken apart, soapy water dripping down his elbows as he wiped the leather with a sponge. From the way the overhead lights reflected off the saddle, I wondered how many times he'd already cleaned it today. It shone like the hood of the silver Mercedes displayed in front of the Gazebo of the Meadowcourt Building—the Mercedes that the lucky winner would drive away with, in addition to the winner's share of the million-dollar prize.

"I think you missed a spot," I said, smiling.

"Well, you're going to be televised, aren't you?"

I had to give it to him—he wasn't giving up.

Derek's hand moved quickly back and forth, polishing every inch of the rich chestnut leather. "Dr. Finlay came to check on him about an hour ago. He's the same." He scratched at the unshaved face around his goatee.

I slumped against Jett's stall door, sliding down to sit on the concrete. Derek moved on to the martingale. I put my head in my hands, my hair falling around me, reminding me of the tent I used to pitch as a child on the back deck in the summer. I'd hide in it all day, playing make-believe with my Breyer horses. What I wouldn't do now to feel that lightness again.

Three pairs of shoes appeared—Derek's paddock boots, a pair of black ballet flats, and a pair of men's dress shoes.

I glanced up. Helena, Derek, and Bill stood in front of me. "What's going on?" I asked.

"C'mon." Derek extended his hand toward me.

Staring at the three of them, I couldn't help noticing a hint of a smile cross Derek's face, and Helena's eyebrow raised in amusement.

"Let's go. We ain't got all day," Derek said, acting stern.

Tentatively I reached my hand toward his, my fingers wrapping around his palm. He tightened his grip and pulled me up. I glanced at Helena, wondering what she was doing here. If Vivian saw her in our barn, she'd probably call a SWAT team to wrestle me down for even talking to one of her clients.

Helena smiled, hesitant, then leaned in and embraced me. I tensed, but tears pooled in my eyes, her familiar Yves Saint Laurent perfume bringing back a flood of memories.

"Let's go," she said, grabbing my other hand. "There's some unfinished business."

As we walked through the next barn, I pulled Derek back and let Helena and Bill walk ahead of us.

"What's Bill doing here?" I whispered.

"We're making up," Derek said and winked. I gave his hand a squeeze.

"I'm so happy for you," I said, giving him a quick hug. "And where the hell are you taking me?"

"You'll see . . ."

They brought me to Seraphim's stall.

"Won't Corinne be furious?" I asked, but Helena and Derek laughed, like kids in on a joke.

"It was Corinne's idea!" Helena said. "She's got Vivian out at some fancy dinner, just so you can ride Sera."

"But why would she do that?" I asked.

Derek and Helena exchanged a glance. Helena leaned in, and played with a button on her shirt before meeting my gaze. "It's time to forgive. To move on. Now hurry up. You have less than an hour before Vivian is back." They turned and left me alone with Seraphim.

I moved in slow motion, getting myself organized. The grooming box, bridle, girth. Derek got my saddle while I spent a long time brushing Seraphim. When I got to her legs, I ran my fingers over the dents and raised lines of the scar tissue. A flash of her coat and tail appeared in my mind as I remembered the night she ran off after coming down on Dad. I forced myself to focus on the present image of her, instead of the one that had been forever imprinted in my memory.

When I finally got on, her flesh quivered, just as a horse's will when it's trying to flick a fly off its sensitive skin. My own skin prickled. I leaned down from my saddle, running my hand down the length of her neck, smoothing the hairs, feeling her warmth under my hand, calming her with my touch. An electric current passed between us, and for a second I had an impulse to get off, put her back in her stall. There was a part of me that was worried that she would take off like she had that night.

"You're such a chickenshit," I scolded myself.

I held her to a slow walk, concentrating on my position as if I were a beginner rider. I rode her out on the back paths of Spruce Meadows, praying no one would see us. A rustle in the bushes startled me, and I held my breath. A buck jumped out toward us, his ivory antlers large, his coat speckled with white. I squeezed a bit too tight with my calves, on the ready for her to take off. But Seraphim didn't falter, her ears alert, yet forward, her step long, her breath slow, like a schoolmaster taking yet another beginner student out for a trail ride. The moon lit our way and the cricket symphony played while I leaned down against her and breathed in her horse and leather scent. And I didn't need to tell her. She knew, and the invisible weight I'd been carrying lifted and disappeared, up with the rising moon.

33

*S*aturday afternoon Jason put his arm around me, and we walked behind the grandstands of the International Ring. I stood in the shade of a tree, drinking a cup of water. First round of the Gold Cup was behind us, and I'd made it into the jump-off.

"Drink it slow, and not too much," Jason warned, then ran off to find Derek, to check on Jett after the first round. Jett wouldn't need much of a warm-up and Jason wanted him to save his energy. Uncle Ian had performed a miracle and Jett had jogged fine. I closed my eyes, listening to the hubbub of fans buzzing about. It was the half-time of show jumping, with people milling around the international food stands buying drinks and food, and the lineup for the restrooms long. The prediction had been right. There were over eighty thousand fans in the grandstands. I still couldn't get over that I'd made it into the jump-off—the only one of five—Vivian, Chris, Roman, Tiffany of Canada, and me.

A light hand brushed my shoulder. "Hi, darling." My mom's face was hidden by large sunglasses.

"Mom! You're here! You took time off?"

"How could I not? My baby's riding in the Gold Cup." Her finger trembled as she reached toward me and tucked a strand of my hair behind my ear. "Actually, I quit the night job. I got full-time work as an editor. It's freed up my evenings for writing. Of course I couldn't have done it without you—believing in us as you do. And look at you. Here you are!" She wrapped her arms around me, held me tight, then said, "It also helps that Aunt Julia and Uncle Ian were generous enough to cover the costs." Her cheeks flushed and she lowered her voice. "They've been so supportive of us."

I guess it would be embarrassing for her to feel like she had to accept their generosity. "We'll figure out a way to pay them back, Mom. This is the first step in our new future."

"Yes. Yes it is. And I know we will. I have faith in you. I have faith in us." Mom pulled me close and all the pain of the past year seemed to lift slightly.

Mom wiped away a tear. "Look who else made it . . ." Chris's mom stood near the stands. The two of us exchanged a smile and I was grateful to see her there for Chris's sake. I hoped they'd made up.

Biting back the sudden tears I felt springing up, I said to Mom, "Did you watch the first round?"

"You and Jett were splendid. I was up in the stands. I didn't want to distract you, but I wanted to come down and wish you good luck before the jump-off."

The announcer's voice boomed, "And now, in the arena, all the way from Germany, the Celle Stallions!"

Six stunning black stallions and their outfitted handlers and riders rode past us through the entrance under the clock tower. They performed carefully choreographed dressage to classical music.

"I'll be riding in fifteen minutes or so," I said.

"I'll be on my way, but I wanted you to know I was here." She brushed the back of her fingers against my cheek and smiled. I'd missed seeing that expression so much. She gave me a kiss on the cheek, then held me at arm's length and said, "Go now. Go show them how it's done, and don't be afraid. You were meant for this— your dad said so the day I first held you in my arms."

Vivian rode Seraphim. Third in the lineup of five. Roman had knocked a rail. Tiffany went clear. Time to beat: 49.5 seconds.

Seraphim's body was tight, contracted. Instead of jumping with vigor and energy, she dragged her hind legs and had lost her spark—her eyes now seemingly filled with pain and sadness. Vivian spurred over and over. Each time Seraphim bucked, my heart clenched, my stomach felt like the bottom was falling out of it.

"Do something," I said aloud.

Jason squeezed his arm around my shoulders, holding me tight.

I closed my eyes not wanting to watch anymore, but I had to. Seraphim fought for her head, but Vivian seized her hands against Sera, forcing her head down, cranking it so that Seraphim couldn't stretch over the jumps.

"The only way she'll beat that time is if she does that last line, the oxer to oxer, in three strides," Jason said as he watched.

As they neared the last combination, Vivian spurred, but Seraphim slowed. I bit my fist, imagining the inevitable crash. They made it over the first jump, and Vivian spurred again, smacking Seraphim hard, four times in a row with the crop.

"She should get disqualified for that!" I cried.

Seraphim slowed more. They had no choice. They had to do the line in four strides: one, two, three—I held my breath—four, but they made it over with no faults. I exhaled. The crowd roared.

I glanced at the scoreboard above the stands. Vivian's name lit up at the top. Her time to beat: 48.6 seconds. I ignored Vivian's proud look as she exited the arena.

"Ready?" Derek asked, leading Jett toward me. He'd been hand-walking him to keep him warm. I nodded, preparing my knee for Derek to give me a leg up. Chris was about to head in, then it was my turn.

"Hold up! You may not want to get on just yet," Vivian called.

Derek let go of my shin abruptly. I stumbled and grabbed Jett's mane. Vivian marched toward us, head high, chin lifted, a smirk playing on her lips.

"Just so you know, the FEI official is on his way over to pull Jett from the show."

"What the . . . ?" It felt like I'd been dunked in ice.

Vivian glanced around in a dramatic gesture, then leaned in toward Derek and me. "Oh, you guys know. I saw you. With Jett. Monday night. I know he's lame. And you know better than I do that he shouldn't be jumping in this competition. There are rules against that sort of thing." She arched her eyebrow. "Someone will be here any second, so don't bother mounting." She pulled her sunglasses off, scanning the crowd.

Derek clenched his fists at his side. "This is bullshit."

"I'm just glad I was here to bring justice to the show. Imagine what might have happened had I not been there that night?"

Derek lunged toward her.

"Don't!" I said, grabbing his arm.

A crowd watched us now, and I saw Helena and Corinne walking closer.

"I know what I'm doing," Derek said to me.

"No, Derek. It's not going to solve anything."

He tried to avoid me, but I pulled on his arm, and even though his eye twitched, his arm relaxed by his side.

Corinne and Helena walked up. "What's going on?" Helena asked.

Derek, with a shaking hand, gestured at Vivian. "She's got some nerve. Coming here, saying Jett's lame."

"Well, you've probably got him drugged to high hell, so he won't show any signs of it now, but I'm sure as soon as the FEI official gets here and does a blood test, we'll find out the truth." Vivian flung her hair over her shoulder. "It's over, Brynn. It's done. *You're* done."

"What unusual circumstances." Corinne faced Vivian, her eyes narrowed. "It really would be unfortunate if Brynn and Jett were disqualified, but"—she glanced up at the scoreboard—"but somewhat beneficial if you had one less rider to compete against."

Vivian eyed Corinne, her smile fading. "Is that what you think this is about?" The vein at Vivian's temple throbbed.

"I'm only noting the facts. And it just so happens, Vivian, that that little fiasco with rapping still hasn't been disclosed. I've never been too happy about it, and actually had cameras installed just a couple of weeks ago back at our barn. I wouldn't have believed it if I hadn't seen it with my own eyes, but sure enough there you were, using your friend the pole. And on Seraphim. Can you imagine how shocked I was? Especially since we had our talk and you promised me you wouldn't do it again."

Corinne stood only inches from Vivian now. "Now, if there is anything I can't stand more than lying, it's hurting my horse, and *then* lying about it."

Vivian leaned farther and farther back as Corinne spoke. Her face took on the color of her white shirt, two bright red spots blooming on her cheeks.

Fourth in the lineup, Chris rode past us on De Salle. Carefully. Purposefully. Chris nodded at me, then smiled, his genuine smile, the one I'd seen the first day I'd met him.

"Now, I know you'll want to make this right," Corinne said.

A shadow loomed in the tunnel below the grandstands. The FEI official stood at the bottom of the ramp, his face dark. He surveyed the area, searching. Spotting Jett and me, the official beelined toward us.

I wrapped my arms around Jett's neck. God no—not now. Everything blurred, and I knew that if he stopped us from showing now, when I'd gotten this far, I wouldn't be able to do it again—I couldn't come back. I squeezed Jett's neck tighter and closed my eyes.

But nothing happened. The official wasn't next to me. He wasn't telling me I had to pull Jett from the competition. I peered around Jett. Vivian was arm in arm with the FEI official, laughing, making light of something. He eyed her up and down, then shrugged. He looked at me, then Vivian again. Vivian clamped her lips as she stared at me, but when he looked toward her, she smiled her flirty smile. The official seemed satisfied, turned and walked down the ramp, his back receding into the shadows.

I glanced at Corinne. She nodded at me, then walked toward the grandstands.

Derek was next to me. "We're set, B. Let's get you on that horse."

34

*Y*ou go get 'em, kid. And don't forget the plan," Jason said.

I bit my lip and nodded, staring out across the International Ring. Everything appeared sharper, bigger, more colorful than I'd ever seen. The sky, the grass, the trees, the jumps. The only sound now was Jason's voice, as he gave me his last tip. "Ride into the void . . . let it carry you." He squeezed my boot, then he gave Jett a pat.

Derek bent down to work on Jett's feet, scraping all the dirt that had accumulated in the warm-up arena. He wiped Jett's froth off the bridle and breastplate, and as I leaned over to adjust his head stall, I smiled at the new brass plate reading Victory by Heart. I smiled to myself. For the first time ever I felt Mom was proud of me, believed in me, wanted me to win.

"You're all set," Derek said, winking up at me, giving me his biggest, most confident smile, the dimple in his cheek deepening.

"Yes. Yes I am."

Inside the arena, Chris had just passed the halfway mark, riding faster and harder than I'd ever seen. The crowd now cheered as Chris jumped De Salle over the water jump. His laser focus honed in on the jumps as he cleared each one with ease. De Salle, the color of dark chocolate, looked graceful and poised, sailing over the jumps as if he were made to fly.

"He has to beat Vivian's time. Watch, he'll try to do that last line in three strides," Jason said.

Chris approached the first oxer of the last line, accelerating, but De Salle wasn't galloping fast enough. Chris spurred, but too late. A hush fell over the crowd, and it seemed that all eighty thousand people held their breath. Chris was almost to the second oxer in the final line now, but instead of clearing it, De Salle jumped headlong into it. I held my breath, watching in slow motion as they crashed straight into the rails. The splitting wood sound resounded across the stands. My stomach clenched and I clamped my hand over my mouth. De Salle fell, Chris tried to roll. The music stopped, and crew members ran across the field.

I saw myself, on the ground, trying to free my foot at the last show. I watched, waiting for Chris to get up, my heart racing. He wasn't moving. Paramedics arrived with their medical golf cart, and then the stretcher. I tried to inhale, but no breath came. I might as well have been winded too. I couldn't help it, but I pulled my feet out of my stirrups, ready to jump down and run to him.

Jason's hand tightened over my knee. "Stay put. He's in good hands."

The jump crew formed a circle around Chris, facing outward, and there was no way to see anything through their tight-knit bodies. The stadium hushed, and the giant screen now played a silent Mercedes-Benz commercial.

Finally the circle around Chris dissolved. Chris lay on the stretcher on the extended golf cart.

"Ladies and gentlemen. An unfortunate event, and something we never like to see happen, but it appears as though Chris Peterson will need emergency care."

The crowd was silent.

The golf cart approached us now. I saw Chris as they passed, his face ashen, his neck in a brace—but he was breathing, and his eyes were open. I let out a sigh of relief. Chris waved for the driver to stop. He looked directly at me, then he mouthed, "I'm sorry."

~

My eyes welled up with tears.

"And now we welcome Brynn Seymour back into the arena for her second round! Two have gone clear, and Vivian Young heads up the lead."

The crowd cheered, the music blared, but I heard nothing after that.

It was down to Vivian, Tiffany, and me. Roman had knocked a rail and Chris was disqualified.

Jett and I entered the arena, Jett electric beneath me. I reached down to pat his shoulder, his black coat shimmering, reflecting the gold of the afternoon sun. I tasted blood in my mouth from having bitten my cheek too hard. I started Jett off at a slow trot, remembering to take a centering breath, feeling light in the stirrups, my body feeling so much stronger than it ever had. Yoga had helped more than just my mind. The jump crew had finished rebuilding the last jump after Chris's crash, and the grass divots had been smoothed, the mirrors of the jump reflecting the setting sun, making it appear as if it were on fire.

"And now, in the arena we have Brynn Seymour, atop Victory by Heart, owned by Redwood Grove Stables!"

The jumbo screen zoomed in on Jett and me, and as I saw us on the screen, I couldn't believe we were finally here.

Victory by Heart and Brynn.

"Let's ride," I said out loud.

Jett moved into a fluid canter. I pressed him forward, opening him up into a gallop. The wind rushed past me as we cleared the first two jumps. Nearing the third fence, I felt out of control. I wanted to rein Jett in, but I heard Jason's voice in my mind, his instructions from before. *Gallop. Give him free rein—here's where you let go. Here's where you repeat Del Mar.* We galloped right at the fence, and even though it had been difficult for several riders, Jett didn't hesitate. We rounded the corner around the tree, and I turned Jett sharply, cutting in between it and the jump standards only four feet apart.

A whoosh resounded in my ear. I collected Jett, just as Jason had told me to, but Jett didn't listen. He kept galloping. I stood in my stirrups, and used my whole body weight to lean back on him. He finally slowed. As if my life depended on it, I jumped the next three jumps. Jett rounded over each, his hooves pounding the ground, only his breath roaring in my ears, the stadium receding to background noise. But we'd lost time. I glanced at the clock. We were too slow. Vivian would win.

I remembered Jason's words in snippets: *The final line—it's big . . . walks a short four strides or a long three, but a long three, not quite four . . . you have to go slow . . . Jett's stride is shorter . . . if he were larger, maybe . . . won't work . . . you have to ride it in four.*

But to win, I *had* to jump it in three. It could work. I didn't have a choice. I knew I should listen to Jason and I should be careful, but I had to let Jett go, to make up lost time. Jett could do this.

As if he'd had read my mind, Jett's ears perked up. His energy increased.

The crowd buzzed. Jett's heart pounded. He drew in deep, powerful breaths. I rounded the corner, and the next jump came up almost immediately. I gave Jett extra leg, and he rose underneath me. My hands reached forward as he stretched his head, and I was at one with him. His body ready, his lungs expanding to their fullest. I was controlling, yet letting myself go, and the colorful jump was below us, but I was already looking ahead to the next one.

I glanced over at Jason. He stood, gripping the edge of the gate, white knuckles bright in the sun.

"It's going to be okay, Jason. Have no fear!" I said under my breath.

And I knew he understood. Jason bowed his head slightly to me. I had his blessing. Fear would not control me anymore, and I fully understood the Abhaya Mudra was not something we talked about—it was part of who I was.

I urged Jett on, leaning over his neck as we galloped toward the final big oxer to oxer line. I made myself as small as I could to give him the advantage. Four strides before we were there I sat back slightly, and slowed Jett, just a hair, and we only had two strides to the fence.

Jett groaned as he landed, his knees buckling, but I used my hands to pull up on the reins, to steady him, and then he was off again, leaping like a cheetah, racing forward. One. Two. Three. And now we were up flying, and I forced my eyes open leaning as far forward as I could.

The sound of the crowd cheering met me on the other side.

"What a round! Brynn Seymour and Victory by Heart in a time of 45.8 seconds! Clear and fastest time to boot!"

The Band of the Grenadier Arms, dressed in their red tunics and white leather belts, their black bearskin caps, and precisely ironed trousers, marched onto the field in a riot of tubas and trumpets and drums.

"You owned it, B!" Derek laughed, clipping a lead rope to Jett's bridle. I smiled, jumping off Jett, giving him a brief hug, my eyes scanning, searching. Then I found the person I needed most. Jason. Walking toward me. His arms outstretched. Tears blurred my vision, my throat clenched. We'd done it.

"And the winner of the renowned million-dollar West Coast Gold Cup is . . . Brynn Seymour, aboard Victory by Heart! Everyone, please put your hands together as Brynn starts us off in the victory gallop!"

Practically every single visitor that day stood, hands clapping, feet stomping, arms waving, calling, whistling, and cheering. As we cantered back into the arena for the victory lap, Jett and I floated over the ground, his hooves pounding in rhythm to my heart. He stretched his neck forward as I let the reins go, standing up in my stirrups. Jett shook his head left and right, foam flying from his mouth. He arched his back like a bucking bronco. We raced around the arena, all the other riders behind us.

I felt lighter than I had in years, my arms buoyant, my body practically levitating above Jett. I grinned up at the crowd, tears wetting my cheeks. I rode with one arm up, the other holding the reins—and we flew.

"This one's for you, Daddy," I said.

Reds and blues and yellows whizzed by as we galloped—advertisements, T-shirts, hats, and banners people waved about.

I knew he was there with me. Just as he'd been there the first day I sat atop my pony. Just like the day he'd taught me to trot, to canter, and to jump my first little X. He was there the day I had my first fall, and the day I had my first win. He was here now. And if I closed my eyes, just for a split second, I could see him. His dark hair, his bright smile, his worn skin, furrowed brow when he was upset, eyes crinkling when he laughed. His long legs curved around Cervantes, and they were here, cantering and soaring with me. And I laughed out loud, as we galloped to victory.

This was Victory. Victory by Heart.

35

$\mathcal{I}$ walked Jason to the front door, my bare feet cooled by the tiles of the foyer. It felt strange having him in our home, since we'd only ever spent time down at the barn or at shows together. As he stood against the backdrop of the glass door, outlined by the greenery and sky behind him, he seemed to belong here. Yet all we'd shared was breakfast together.

He held his hat in both hands, spinning it around, letting the brim fall between his fingers, then deftly catching it. I fixated on the hat, not wanting to look him in the eye, suddenly shy, feeling like I did that first day I met him.

"Thanks for breakfast," he said. "You're catching on to all this Ayurvedic stuff."

"I went over the top, didn't I?" I'd cooked enough for at least five more. "I'm glad you're taking some home with you."

"And I'm sure Derek and your mom and the clients will all enjoy some too."

I swallowed down the lump in my throat, feeling cheated out of time with him. "So, how long will you be gone?" I asked, trying to be casual but wanting to throw my arms around him, to beg him to stay.

"We're going to spend some time up in B.C. A little town on Vancouver Island. Tyler leaves for Afghanistan today. Ashley and I will take Eve there, keep her away from crowds while her immune system strengthens. She's in remission, but she's weak. Being up there, well, you'd have to see it. It's so serene and healing. That's what they both need, especially after being in the hospital for much of this past year. We'll probably stay a couple of months. Now that she's better I want Ashley to take a break, to rest and spend time with Eve outdoors, in the fresh air."

"Why Canada?"

"My mother was Canadian, my grandma was from the Tsimshian tribe. We're going to spend time with relatives, ones neither Ashley nor I have met before. Our mother had kept us separate from our relatives, trying to assimilate us into Los Angeles culture."

"I see," I mumbled. He'd shared snippets of his life with me, but I'd been so self-absorbed in saving the barn and winning, I felt bad I hadn't asked him more about himself.

As if he'd read my mind, he leaned forward and lifted my chin with his finger. "It's okay. We haven't had much time together—like this."

I nodded, wishing the words would come easier. "I'm so thankful Eve's doing better. I'd love to come say goodbye to her before you go up to Canada."

He shook his head. "We're leaving tonight. And it's probably best not to." My heart sank, and as if sensing that he quickly added, "For Eve's sake. It's a confusing time for her and we're trying to minimize how many people she sees."

I nodded again, biting my lips, pushing down the immediate sense of disappointment at not being close enough to Jason to be in Eve's circle of approved visitors.

"I'll write you a letter," he said.

I laughed. "A letter? I don't think I've ever received one before."

"I'd like to be the first." He wound a strand of my hair that had fallen in my face around his finger, tucking it behind my ear, his hand pausing to cradle my cheek. The warmth spread like a radiant sun. I reached up and held his hand in place, then kissed the back of his fingers. I raised my eyes to his, and I knew. He understood me—better than anyone ever had.

His fingers weaved through my hair, tugging gently, bringing my mouth closer. I reached up, clutching his shirt, pulling him toward me, wanting to feel him, taste him.

Jason broke away, resting his forehead against mine. I stood on tiptoes, breathing his breath, strawberries and tea. He gave me a light, fleeting kiss on my forehead, brushing against my sensitive skin.

"Goodbye, my Brynn."

Jason walked down the winding stone steps toward his old Chevy truck. His shirt, the color of the sky behind him, billowed in the breeze. His faded jeans, worn and comfortable, accentuated his legs. As he ducked his head to get into his old truck, I grabbed at a sharp pain in my side. He stretched out his arm through the open window, his hand in an Abhaya Mudra. I wanted to run after the truck, but this was my last test of bravery. I put my hand out in response. No fear.

His truck turned onto the road, and I watched until it was nothing more than a blur merging with the asphalt of the road.

I headed down the steps, leaving the front door open behind me, inhaling the crisp air into the deepest recesses of my lungs, gazing up at the sky. Chris was out of the hospital today. He'd suffered a concussion, a broken pelvis, and a couple of cracked ribs, but was doing well overall. I texted him that I'd swing by to check on him later. A few clouds whirred by, turning the driveway into patches of bright and light puddles as they passed.

I brushed my fingers against the lavender that grew along the side of the house, filling the air with its sweet, rich scent. The path sloped and curved around the back of the house, toward the barn. Enjoying the silence of the quiet morning, I stood at the top of the hill gazing down toward the barn and the large semi-transport truck trailer parked in front. New horses were moving in today, including Helena's and Corinne's.

I had used the check from the Gold Cup win to pay down all of our revolving debt, and had put the rest of the money toward the mortgage on the house. We would be fine for another two years—longer if business picked up. I still wasn't sure what to do with the Mercedes. It wasn't me. I thought I'd give it to Mom—she deserved to drive in style.

Derek came into view from behind the trailer doors. He walked an extraordinary bay out of the trailer, the horse's coat shimmering like dark chocolate. Derek smiled and said something to the short, heavyset man carrying a bin. They laughed, Derek perfectly at ease. At home. He belonged here. We belonged here.

I knew the path that I would now take. I had a couple of phone calls to make. One to Uncle Ian, one to Professor Dixon. And then I'd have a conversation with Derek.

But there was one place I needed to go first. I grabbed my car keys and sweater, and headed out the door. Mom walked down her hall-way toward me. "Where are you off to?"

"To visit Dad."

Her silence rang loud in my ears.

I reached for the doorknob.

"Can I come? I haven't been to see him." She brushed her hands down the front of her pants.

The light streamed in through the glass door, illuminating her. She wore her hair up and wispy blonde waves fell around her face. She looked more hopeful than I'd ever seen her look.

"I haven't either."

We took the new Mercedes, the sun shining through the sun-roof, the air crystal clear. Everything looked like it had been washed clean after a good rain. We neared the Devon Creek cemetery. Mom's voice broke the silence. "How different it all seems."

The place was deserted. I inhaled the scent of fresh-cut grass and rich soil. The little white stucco church needed a paint job, the red tile roof had faded and cracked. We parked and walked around back to the small plot, corralled by a low picket fence.

We walked along a rocky path, our shoes sinking into the patchy brown grass. The gray tombstones, marbled with white from the Pacific rains, matched the gray rocks of Marin County's coast side. Blending in, as if Nature herself had a hand in placing the rocks to mark the place where her children lay.

My father's grave was still one of the newest in the tiny cemetery, and when we first stood in front of it, I wasn't sure what to do. A few colorless carnations spilled over from the plastic vase. I closed my eyes, hung my head, embarrassed that I hadn't stopped in before.

Mom slid her hand in mine, her hand cold and damp. "I feel terrible I haven't been here," she said, reading my thoughts.

"Let's fix this up," I said, kneeling, pulling at the weeds. I picked out twigs and rocks from around the plot. It felt good to handle the dirt, to smell the soil, the earth under my nails.

"I'll be right back!" Mom said, renewed vigor in her voice. Then she turned back. "Can I have the keys?"

I pulled them out of my jacket pocket and continued to work around Dad's grave.

Within ten minutes, she returned, carrying a fresh bouquet of yellow roses and a stained glass vase. She dangled a paper bag in the other hand. "Candles." She lifted the bag toward me.

We found a tap and filled the vase with water. Mom arranged the flowers while I found matches in the bag. We took our time lighting the candles. Each one was about five inches tall, encased in red glass.

"To Dad's amazing love of horses," I said as I lit the first one.

"To Luke, who brought light into my life." Mom turned her eyes down as she lit her candle.

"To his ability to find humor in everything," I continued.

"To his resilient spirit."

"To his strength."

"And courage."

At the last two, Mom's eyes found mine and held steady. "To Luke, the father of the best daughter I could ever have."

My hand shook as I lit the last one. "To Dad, for finding you, the perfect mother." A silent tear slid down her face.

We placed all the candles around the grave. They glowed and flickered and we continued to kneel. It felt right, to have the earth against my knees, to bow my head. I prayed for strength. I prayed for forgiveness.

A hawk flew overhead, his shadow flitting across the grave, dark contrasting with light. He circled, glided, soared, and then disappeared behind the hilltop. Mom's reflection, and mine, merged in the granite of the tombstone, green and white, like the mountains and clouds reflecting across a lake, our imperfections a blur. Jason's words rang through me. *The best of intentions.* That's when I realized that I didn't need to pray for forgiveness anymore. It was always me, the one whose forgiveness I sought. I had to forgive myself.

And I had.

Acknowledgments

$\mathcal{W}$riting a novel is something I've always dreamed of. When I was young, I convinced myself I first had to own a laptop before I could be considered a writer. I worked in academia and in biotech, and it wasn't until I started my MBA, following the birth of my two girls, that my father presented me with a gift: a white Mac-Book. I said, "Now, then, I can finally write a novel." It wasn't for a couple of more years that nuggets took hold and the first scenes of *Learning to Fall* came to be. I've read that writing a novel is a lonely, solitary endeavor, yet it requires much support from others. This most certainly was my experience.

Each and every person who came into my life between 2010 and 2016 affected me in some way, taught me something, helped me become who I was: in essence, helped me create this novel. For the following I am most grateful:

Karen Bjorneby, for your kind and gentle guidance in the very first (secretive days) of my writing; Karen Dion, for Salt Cay and Backspace; the wonderful Backspace community members; Sandra Kring, for giving so freely of yourself. For everyone who read the many early drafts. For Betsy Johnson, one of the first readers and my huge supporters; Nancy Benovich-Gilby, for telling me you wanted more; Renata Nordell; Bonnie Glick, for those e-mail exchanges and walks at Filoli; Amy Hartman, for your friendship and support; Kris Waldherr and Atossa Shafaie, for your detailed notes and edits; Emma Sweeney, who initially signed me on and helped guide me. To

Heather Lazare—I'm still wowed by your talent. Jim Thomsen, for helping me go the distance.

To Jacquelyn Mitchard, who made me believe that I am a writer and that I can. To Ellen Sussman—I learned so much from you. To Robert Goolrick—thank you for believing in me.

To my wonderful literary agent, Kevan Lyon, for keeping the faith.

To Emily Smith, for helping me find forgiveness, and to Jen Breen and the community at the Bainbridge Yoga House, for helping me during a tough transitionary year.

To Brooke Warner, Crystal Patriarche, Lauren Wise, and everyone else at SparkPress, for making this dream a reality.

A special thanks to my parents, who read several drafts and never gave up on me; to my daughters, Natalia and Alexandra, who've lived with this novel way longer than any child should; and to my husband, Craig, without whom this never would have come to be.

Lastly, to all the show jumpers and horse lovers and writers who aspire to do something courageous and new! Be brave. Follow your dreams. This is my gift, as small as it is, and I share it with you.

ABOUT THE AUTHOR

Lisa Dunham of LSD Photography

Anne Clermont, born in Kraków and raised outside of Toronto, spent fifteen years in California before relocating to the beautiful Pacific Northwest. She holds a BS in animal biology, and an MBA. Her background ranges from studying animal behavior to carrying out pancreatic cancer research at one of the world's largest and most innovative biotech companies. Inspired to write *Learning to Fall* in part by her own experience of running a show jumping business, she now devotes her time to writing and working as an editor and website designer. She lives on an island in the middle of Puget Sound with her husband and two children.

SELECTED TITLES FROM SPARKPRESS

SparkPress is an independent boutique publisher delivering high-quality, entertaining, and engaging content that enhances readers' lives, with a special focus on female-driven work. Visit us at **www.gosparkpress.com**.

The Year of Necessary Lies, by Kris Radish. $17, 978-1-94071-651-0. A great-granddaughter discovers her ancestor's secrets—inspirational forays into forbidden love and the Florida Everglades at the turn of the last century.

Rooville, by Julie Long. $17, 978-1-94071-660-2. Even after thirteen years in California, TV weatherman Owen Martin can feel the corners of his squareness still evident. When he's fired from his job, he heads home to Iowa—but in his absence, Martinville has become the center of the Transcendental Meditation movement. With old customs and open-mindedness clashing like warm and cold fronts, Owen gets caught in a veritable tornado.

So Close, by Emma McLaughlin and Nicola Kraus. $17, 978-1-940716-76-3. A story about a girl from the trailer parks of Florida and the two powerful men who shape her life—one of whom will raise her up to places she never imagined, the other who will threaten to destroy her. Can a girl like her make it to the White House? When her loyalty is tested will she save the only family member she's ever known—even if it means keeping a terrible secret from the American people?

First Rodeo, by Judith Hennessey. $16.95, 978-1943006038. Fast-paced and wildly entertaining, *First Rodeo* is filled with humorous scenes of city girl gone country, encounters with handsome cowboys, the struggles of the creative process, and a powerful message: the greatest love of all is the love you have for yourself.

Hostile Takeover, by Phyllis Piano, $16.95, 978-1940716824. Long-lost love, a hostile corporate takeover, and the death of her beloved husband turn attorney Molly Parr's life into a tailspin that threatens to ruin everything she has worked for. Molly's all-consuming job is to take over other companies, but when her first love, a man who she feels betrayed her, appears out of nowhere to try and acquire her business, long-hidden passions and secrets are exposed.